Death is Now My Neighbour
'Dexter . . . has created a giant among fictional
detectives and has never short-changed his readers.'
The Times

The Daughters of Cain
'This is Colin Dexter at his most excitingly devious.'
Daily Telegraph

The Way Through the Woods
'Morse and his faithful Watson, Sergeant Lewis,
in supreme form . . . Hallelujah.'
Observer

The Jewel That Was Ours
'Traditional crime writing at its best; the kind
of book without which no armchair is complete.'
Sunday Times

The Wench is Dead
'Dextrously ingenious.'
Guardian

THE SECRET OF ANNEXE 3

Colin Dexter graduated from Cambridge University in 1953 and has lived in Oxford since 1966. His first novel, *Last Bus to Woodstock*, was published in 1975. There are now thirteen novels in the series, of which *The Remorseful Day* is, sadly, the last.

Colin Dexter has won many awards for his novels, including the CWA Silver Dagger twice, and the CWA Gold Dagger for *The Wench is Dead* and *The Way Through the Woods*. In 1997 he was presented with the CWA Diamond Dagger for outstanding services to crime literature, and in 2000 was awarded the OBE in the Queen's Birthday Honours List.

The Inspector Morse novels have, of course, been adapted for the small screen with huge success by Carlton/Central Television, starring John Thaw and Kevin Whately.

The Inspector Morse Novels

LAST BUS TO WOODSTOCK
LAST SEEN WEARING
THE SILENT WORLD OF NICHOLAS QUINN
SERVICE OF ALL THE DEAD
THE DEAD OF JERICHO
THE RIDDLE OF THE THIRD MILE
THE SECRET OF ANNEXE 3
THE WENCH IS DEAD
THE JEWEL THAT WAS OURS
THE WAY THROUGH THE WOODS
THE DAUGHTERS OF CAIN
DEATH IS NOW MY NEIGHBOUR
THE REMORSEFUL DAY

Also available in Pan Books

MORSE'S GREATEST MYSTERY AND OTHER STORIES
THE FIRST INSPECTOR MORSE OMNIBUS
THE SECOND INSPECTOR MORSE OMNIBUS
THE THIRD INSPECTOR MORSE OMNIBUS
THE FOURTH INSPECTOR MORSE OMNIBUS

COLIN DEXTER

THE SECRET
OF ANNEXE 3

PAN BOOKS

First published 1986 by Macmillan London

First published in paperback 1987 by Pan Books

This edition published 2011 by Pan Books
an imprint of Pan Macmillan, a division of Macmillan Publishers Limited
Pan Macmillan, 20 New Wharf Road, London N1 9RR
Basingstoke and Oxford
Associated companies throughout the world
www.panmacmillan.com

ISBN 978-0-330-47967-7

1 3 5 7 9 8 6 4 2

A CIP catalogue record for this book is available from
the British Library.

Typeset by SetSystems Ltd, Saffron Walden, Essex
Printed and bound by CPI Group (UK) Ltd, Croydon, CR0 4YY

Visit **www.panmacmillan.com** to read more about all our books
and to buy them. You will also find features, author interviews and
news of any author events, and you can sign up for e-newsletters
so that you're always first to hear about our new releases.

for

Elizabeth, Anna, and Eve

ACKNOWLEDGEMENTS

The author and publishers wish to thank the following who have kindly given permission for the use of copyright material:

George Allen & Unwin (Publishers) Ltd, for a quotation by Bertrand Russell.

Curtis Brown Group Ltd, London, on behalf of the Estate of Ogden Nash for a quotation by him.

Peter Champkin for an extract from his book *The Waking Life of Aspern Williams*.

Faber and Faber Ltd, for an extract from 'La Figlia Che Piange' in *Collected Poems* by T. S. Eliot.

A. M. Heath & Company Ltd, on behalf of the Estate of the late Sonia Brownell Orwell for an extract from *Shooting an Elephant* by George Orwell, published by Secker & Warburg Ltd.

Henry Holt & Company Inc, for a quotation by Robert Frost.

A. D. Peters & Company and Jonathan Cape Ltd, on behalf of the Executors of the Estate of C. Day Lewis, for an extract from 'Departure in the Dark' in *Collected Poems*, 1954, published by the Hogarth Press.

The Society of Authors on behalf of the Bernard Shaw Estate for a quotation by Bernard Shaw.

A. P. Watt Ltd, on behalf of *The National Trust for*

CHAPTER ONE

November

The pomp of funerals has more regard to the vanity of
the living than to the honour of the dead.

(LA ROCHEFOUCAULD, *Maxims*)

WHEN THE OLD man died, there was probably no
great joy in heaven; and quite certainly little if any real
grief in Charlbury Drive, the pleasantly unpretentious
cul-de-sac of semi-detached houses to which he had
retired. Yet a few of the neighbours, especially the
womenfolk, had struck up some sort of distanced
acquaintance with him as they pushed prams or shopping trolleys past his neatly kept front lawn; and two of
these women (on learning that things were fixed for a
Saturday) had decided to be present at the statutory
obsequies. Margaret Bowman was one of them.

'Do I look all right?' she asked.

'Fine!' His eyes had not left the racing page of the
tabloid newspaper, but he knew well enough that his
wife would always be an odds-on favourite for looking
all right: a tall, smart woman upon whom clothes
invariably hung well, whether for dances, weddings,
dinners – or even funerals.

'Well? Have a *look* then! Yes?'

So he looked up at her and nodded vaguely as he surveyed the black ensemble. She *did* look fine. What else was there to say? 'You look fine,' he said.

With a gaiety wholly inappropriate she twirled round on the points of her newly purchased black leather court shoes, fully aware, just as he was, that she did look rather attractive. Her hips had filled out somewhat alarmingly since that disappointing day when as a willowy lass of twenty (a year before marrying Tom Bowman) her application to become an air hostess had proved unsuccessful; and now, sixteen years later, she would have more than a little trouble (she knew it!) in negotiating the central aisle of a Boeing 737. Yet her calves and ankles were almost as slender as when she had slipped her nightgowned body between the stiff white sheets of their honeymoon bed in a Torquay hotel; it was only her feet, with a line of whitish nodules across the middle joints of her slightly ugly toes, that now presaged the gradual approach of middle age. Well, no. It wasn't *only* that – if she were being really honest with herself. There was that hebdomadal visit to the expensive clinic in Oxford ... But she cast that particular thought from her mind. ('Hebdomadal' was a word she'd become rather proud of, having come across it so often in her job in Oxford with the University Examining Board.)

'Yes?' she repeated.

He looked at her again, more carefully this time. 'You're going to change your shoes, aren't you?'

'What?' Her hazel eyes, with their markedly flecked

irises, took on a puzzled, appealingly vulnerable aspect. Involuntarily her left hand went up to the back of her freshly brushed and recently dyed blonde hair, whilst the fingers of her right hand began to pluck fecklessly at some non-existent speck that threatened to jeopardize her immaculate, expensive nigritude.

'It's bucketing down – hadn't you noticed?' he said.

Little rivulets were trickling down the outside of the lounge window, and even as he spoke a few slanted splashes of rain re-emphasized the ugly temper of the windswept sky.

She looked down at the specially purchased black leather shoes – so classy-looking, so beautifully comfortable. But before she could reply he was reinforcing his line of argument.

'They're going to inter the poor sod, didn't you say?'

For a few moments the word 'inter' failed to register adequately in her brain, sounding like one of those strangely unfamiliar words that had to be sought out in a dictionary. But then she remembered: it meant they wouldn't be cremating the body; they would be digging a deep, vertically sided hole in the orange-coloured earth and lowering the body down on straps. She'd seen the sort of thing on TV and at the cinema; and usually it had been raining then, too.

She looked out of the window, frowning and disappointed.

'You'll get your feet drenched – that's all I'm trying to say.' He turned to the centre pages of his newspaper and began reading about the extraordinary sexual prowess of a world-famous snooker player.

For a couple of minutes or so at that point the course of events in the Bowman household could perhaps have continued to drift along in its normal, unremarkable neutral gear. But it was not to be.

The last thing Margaret wanted to do was ruin the lovely shoes she'd bought. All right. She'd bought them *for* the funeral; but it was ridiculous to go and waste more than £50. It wasn't necessary to go and trample all over the muddy churchyard of course; but even going out in them in this weather was pretty foolish. She looked down again at her expensively sheathed feet, and then at the clock on the mantelpiece. Not much time. But she *would* change them, she decided. Most things went reasonably well with black, and that pair of grey shoes with the cushioned soles would be a sensible choice. But if she was going to be all in black apart from just her shoes, wouldn't it be nicely fashionable to change her handbag as well? Yes! There was that grey leather handbag that would match the shoes almost perfectly.

She tripped up the stairs hurriedly.

And fatefully.

It was no more than a minute or so after this decision – not a decision that would strike anyone as being particularly momentous – that Thomas Bowman put down his newspaper and answered the confidently repeated stridencies at the front door, where in friendly fashion he nodded to a drably clad young woman standing at the porch in the pouring rain under a garishly multicoloured golf umbrella, and wearing knee-length boots of bright yellow plastic that took his thoughts back to the Technicolor broadcasts of the first manned landing on the moon. Some of the women on the estate, quite clearly, were considerably less fashion-conscious than his wife.

'She's nearly ready,' he said. 'Just putting on her ballet shoes for your conducted tour across the ploughed fields.'

'Sorry I'm a bit late.'

'You coming in?'

'Better not. We're a bit pushed for time. Hello Margaret!'

The chicly clad feet which moments ago had flitted lightly up the stairs were now descending more sombrely in a pair of grey, thickish-soled walking shoes. A grey-gloved hand hurriedly pushed a white handker-chief into the grey handbag – and Margaret Bowman was ready, at last, for a funeral.

CHAPTER TWO

November

'Nobody ever notices postmen, somehow,' said he thoughtfully; 'yet they have passions like other men.'

(G.K. CHESTERTON, *The Invisible Man*)

IT WAS A little while after the front door had closed behind the two women that he allowed himself an oblique glance across the soggy lawn that stretched between the wide lounge window and the road. He had told Margaret that she could have the car if she wanted it, since he had no plans for going anywhere himself. But clearly they had gone off in the other woman's since the maroon Metro still stood there on the steepish slope that led down to the garage. Charlbury Drive might just as well have been uninhabited, and the rain poured steadily down.

He walked upstairs and went into the spare bedroom, where he opened the right-hand leaf of the cumbrous, dark mahogany wardrobe that served to store the overflow of his wife's and his own clothing. Behind this leaf, stacked up against the right-hand side of the wardrobe, stood eight white shoe boxes, one atop the other; and from this stack he carefully withdrew the third box from the bottom. Inside lay a bottle of malt whisky about two-thirds empty – or about one-third full, as a man who is thirsting for a drink would probably have described it. The box was an old one, and had been the secret little hiding place for two things since his marriage to Margaret. For a week, in the days when he was still playing football, it had hidden a set of crudely pornographic photographs which had circulated from the veteran goalkeeper to the fourteen-year-old outside-left. And now (and with increasing frequency) it had become the storage space for the whisky of which he was getting, as he knew, rather dangerously over-fond. Guilty secrets both, assuredly; yet hardly sins of cosmic proportions. In fact, he had slowly grown towards the view that the lovely if some-what overweight Margaret would perhaps have forgiven him readily for the photographs; though not for the whisky, perhaps. Or *would* she have forgiven him for the whisky? He had sensed fairly early on in their married life together that she would probably always have preferred unfaithful sobriety to intoxicated fidelity. But had she changed? Changed recently? She must have smelled the stuff on his breath more than once, although their intimacy over the past few months had been unromantic, intermittent, and wholly unremarkable. Not that any such considerations were bothering his mind very much, if at all, at this particular juncture. He took out the bottle, put the box back, and was just pushing two of his old suits back into place along the rail when he caught sight of it – standing on the floor immediately behind the left-hand leaf of the wardrobe, a leaf which in his own experience was virtually never opened: it was the black handbag which his wife had at the very last minute decided to leave behind.

At first this purely chance discovery failed to register in his mind as an incident that should occasion any interest or surprise; but after a few moments he frowned a little – and then he frowned a lot. Why had she put the handbag behind the door of the wardrobe? He had never noticed any of her accessories there before. Normally she would keep her handbag on the table beside the twin bed that stood nearer the window – her bed. So why . . .? Still frowning, he walked across the landing into their bedroom and looked down at the two black leather shoes, one toppled on to its side, which had been so hurriedly taken off and carelessly left at the foot of her bed.

Back in the spare bedroom he picked up the handbag. An incurious man who had seldom felt any fascination for prying into others' affairs, he would never have thought of opening one of his wife's letters – or opening one of her handbags. Not in normal circumstances. But why had she tried to conceal her handbag? And the answer to that question now seemed very obvious indeed. There was something, perhaps more than one thing, *inside* the handbag that she didn't want him to see; and in her rush she hadn't had the time to transfer all its contents to the other one. The catch opened easily and he found the letter, four pages of it, almost immediately.

You are a selfish thankless bitch and if you think you
can just back out of things when *you* like you'd better

8

realize that you've got another big thick headaching think coming because it could be that I've got some ideas about what *I* like. You'd better understand what I'm saying. If you can act like a bitch you'd better know I can be a bit of a sod too. You were glad enough to get what you wanted from me and just because I wanted to give it to you you think that we can just drop everything and go back to square one. Well this letter is to tell you we can't and like I say you'd better understand what I'm telling you. You can be sure I'll get my own back on you...

His throat was dry as he rapidly skimmed the rest of the letter: it had no salutation on page one, no subscription on page four. But there was no doubt about the message of the letter – a message that screamed so loudly at him that even some under-achieving idiot would require no prompting about its import: *his wife was being unfaithful to him* – probably had been for a period of several months.

A sharp pain throbbed in the centre of his forehead, the blood was pounding in his ears, and for several minutes his thought processes were utterly incapable of any sharp tuning. Yet curiously enough he appeared to be adequately in control of the rest of his body, for his hands trembled not the merest millimetre as he filled the shabby little cylindrical glass he always used for the whisky. Sometimes he added a little cold tap water; sometimes not. Now he sipped the whisky neat: first just a small sip; then a large sip; then two large gulps of the burning liquor, and the glass was empty. He refilled his glass and soon had drained that, too. The last drops from the bottle just filled the third glass to the brim and this he sipped more slowly, feeling as he did so the familiar surge of warmth that slowly suffused his brain. And now it happened, paradoxically and totally unexpectedly, that instead of the vicious jealousy which a few minutes ago had threatened to swamp his foundering senses he was gradually becoming ever more conscious of the love he felt for his wife. This renewed consciousness reminded him vividly of the day when, under-prepared and over-confident, she had failed her first driving test; and when, as she sadly and quietly explained to him where she thought she had gone wrong, he had felt an overwhelming surge of sympathy for her. Indeed such had been his awareness of her vulnerability that day, so fierce his determination to protect her whenever possible from future disappointment, that he would willingly have shot the examiner who had been allotted the unavoidable task of reporting adversely on his wife's incompetence.

The glass was empty – the bottle was empty; and Thomas Bowman walked slowly but steadily down the stairs, the empty bottle in his left hand, the letter in his right. The car keys were on the kitchen table, and he picked them up and put on his mackintosh. Before getting into the Metro, he inserted the bottle beneath the four or five bundles of kitchen refuse which almost filled the larger of the two dustbins standing beside the garden shed. Then he drove off: there was one very simple little job he would do immediately.

It was only a mile or so to his place of work in

Chipping Norton, and as he drove he was conscious of the surprisingly clear-cut logicality of what he was proposing to do. It was only when he'd returned some fifteen minutes later to Charlbury Drive and replaced the letter in the handbag that he became fully aware of the blazing hatred he was feeling against the man, whoever he was, who had robbed him of his wife's affection and fidelity; a man who hadn't even got the guts to sign his name.

The woman with the grey handbag stood at the grave-side, the purplish-yellow clay sucking and clinging to her sensible shoes. The rain had now almost stopped, and the fresh-faced young vicar intoned the interment rites with unrushed and edifying dignity. From the snatches of conversation she had heard, Margaret Bowman learned that the old fellow had been with the Allied spearhead on the Normandy beaches and that he had fought right through to VE Day. And when one of his old colleagues from the British Legion had thrown a Remembrance Day poppy down on to the top of the coffin lid, she had felt the tears welling up at the back of her eyes; and before she could turn her head away (though no one noticed it) a great blobby tear had splashed down on her gloves.

'That's it, then!' said the woman in the yellow boots. 'No port and ham sandwiches today, I'm afraid.'

'Do they usually have that after funerals?'

'Well, you need something to cheer you up. Specially on a day like this.'

Margaret was silent, and remained so until she got into the car.

'Would you like to nip along to the pub?' asked her companion.

'No. I'd better not. I'd better get home I think.'

'You're not going to cook him a meal, are you?'

'I said I'd get us a snack when I got in,' she said, rather weakly.

The yellow-booted driver made no further attempt to influence the course of events: it would be sensible, she knew, to get her nervous-looking passenger home as quickly as possible and then go and join some of the others at the local.

Margaret Bowman wiped her shoes on the front door mat and slid her latchkey into the Yale lock.

'I'm ho-ome,' she called.

But she received no reply. She looked quickly into the kitchen, the lounge, the bedroom – and then the spare room: but he wasn't there, and she was glad. The Metro hadn't been in the drive when she had come in; but he might of course have driven it into the garage out of the rain. More likely though he'd driven down to the local for a drink – and if he had, she was glad about that, too. In the spare room she opened the door of the wardrobe, picked up her handbag, and looked inside it: obviously she needn't have worried at all, and she began to wish she'd agreed to join her fellow mourners for a consolatory gin at the Black Horse. But that didn't really matter. The pile of shoe boxes on the right looked rather precariously askew and she squared them into a neater stack. In all, it was a great relief, and she promised herself that she would be far more careful in the future.

She reheated the leftovers from the chicken risotto she'd cooked the previous evening, but the few mouthfuls she managed to swallow tasted like the Dead Sea apples. What a mess she was in! What an unholy, desperate mess she'd landed herself in! She sat in the lounge and listened to the one o'clock news, and learned that the pound had perked up a little overnight on the Tokyo Stock Exchange. Unlike her heart. She turned on the television and watched the first two races from Newbury without having any recollection whatsoever of which horses had been first past the post. It was only after the third race had similarly bypassed her consciousness that she heard the squeak of the Metro's brakes on the drive. He kissed her lightly on the cheek, and his voice sounded surprisingly sober as he asked a few perfunctory questions about the funeral. But he had been drinking heavily, she could tell that; and she was not one whit surprised when he declared that he would have a lie-down for the remainder of the afternoon.

But Thomas Bowman rested little that Saturday afternoon, for a plan of action had already begun to form in his mind. The room at the post office housing the Xerox machine had been empty; and after copying the letter he had stood there looking out at the fleet of postal vans in the rear park. A small post office van (he had never quite seen things this way before) was as anonymous as any vehicle could be: no passer-by was interested in the identity of its driver, hemmed in as the latter was (from all but a directly frontal encounter) by the closed side of the secretive little red van that could creep along unobtrusively from one parking point to the next, immune from the tickets of the predatory traffic wardens who prowled the busier streets of Oxford. In the letter, the man who was making such a misery of Margaret's life had begged her to meet him at ten minutes to one on Monday outside the Summertown Library in South Parade – and yes! he, Tom Bowman, would be there too. There would be no real problem about borrowing one of the vans; he could fix that. Furthermore, he had often picked up Margaret, before she had passed her test, along exactly that same road, and he remembered perfectly clearly that there was a little post office right on the corner of South Parade and Middle Way, with a post-box just outside. There could hardly have been a more suitable spot . . .

Suddenly the thought struck him: how long had the letter been in her bag? There was no date on the letter – no way at all of telling which particular Monday was meant. Had it been *last* Monday? There was no way he could be certain about things; and yet he had the strong conviction that the letter, presumably addressed to her at work, had been received only a day or so previously. Equally, he felt almost certain that Margaret was going to do exactly what the man had asked her. On both counts, Thomas Bowman was correct.

*

In the wing-mirror at ten minutes to one the following Monday he could see Margaret walking towards him and he leaned backwards as she passed, no more than two or three yards away. A minute later a Maestro stopped very briefly just ahead of him, outside the Summertown Library, the driver leaning over to open the passenger door, and then to accelerate away with Margaret Bowman seated beside him.

The post office van was three cars behind when the Maestro came to the T-junction at the Woodstock Road, and at that moment a train of events was set in motion which would result in murder – a murder planned with slow subtlety and executed with swift ferocity.

CHAPTER THREE

December

'I have finished another year,' said God,
'In grey, green, white, and brown;
I have strewn the leaf upon the sod,
Sealed up the worm within the clod,
And let the last sun down.'

(THOMAS HARDY, *New Year's Eve*)

THE TREE-LINED BOULEVARD of St Giles' is marked at three or four points by heavy cast-iron street-plaques (the latter painted white on a black background) that were wrought at Lucy's foundry in nearby Jericho. And Oxford being reckoned a scholarly city, the proper apostrophe appears after the final 's': indeed, if a majority vote were to be taken in the English Faculty, future signwriters would be exhorted to go for an extra 's', and print 'St Giles's'. But few of the leading characters who figure in the following chronicle were familiar with Fowler's advice over the difficulties surrounding the possessive case, for they were people who, in the crude distinction so often drawn in the city, would be immediately – and correctly – designated as 'Town' rather than 'Gown'.

At the northern end of St Giles', where in a triangle of grass a stone memorial pays tribute to the dead of two world wars, the way divides into the Woodstock Road, to the left, and the Banbury Road, to the right. Taking the second of these two roads (the road, incidentally, in which Chief Inspector Morse has lived these many years) the present-day visitor will find, after he has walked a few hundred yards, that he is viewing a fairly homogeneous stretch of buildings – buildings which may properly be called 'Venetian Gothic' in style: the houses have pointed arches over their doorways, and pointed arches over their clustered windows which are themselves vertically bisected or trisected by small columns of marble. It is as though Ruskin had been looking over the shoulders of the architects as they ruled and compassed their designs in the 1870s. Most of these houses (with their yellowish-beige bricks and the purple-blue slates of their roofs) may perhaps appear to the modern eye as rather severe and humour-less. But such an assessment would be misleading: attractive bands of orange brick serve to soften the ecclesiastical discipline of many of these great houses, and over the arches the pointed contours are re-emphasized by patterns of orange and purple, as though the old harlot of the Mediterranean had painted on her eye-shadow a little too thickly.

This whole scene changes as the visitor walks further northwards past Park Town, for soon he finds houses built of a cheerful orange-red brick that gives an immediate impression of warmth and good fellowship after the slightly forbidding façades of the Venetian wedge. Now the roofs are of red tile, and the paint-work around the stone-plinthed windows of an almost uniform white. The architects, some fifteen years older now, and no longer haunted by the ghost of Ruskin, drew the tops of their windows, sensibly and simply, in a straight horizontal. And thus it is that the housing for about half a mile or so north of St Giles' exhibits the influences of its times – times in which the first batches of College Fellows left the cloisters and the quads to marry and multiply, and to employ cohorts of maids and under-maids and tweeny maids in the spacious suburban properties that slowly spread northward along the Banbury and Woodstock Roads in the last decades of the nineteenth century – their annual progress leaving its record no less surely than the annular tracings of a sawn-through tree of mighty girth.

Betwixt the two rings sketched briefly above, and partaking something of each, stands the Haworth Hotel. It will not be necessary to describe this building – or, rather, these buildings – in any great detail at this point, but a few things should be mentioned immedi-ately. When (ten years since) the house had been put on the market, the successful purchaser had been one John Binyon, an erstwhile factory-hand from Leeds who had one day invested a £1 Treble Chance stake on the Pools, and who (to the incredulity of the rest of the nation) had thought fit to presume, in an early round of the FA Cup, that the current leaders of the First Division would be unable to defeat a lowly bunch of non-league part-time no-hopers from the Potteries –

Binyon's reward for such effrontery being a jackpot prize of £450,000 from Littlewoods. The large detached residence (first named the Three Swans Guest House and then the Haworth Hotel) had been his initial purchase – a building that paid tribute both to the staid Venetian planner of the 1880s and to his gayer rosy-fingered colleague of the 1890s. Yellow-bricked, red-roofed, the tops of doors and windows now compromised to gentle curves, the house openly proclaimed its divided loyalties in a quietly genteel manner, standing back from the road some ten yards or so with a slightly apologetic air, as if awaiting with only partial confidence the advent of social acceptability. After a few disappointing months, trade began to pick up for Binyon, and then to prosper most satisfactorily; after two years of a glorified B & B provision, the establishment was promoted to the hotel league, boasting now a fully licensed restaurant, colour-TV'd and showered or bathroomed accommodation, and a small exercise room for fitness fanatics; and four years after this, the proprietor had been able to stand under his own front porch and to look up with pride at the yellow sign which proclaimed that the AA had deemed it appropriate to award the Haworth Hotel one of its stars. Thereafter such was mine host's continued success that he was soon deciding to expand his operations – in two separate directions. First, he was able to purchase the premises immediately adjacent on the south side, in order to provide (in due course and after considerable renovation) a readily accessible annexe for the increasingly large number of tourists during the spring and summer seasons. Second, he began to implement his growing conviction that much of the comparatively slack period (especially weekends and holidays) from October to March could be revitalized by a series of tastefully organized special-rate functions. And it was for this reason that a half-page advertisement for the Haworth Hotel appeared (now for the third year running) in the 'Winter Breaks with Christmas and New Year Bonanzas' brochures which were to be seen on the racks of many a travel agent in the autumn of the year in which our story begins. And in order that the reader may get the flavour of the special features which attracted those men and women we are to meet in the following pages we reproduce below the prospectus in which the hotel was willing to offer 'at prices decidedly too difficult to resist' for a three-day break over the New Year.

TUESDAY

NEW YEAR'S EVE

I2.30 p.m. Sherry reception! John and Catherine Binyon extend a happy welcome to as many of their guests as can make this early get-together.

I.00 p.m. Buffet lunch: a good time for more introductions – or reunions.

The afternoon will give you the opportunity for strolling down – only ten minutes' walk to Carfax! – into the centre of our beautiful University City. For those who prefer a little lively competition to keep them busy and amused, tournaments are arranged for anyone fancying his (her!) skills at darts, snooker, table-tennis, Scrabble, and video games. Prizes!

5.00 p.m.   Tea and biscuits: nothing — but nothing! — else will be available. Please keep a keen edge on your appetite for...

7.30 p.m.   OUR GRAND FANCY DRESS DINNER PARTY.

It will be huge fun if everyone — yes, everyone! — comes to the dinner in fancy dress. But *please* don't think that we shall be any less liberal with the pre-prandial cocktails if you can't. This year's theme is 'The Mystery of the East', and for those who prefer to improvise their costumes our own Rag Bag will be available in the games room throughout the afternoon.

10.00 p.m.   Fancy Dress Judging: Prizes!! — continuing with live Cabaret and Dancing to keep you in wonderful spirits until...

Midnight —   Champagne! Auld Lang Syne! Bed!!!
1.00 a.m.

WEDNESDAY

NEW YEAR'S DAY

8.30–   Continental Breakfast (quietly please, for the
10.30 a.m. benefit of any of us — all of us! — with a mild hangover).

10.45 a.m.   CAR TREASURE-HUNT, with clues scattered round a care-free, car-free (as we hope) Oxford. There are plenty of simple instructions, so you'll never get lost. Be adventurous! And get out for a breath of fresh air! (Approximately one and a half hours to complete.) Prizes!!

1.00 p.m.   English Roast Beef Luncheon.

2.00 p.m.   TOURNAMENTS once more for those who have the stamina; and the chance of an afternoon nap for those who haven't.

4.30 p.m.   Devonshire Cream Tea.

6.30 p.m.   Your pantomime coach awaits to take you to *Aladdin* at the Apollo Theatre.
        There will be a full buffet awaiting you on your return, and you can dance away the rest of the evening at the DISCO (live music from Paper Lemon) until the energy (though not the bar!) runs out.

THURSDAY

9.00 a.m.   Full English Breakfast — available until 10.30 a.m. The last chance to say your farewells to your old friends and your new ones, and to promise to repeat the whole enjoyable process again next year!

Of course (it is agreed) such a prospectus would not automatically appeal to every sort and condition of humankind. Indeed, the idea of spending New Year's

Eve being semi-forcibly cajoled into participating in a darts match, or dressing up as one of the Samurai, or even of being expected *de rigueur* to wallow in the company of their fellow men, would drive some solid citizens into a state of semi-panic. And yet, for the past two years, many a couple had been pleasingly surprised to discover how much, after the gentlest nudge of persuasion, they had enjoyed the group activities that the Binyons so brashly presented. Several couples were now repeating the visit for a second time; and one couple for a third – although it is only fair to add that neither member of this unattractive duo would ever have dreamed of donning a single item of fancy dress, delighting themselves only, as they had done, in witnessing what they saw as the rather juvenile imbecilities of their fellow guests. For the simple truth was that almost all the guests required surprisingly little, if any, persuasion to dress up for the New Year's Eve party – not a few of them with brilliant, if bizarre effect. And such (as we shall see) was to be the case this year, with several of the guests so subtly disguised, so cleverly bedecked in alien clothing, that even long-standing acquaintances would have recognized them only with the greatest difficulty.

Especially the man who was to win the first prize that evening.

Yes, especially him.

CHAPTER FOUR

December 30th/31st

The feeling of sleepiness when you are not in bed, and can't get there, is the meanest feeling in the world.

(E.W. HOWE, *Country Town Sayings*)

WHENEVER SHE FELT tired – and that was usually in the early hours of the evening – the almost comically large spherical spectacles which framed the roundly luminous eyes of Miss Sarah Jonstone would slowly slip further and further down her small and neatly geometrical nose. At such times her voice would (in truth) sound only perfunctorily polite as she spoke into whichever of the two ultramodern phones happened to be purring for her expert attention; at such times, too, some of the belated travellers who stood waiting to sign the register at the Haworth Hotel would perhaps find her expression of welcome a thing of somewhat mechanical formality. But in the eyes of John Binyon, this same slightly fading woman of some forty summers could do little, if anything, wrong. He had appointed her five years previously: first purely as a glorified receptionist; subsequently (knowing a real treasure when he spotted one) as his unofficial 'manageress' –

although his wife Catherine (an awkward, graceless woman) had still insisted upon her own name appearing in that senior-sounding capacity on the hotel's general literature, as well as in the brochures announcing bargain breaks for special occasions.

Like Easter, for example.

Or Whitsun.

Or Christmas.

Or, as we have seen, like New Year.

With Christmas now over, Sarah Jonstone was looking forward to her official week's holiday – a whole week off from everything, and especially from the New Year festivities – the latter, for some reason, never having enthused her with rapture unconfined.

The Christmas venture was again likely to be oversubscribed, and this fact had been the main reason – though not quite the only reason – why John Binyon had strained every nerve to bring part of the recently purchased, if only partially developed, annexe into premature use. He had originally applied for planning permission for a single-storey linking corridor between the Haworth Hotel and this adjoining freehold property. But although the physical distance in question was only some twenty yards, so bewilderingly complex had proved the concomitant problems of potential subsidence, ground levels, drains, fire exits, goods access and gas mains, that he had abandoned his earlier notions of a formal merger and had settled for a self-standing addendum physically separated from the parent hotel. Yet even such a limited ambition was proving (as Binyon saw it) grotesquely expensive; and a long-term token of such expenditure was the towering yellow crane which stood like some enormous capital Greek Gamma in what had earlier been the chrysanthemumed and foxgloved garden at the rear of the newly acquired property. From late August, the dust ever filtering down from the planked scaffolding had vied, in degrees of irritation, with the daytime continuum of a revolving cement mixer and the clanks and hammerings which punctuated all the waking and working hours. But as winter had drawn on – and especially during the record rainfall of November – such inconveniences had begun to appear, in retrospect, as little more than the mildest irritancies. For now the area in which the builders worked day by day was becoming a morass of thick-clinging, darkish-orange mud, reminiscent of pictures of Passchendaele. The mud was getting everywhere: it caked the tyres of the workmen's wheelbarrows; it plastered the surfaces of the planks and the duckboards which lined the site and linked its drier spots; and (perhaps most annoying of all) it left the main entrance to the hotel, as well as the subsidiary entrance to the embryo annexe, resembling the approaches to a milking parlour in the Vale of the Great Dairies. A compromise was clearly called for over the hotel tariffs, and Binyon promptly amended the Christmas and New Year brochures to advertise the never-to-be-repeated bargain of 15 per cent off rates for the rooms in the main hotel, and 25 per cent (no less!) off the rates for the three double rooms and the one single room now available on the ground floor of the semi-completed annexe. And indeed it *was* a bargain: no workmen; no noise; no real inconvenience whatsoever over these holiday periods – except for that omnipresent mud . . .

The net result of these difficulties, and of further foul weather in early December, had been that, in spite of daily Hooverings and daily scrapings, many rugs and carpets and stretches of linoleum were so sadly in need of a more general shampoo after the departure of the Christmas guests that it was decided to put into operation a full-scale clean-up on the 30th in readiness for the arrival of the New Year contingent – or the majority of it – at lunchtime on the 31st. But there were problems. It was difficult enough at the best of times to hire waitresses and bedders and charladies. But when, as now, extra help was most urgently required; and when, as now, two of the regular cleaning women were stricken with influenza, there was only one thing for it: Binyon himself, his reluctant spouse Catherine, Sarah Jonstone, and Sarah's young assistant-receptionist, Caroline, had been called to the colours early on the 30th; and (armed with their dusters, brushes, squeegees, and Hoovers) had mounted their attack upon the blighted premises to such good effect that by the mid-evening of the same day all the rooms and the corridors in both the main body of the hotel and in the annexe were completely cleansed of the quaggy, mire-caked traces left behind by the Christmas revellers, and indeed by their predecessors. When all was done, Sarah herself had seldom felt so tired, although such unwonted physical labour had not – far from it! – been wholly unpleasant for her. True, she ached in a great many areas of her body which she had forgotten were still

potentially operative, especially the spaces below her
ribs and the muscles just behind her knees. But such
physical activity served to enhance the delightful prospect of her imminent holiday; and to show the world
that she could live it up with the rest and the best of
them, she had wallowed in a long 'Fab-Foam' bath
before ringing her only genuine friend, Jenny, to say
that she had changed her mind, was feeling fine and
raring to go, and would after all be delighted to come
to the party that same evening at Jenny's North Oxford
flat (only a stone's throw, as it happened, from Morse's
own small bachelor property). Jenny's acquaintances,
dubiously moral though they were, were also (almost
invariably) quite undoubtedly interesting; and it was at
1.20 a.m. precisely the following morning that a paun-
chy, middle-aged German with a tediously repeated
passion for the works of Thomas Mann had suddenly
asked a semi-intoxicated Sarah (yes, just like that!) if
she would like to go to bed with him. And in spite of
her very brief acquaintance with the man, it had been
only semi-unwillingly that she had been dragged off to
Jenny's spare room where she had made equally brief
love with the hirsute lawyer from Bergisch Gladbach.
She could not remember too clearly how she had finally
reached her own flat in Middle Way – a road (as the
careful reader will remember) which stretches down
into South Parade, and at the bottom of which stands a
post office.

At nine o'clock the same morning, the morning of
the 31st, she was awakened by the insistent ringing of
her doorbell; and drawing her dressing gown round

her hips, she opened the door to find John Binyon on the doorstep: Caroline's mother (Sarah learned) had just rung to say that her daughter had the flu, and would certainly not be getting out of bed that day – let alone getting out of the house; the Haworth Hotel was in one almighty fix; could Sarah? would Sarah? it would be well worth it – very much so – if Sarah could put in a couple of extra days, please! And stay the night, of course – as Caroline had arranged to do, in the nice little spare room at the side, the one overlooking the annexe.

Yes. If she could help out, of course she would! The only thing she *couldn't* definitely promise was to stay awake. Her eyelids threatened every second to close down permanently over the tired eyes, and she was only half aware, amidst his profuse thanks, of the palms of his hands on her bottom as he leaned forward and kissed her gently on the cheek. He was, she knew, an inveterate womanizer; but curiously enough she found herself unable positively to dislike him; and on the few occasions he had tested the temperature of the water with her he had accepted without rancour or bitterness her fairly firm assurance that for the moment it was little if anything above freezing point. As she closed the door behind Binyon and went back to her bedroom, she felt a growing sense of guilt about her early morning escapade. It had been those wretched (beautiful!) gins and Campari that had temporarily loosened the girdle round her robe of honour. But her sense of guilt was, she knew, not occasioned just by the lapse itself, but by the anonymous, mechanical nature of that lapse. Jenny had been utterly delighted, if wholly flab-bergasted, by the unprecedented incident; but Sarah herself had felt immediately saddened and diminished in her own self-estimation. And when finally she had returned to her flat, her sleep had been fitful and unrefreshing, the eiderdown perpetually slipping off her single bed as she had tossed and turned and tried to tell herself it didn't matter.

Now she took two Disprin, in the hope of dispelling her persistent headache, washed and dressed, drank two cups of piping hot black coffee, packed her toilet bag and night-clothes, and left the flat. It was only some twelve minutes' walk down to the hotel, and she decided that the walk would do her nothing but good. The weather was perceptibly colder than the previous day: heavy clouds (the forecasters said) were moving down over the country from the north, and some moderate falls of snow were expected to reach the Midlands by the early afternoon. During the previous week the bookmakers had made a great deal of money after the tenth consecutive non-white Christmas; but they must surely have stopped taking any more bets on a white New Year, since such an eventuality was now beginning to look like a gilt-edged certainty.

Not that Sarah Jonstone had ever thought of laying a bet with any bookmaker, in spite of the proximity of the Ladbrokes office in Summertown which she passed almost daily on her way to work. Passed it, indeed, again now, and stared (surely, far too obviously!) at the man who had just emerged, eyes downcast, from one of the swing-doors folding a pink, oblong betting slip into his wallet. How extraordinarily strange life could become on occasions! It was just like meeting a word in the English language for the very first time, and then – lo and behold! – meeting exactly the same word for the *second* time almost immediately thereafter. She had seen this same man, for the first time, the previous evening as she had walked up to Jenny's flat at about 9.30 p.m.: middle-aged; greyish-headed; balding; a man who once might have been slim, but who was now apparently running to the sort of fat which strained the buttons on his shabby-looking beige raincoat. *Why* had she looked at him so hard on that former occasion? *Why* had she recorded certain details about him so carefully in her mind? She couldn't tell. But she did know that this man, in his turn, had looked at *her*, however briefly, with a look of intensity which had been slightly (if pleasurably) disturbing.

Yet the man's cursory glance had been little more than a gesture of approbation for the high cheekbones that had thrown the rest of her face into a slightly mysterious shadow under the orange glare of the street lamp which illuminated the stretch of road immediately outside his bachelor flat. And after only a few yards, he had virtually forgotten the woman as he stepped out with a purpose in his stride towards his nightly assigna-tion at the Friar.

CHAPTER FIVE

Tuesday, December 31st

Serious sport has nothing to do with fair play. It is
bound up with hatred, jealousy, boastfulness, and disre-
gard of all the rules.

(GEORGE ORWELL, *Shooting an Elephant*)

IN VIEW OF the events described in the previous
chapter, it is not surprising that from the start of
subsequent police investigations Sarah Jonstone's memories should have resembled a disorderly card index,
with times and people and sequences sometimes hopelessly confused. Interview with one interrogator had
been followed by interview with another, and the truth
was that her recollection of some periods of December
31st had grown as unreliable as a false and faithless
lover.

Until about 11.30 a.m. she spent some time in the
games room: brushing down the green baize on the
snooker table; putting up the ping-pong net; rep-
olishing the push-penny board; checking up on the
Monopoly, Scrabble and Cluedo sets; and putting into
their appropriate niches such items as cues, dice, bats,
balls, chalk, darts, cards, and scoring pads. She spent

some time, too, in the restaurant; and was in fact helping to set up the trestles and spread the tablecloths for the buffet lunch when the first two guests arrived – guests signed in, as it happened, by a rather poorly and high-temperatured Mrs Binyon herself in order to allow Sarah to nip upstairs to her temporary bedroom and change into regulation long-sleeved cream-coloured blouse, close-buttoned to the chin, and regulation mid-calf, tightly fitting black skirt which (Sarah would have been the first to admit) considerably flattered waist, hips, thighs and calves alike.

From about noon onwards, guests began to arrive regularly, and there was little time, and little inclination, for needless pleasantries. The short-handed staff may have been a little short-tempered here and there – particularly with each other; but the frenetic to-ings and fro-ings were strangely satisfying to Sarah Jonstone that day. Mrs Binyon kept out of the way for the most part, confining her questionable skills to restaurant and kitchen before finally retiring to bed; whilst Mr Binyon, in between lugging suitcases along corridors and up stairs, had already repaired one squirting radiator, one flickering TV and one noisily dripping bath tap, before discovering in early afternoon that some of the disco equipment was malfunctioning, and spending the next hour seeking to beg, cajole and bribe anyone with the slightest knowledge of circuits and switches to save his hotel from imminent disaster. Such (not uncommon) crises meant that Sarah was called upon to divide her attention mainly between Reception – a few guests had rung to say that the bad weather might delay their arrival – and the games room.

Oh dear – the games room!

The darts (Sarah soon saw) was not going to be one of the afternoon's greater successes. An ex-publican from East Croydon, a large man with the facility of lobbing his darts into the treble-twenty with a sort of languid regularity, had only two potential challengers for the championship title; and one of these could hardly be said to pose a major threat – a small, ageing charlady from somewhere in the Chilterns who shrieked with juvenile delight whenever one of her darts actually managed to stick in the board instead of the wooden surround. On the other hand, the Cluedo players appeared to be settling down quite nicely – until one of the four children booked in for the festivities reported a 'Colonel Mustard' so badly dog-eared and a 'Conservatory' so sadly creased that each of the two cards was just as easily recognizable from the back as from the front. Fortunately the knock-out Scrabble competition, which was being keenly and cleanly played by a good many of the guests, had reached the final before any real dissension arose, and that over both the spelling and the admissibility of 'Caribbean'. (What an unpropitious omen *that* had been!) But these minor worries could hardly compare with the consternation caused on the Monopoly front by a swift-fingered checker-out from a Bedford super-market whose palm was so extraordinarily speedy in the recovery of the two dice thrown from the cylindrical cup that her opponents had little option but to accept,

without ever seeing the slightest evidence, her instanta-
neously enunciated score, and then to watch helplessly
as this sharp-faced woman moved her little counter
along the board to whichever square seemed of the
greatest potential profit to her entrepreneurial designs.
No complaint was openly voiced at the time; but the
speed with which she bankrupted her real-estate rivals
was later a matter of some general dissatisfaction – if
also of considerable amusement. Her prize, though,
was to be only a bottle of cheap, medium-sweet sherry;
and since she did not look the sort of woman who
would ever own a real-life hotel in Park Lane or
Mayfair, Sarah had said nothing, and done nothing,
about it. The snooker and the table-tennis tournaments
were happily free from any major controversy; and a
friendly cheer in mid-afternoon proclaimed that the
ageing charlady from the Chilterns (who appeared to
be getting on very nicely thank-you with the ex-publican
from East Croydon) had at last managed to hit the
dartboard with three consecutive throws.

Arbiter, consultant, referee, umpire – Sarah Jonstone was acquitting herself well, she thought, as she
emulated the impartiality of Solomon that raw but not
unhappy afternoon. Especially so since she had been
performing, indeed was still performing, a contempor-
aneous role at the reception desk.

In its main building, the Haworth Hotel boasted
sixteen bedrooms for guests – two family rooms, ten
double rooms and four single rooms – with the now
partially opened annexe offering a further three double
rooms and one single room. The guest-list for the New

Year festivities amounted to thirty-nine, including four children; and by latish afternoon all but two couples and one single person had registered at the desk, just to the right of the main entrance, where Sarah's large spectacles had been slowly slipping further and further down her nose. She'd had one glass of dry sherry, she remembered that; and one sausage roll and one glass of red wine – between half-past one and two o'clock, that had been. But thereafter she'd begun to lose track of time almost completely (or so it appeared to those who questioned her so closely afterwards). Snow had been falling in soft, fat flakes since just before midday, and by dusk the ground was thickly covered, with the white crystalline symbols of the TV weatherman portending further heavy falls over the whole of central and southern England. And this was probably the reason why very few of the guests – none, so far as Sarah was aware – had ventured out into Oxford that afternoon, although (as she later told her interrogators) it would have been perfectly possible for any of the guests to have gone out (or for others to have come in) without her noticing the fact, engaged as she would have been for a fair proportion of the time with form-filling, hotel documentation, directions to bedrooms, general queries, and the rest. Two new plumbing faults had further exercised the DIY skills of the proprietor himself that afternoon; yet when he came to stand beside her for a while after the penultimate couple had signed in, he looked reasonably satisfied.

'Not a bad start, eh, Sarah?'

'Not bad, Mr Binyon,' she replied quietly.

She had never taken kindly to *too* much familiarity over Christian names, and 'John' would never have fallen easily from those lips of hers – lips which were slightly fuller than any strict physiognomical proportion would allow; but lips which to John Binyon always looked softly warm and eminently kissable.

The phone rang as he stood there, and she was a little surprised to note how quickly he pounced upon the receiver.

'Mr Binyon?' It was a distanced female voice, but Sarah could hear no more: the proprietor clamped the receiver tight against his ear, turning away from Sarah as he did so.

'But you're not as sorry as I am!' he'd said . . .

'No – no chance,' he'd said . . .

'Look, can I ring you back?' he'd said. 'We're a bit busy here at the minute and I could, er, I could look it up and let you know . . .'

Sarah thought little about the incident.

It was mostly the *names* of the people, and the association of those names with the *faces*, that she couldn't really get fixed in her mind with any certitude. Some had been easy to remember: Miss Fisher, for example – the embryo property tycoon from Bedford; Mr Dods, too ('Ornly t'one "d" in t'middle, lass!') – she remembered *his* face very clearly; Fred Andrews – the mournful-visaged snooker king from Swindon; Mr and Mrs J. Smith from Gloucester – a marital appellation not unfamiliar to anyone who has sat at a hotel reception desk for more than a few hours. But the others? It really was very difficult for her to match the names with

37

the faces. The Ballards from Chipping Norton? *Could* she remember the Ballards from Chipping Norton? They must, judging from the register, have been the very last couple to sign in, and Sarah *thought* she could remember Mrs Ballard, shivering and stamping her snow-caked boots in front of Reception, looking not unlike an Eskimo determined to ward off frostbite. Names and faces ... faces and names ... names which were to echo again and again in her ears as first Sergeant Phillips, then Sergeant Lewis, and finally a distinctly brusque and hostile Chief Inspector Morse, had sought to reactivate a memory torpid with shock and far-spent with weariness. Arkwright, Ballard, Palmer, Smith ... Smith, Palmer, Ballard, Arkwright.

It was funny about names, thought Sarah. You could often tell what a person was like from a name. Take the Arkwright woman, for instance, who had cancelled her room, Annexe 4 – the drifting snow south of Solihull making motoring a perilous folly, it appeared. Doris Arkwright! With a name like that, she just had to be a suspicious, carefully calculating old crab-crumpet! And she wasn't coming – Binyon had just brought the message to her.

Minus one: and the number of guests was down to thirty-eight.

Oddly enough, one of the things very much on Sarah Jonstone's mind early that evening was the decision she had made (so authoritatively!) to allow 'Caribbean' in the Scrabble final. And she could hardly forget the matter, in view of a most strange coincidence. Later on in the evening, the judge for the fancy-dress competition would be asking whether another 'Caribbean' should be allowed, since one of the male entrants had gaily bedecked himself in a finely authentic Rastafarian outfit. 'The Mystery of the East' (the judge suggested) could hardly accommodate such an obviously West Indian interpretation? Yet (as one of the guests quietly pointed out) it wasn't really 'West Indian' at all – it was 'Ethiopian'; and Ethiopia had to be East in anyone's atlas – well, Middle East, anyway. Didn't it all depend, too (as another of the guests argued with some force), on exactly what this 'East' business meant, anyway: didn't it depend on exactly whereabouts on the globe one happened to be standing at any particular time? The upshot of this difference of opinion was that 'Caribbean' was accepted for a second time in the Haworth Hotel that New Year's Eve.

It would be a good many hours into New Year's Day itself before anyone discovered that the number of guests was down to thirty-seven.

CHAPTER SIX

December 31st/January 1st

Beware of all enterprises that require fancy clothes.

(THOREAU)

DURING THE TIMES in which these events are set, there occurred a quite spectacular renaissance in fancy-dress occasions of all types. In pubs, in clubs, in ballrooms, at discos, at dinner parties – it was as if a collective mania would settle upon men and women wherever they congregated, demanding that at fairly regular intervals each of them should be given an opportunity to bedeck the body in borrowed plumes and for a few hours to assume an entirely alien personality. Two years previously (the Haworth's first such venture) the New Year's party had taken 'What we were wearing when the ship went down' as its theme, with the emphasis very much upon the degree of imagination, humour and improvisation that could be achieved with a very minimum of props. The theme for the following New Year's Eve had been 'This Sporting Life'; and since this theme had been announced in the brochure, some of the guests had taken the challenge most seriously, had turned their backs on improvisation, and had brought appropriate costumes with them. This year, in accord with the temper of the times, participants had been given even wider scope than before, with ample time and opportunity to hire their chosen outfits and to acquire suitable make-up and accessories – in short, to take the whole thing far too seriously. The hotel's 'Rag Bag' still stood in the games room, but only one or two had rummaged through its contents that afternoon. After all, the current theme had been likewise pre-announced, and all the guests knew exactly what was coming; and, to be fair, in many cases the fancy-dress evening was one of the chief reasons for them choosing the Haworth Hotel in the first place. On such occasions, the greatest triumph would be registered when a person went through the first part of the evening – sometimes a good deal longer – totally unrecognized even by close acquaintances: a feat which Binyon himself had accomplished the previous year when only by a process of elimination had even his hotel colleagues finally recognized the face of their proprietor behind the bushy beard and beneath the Gloucestershire cricket-cap of Dr W.G. Grace.

This year the enthusiasm of the guests was such – all but six had presented themselves in various guises – that even Sarah, not by nature one of the world's obvious have-a-go extroverts, found herself wishing that she were one of the happy band drinking red or blue cocktails in the restaurant-cum-ballroom on the ground floor at the back of the hotel, where everything was now almost ready. The whole of the area was surprisingly warm, the radiators round the walls turned up to their maximum readings, and a log fire burning brightly in a large old grate that was simultaneously the delight of guests and the despair of management. But tonight the fire was dancing smokelessly and merrily, and the older folk there spoke of the times when their shadows had passed gigantic round the walls of their childhood, and when in the late hours of the night the logs had collapsed of a sudden in a firework of sparks. Abetting this fire, in a double illumination, were tall red candles, two on each of the tables, and all already lit, with the haloes that formed around them creating little pools of warm light amid the darkling, twinkling dining room, and reflecting their elongated yellow flames in the gleaming cutlery.

It would have been easiest to divide the original guest-list into three tables of thirteen; but in deference to inevitable superstition Binyon had settled for two tables of fourteen and one of eleven, with each place set only for two courses. At each place, a small white card denoted the seating arrangements for these first two courses, spouse duly positioned next to spouse; but each of these cards also had two numbers printed on it, denoting a different table for the third and fourth courses, and a different table again for the fifth and sixth. This system had been tried out the previous year; and although on that occasion one or two of the couples had failed to follow instructions too carefully, the social mix effected thereby had proved a huge success. The only real problem attendant upon such a system was the awkwardness of transferring side plates from one seat to another, but this had been solved by the supremely simple expedient of dispensing with rolls and butter altogether.

It was at about a quarter to eight (eating would begin at eight o'clock) when the nasty little episode occurred: Sarah could vouch for the time with reasonable confidence. One of the women guests from the annexe, one dressed in the black garb of a female adherent of the Ayatollah, informed Sarah in a voice muffled by the double veil of her yashmak that there was something rather unpleasant written on the wall of the Ladies' lavatory, and Sarah had accompanied this woman to inspect the offending graffito. And, yes, she agreed with the voice behind the veils that it was not really very nice at all: 'I'm nuts' had been daubed on the wall over one of the washbasins in a black felt pen; and underneath had been added 'So are Binyon's B—'. Oh dear! But it had taken only a few minutes with sponge and detergent to expunge these most distressing words – certainly to the point of illegibility.

The cocktails turned out to be a huge success, for even the most weirdly bedizened strangers were already beginning to mix together happily. Binyon himself, gaudily garbed as the Lord High Executioner, was making no attempt this year to cloak his identity, and in a kindly way (so Sarah thought, as she looked in briefly) was making a successful fuss of one of the children, a small-boned nervous little girl dressed up prettily in Japanese costume. The mystical lure of the Orient had clearly provoked a colourful response, and there were one or two immediate hits – the most stunning being a woman with a lissomly sinuous figure, whose Turkish belly-dancer's outfit (what little there was of it) was causing several pairs of eyes (besides Binyon's) to sparkle widely with fornicatory intent. There was, as far as Sarah could see, only one real embarrassment amongst the whole lot, and that in the form of the gaunt-faced snooker king from Swindon, who had turned up as a rather too convincing version of Gandhi – a Gandhi, moreover, clearly in the latter stages of one of his emaciating fasts. But even he appeared happy enough, holding a cocktail in one hand, and ever hitching up his loin-cloth with the other.

It would not be long now before the guests began to drift to their places, to start on the Fresh Grapefruit Cerisette – already laid out (to be followed by the Consommé au Riz); and Sarah picked up a Tequila Sunrise and walked back through to Reception, where she locked the front door of the hotel. Her head was aching slightly, and the last thing she wanted was a six-course meal. An early night was all she really craved for; and that (she told herself) was what she *would* have, after giving a hand (as she'd promised) with the Grilled Trout with Almonds and then with the Pork Chop Normandy. (The Strawberry Gâteau, the cheese and biscuits and the coffee, Binyon had assured her, would be no problem.) She had never herself been a big eater, and for this reason she was always a little vexed that she could put on weight so easily; and unlike the Mahatma, perhaps, she most certainly did not wish to face the new year with a little extra poundage.

The cocktail tasted good; and with ten or fifteen

minutes to spare before the grapefruit plates would need to be cleared Sarah lit one of the half-dozen cigarettes she allowed herself each day, enjoying the sensation as she sat back in her chair and inhaled deeply.

Ten minutes to eight.

It could have been only some two or three minutes later that she heard the noise, fairly near her. And suddenly, illogically – with the stillness of the half-lit, empty entrance hall somehow emphasized by the happy voices heard from the dining room – she experienced a sense of fear that prickled the roots of her honey-coloured hair. And then, equally suddenly, everything was normal once again. From the door of the Gents' lavatory there emerged a gaily accoutred personage who on any normal evening might justifiably have been the cause of some misgiving on her part; but upon whom she now bestowed a knowingly appreciative smile. It must have taken the man some considerable time to effect such a convincing transformation into a coffee-coloured, dreadlocked Rastafarian; and perhaps he hadn't quite finished yet, for even as he walked across to the dining room he was still dabbing his brown-stained hands with a white handkerchief that was now more chocolate than vanilla.

Sarah drank some more of the liberally poured cocktail – and began to feel good. She looked down at the only letter that had found its way into her tray that morning: it was from a Cheltenham lady thanking the hotel for the fact that her booking of a room had been answered with 'laudable expedition' ('very quickly', translated Sarah), but at the same time deploring the etiquette of these degenerate days that could allow the 'Dear Madam' of the salutation to be complemented by the 'Yours sincerely' of the valediction. Again, Sarah smiled to herself – the lady would probably turn out to be a wonderful old girl – and looked up to find the Lord High Executioner smiling down, in turn, at her.

'Another?' he suggested, nodding to the cocktail.

'Mm – that would be nice,' she heard herself say.

What had she remembered then? She could recall, quite certainly, clearing away after the soup course; picking up the supernumerary spoons and forks that marked the place of that pusillanimous spirit from Solihull, Doris Arkwright; standing by in the kitchen as a Pork Chop Normandy had slithered off its plate to the floor, to be replaced thither after a perfunctory wipe; drinking a third cocktail; dancing with the Lord High Executioner; eating two helpings of the gâteau in the kitchen; dancing, in the dim light of the ballroom, a sort of chiaroscuro cha-cha-cha with the mysterious 'Rastafarian' – the latter having been adjudged the winner of the men's fancy-dress prize; telling Binyon not to be so silly when he'd broached the proposition of a brief dive beneath the duvet in her temporary quarters; drinking a fourth cocktail, the colour of which she could no longer recall; feeling slightly sick; walking up the stairs to her bedroom before the singing of 'Auld Lang Syne'; feeling *very* sick; and finally finding herself in bed. Those were the pretty definite events of a crowded evening. ('But there must have been so many other little things, Miss Jonstone?') And there *were* other things, yes. She remembered, for example, the banging of so many doors once the music and the singing had finally ended – half-past midnight, it must have been – when standing by her window (alone!) she had seen the guests from the annexe walking back to their rooms: two of the women, their light-coloured raincoats wrapped around them, with the prize-winning Rastafarian between them, a hand on either shoulder; and behind that trio, another trio – the yashmak'd, graffiti-conscious woman, with a Samurai on one side and Lawrence of Arabia on the other; and bringing up the rear the Lord High Executioner, with a heavy, dark coat over his eastern robes. Yes! And she remembered quite clearly seeing all of them, including Binyon, go *into* the annexe, and then Binyon, fairly shortly afterwards, coming *out*, and fiddling for a moment or two with the Yale lock on the side door of the annexe – presumably to secure the inmates against any potential intruders.

It was just before 7 a.m. when Sarah woke, for a few seconds finding some difficulty in recalling exactly where she was. Then, it had been with a wholly childlike delight that on opening her curtains she saw the canopy of snow that enveloped everything – four or five inches of it on the ledge outside her window, and lodging heavily along the branches of the trees. The world outside looked so bitterly chill. But she was happily conscious of the square little radiator, now boiling hot, that made her room under the eaves so snugly warm; and through the frost-whorled window-panes she looked out once more at the deep carpet of snow: it was as if the Almighty had taken his brush, after the last few hours of the death-struck year, and painted the earth in a dazzling Dulux Super-White. Sarah wondered about slipping back into bed for a brief while, but decided against it. Her head was beginning to ache a little, and she knew there were some aspirin in the kitchen. In any case she'd promised to help with the breakfasts. Much better to get up – even to go out and walk profanely across the virgin snow. As far as could be seen, there were no footprints, no indentations whatsoever, in the smooth surface of snow that surrounded the strangely still hotel, and a line from a poem she'd always loved came suddenly to mind: 'All bloodless lay the untrodden snow . . .'

The water in the washbasin became very hot indeed after only ten or fifteen seconds, and she was taking her flannel from her washing bag when she noticed a creosote-looking stain on the palm of her right hand; and then noticed the same sort of stain on one of the fluffy white towels she must have used before going to bed. And, of course, she knew immediately where *that* had come from. Had that wretched Rastafarian stained her blouse as well, when his left hand had circled her waist (perhaps a fraction too intimately) above her black tight-fitting skirt? Yes! He had! Blast it! For a few minutes as her headache became gradually worse she moistened the offending patch on her cream blouse and cleaned off the stain as best she could. No one would notice it, anyway.

It was seven forty-five when she walked into the kitchen. Seemingly, she was the only person stirring in the whole hotel. And, had Sarah Jonstone known it at that time, there was a person in the same hotel who never would be seen to stir again. For in the room designated, on the key-hook board behind Reception, as 'Annexe 3', a man lay stiffly dead – the window of his ground-floor room thrust open, the radiator switched completely off, and the temperature around the body as icily frigid as an igloo's.

The end of the year had fallen cold; and the body that lay across the top of the coverlet on one of the twin beds in Annexe 3 was very, very cold indeed.

CHAPTER SEVEN

Wednesday, January 1st: p.m.

> But if he finds you and you find him,
> The rest of the world don't matter;
> For the Thousandth Man will sink or swim
> With you in any water.
>
> (RUDYARD KIPLING, *The Thousandth Man*)

FOR THE CHIEF Constable of Oxfordshire, a man internationally renowned for his handling of terrorist sieges, the new year dawned upon fewer problems than had been anticipated. With the much-publicized CND march from Carfax to Greenham Common badly hit by the weather, and with the First Division game between Oxford United and Everton inevitably postponed, many of the extra police drafted in for special duties in both the city and the county had not been required. There had been, it was true, a whole string of minor accidents along the A40, but no serious injuries and no serious hold-ups. Indeed, it had been a very gentle New Year's Day; and at 6.30 p.m. the Chief Constable was just about to leave his office on the second floor of the Kidlington Police HQ when Superintendent Bell rang from the City Police HQ in St

Aldates to ask whether among extra personnel available that day there happened to be any spare inspectors from the CID division.

The phone had been ringing for a good while before the sole occupant of the bachelor flat at the top of the Banbury Road in North Oxford turned down the mighty volume of the finale of *Die Walküre* and answered it.

'Morse!' he said curtly.

'Ah, Morse!' (The Chief Constable expected his voice to be instantly recognized, and it almost always was.) 'I suppose you've just staggered out of bed all ready for another night of debauchery?'

'A Happy New Year to you, too, sir!'

'Looks like being a pretty good new year for the crime rate, Morse: we've got a murder down at the bottom of your road. I'm assuming you had nothing to do with it, of course.'

'I'm on furlough, sir.'

'Well, never mind! You can make up the days later in January.'

'Or February,' mumbled Morse.

'Or February!' admitted the Chief Constable.

'Not tonight, I'm afraid, sir. I'm taking part in the final of the pub quiz round at the Friar.'

'I'm glad to hear others have got such confidence in your brains.'

'I'm quite good, really – apart from Sport and Pop Music.'

'Oh, I know that, Morse!' The Chief Constable was speaking very slowly now. 'And *I* have every confidence in your brains, as well.'

Morse sighed audibly into the phone and held his peace as the Chief Constable continued: 'We've got dozens of men here if you need 'em.'

'Is Sergeant Lewis on duty?' asked a Morse now fully resigned.

'Lewis? Ah yes! As a matter of fact he's on his way to pick you up now. I thought, you know, that er . . .'

'You're very kind, sir.'

Morse put down the phone and walked to the window where he looked down on the strangely quiet, muffled road. The Corporation lorries had gritted for a second time late that afternoon, but only a few carefully driven cars were intermittently crawling past along the icy surfaces. Lewis wouldn't mind coming out, though. In fact, thought Morse, he'd probably be only too glad to escape the first night of the new year television.

And what of Morse himself? There was perhaps just a hint of grim delight to be observed on his features as he saw the police car pull into the gutter in a spurt of deep slush, and waved to the man who got out of it – a thick-set, slightly awkward-looking man, for whom the only blemishes on a life of unexciting virtuousness were a gluttonous partiality for egg and chips, and a passion for fast driving.

Sergeant Lewis looked up to the window of the flat, and acknowledged Morse's gesture of recognition. And had Lewis been able to observe more closely at that moment he might have seen that in the deep shadows of Morse's rather cold blue eyes there floated some reminiscences of an almost joyful satisfaction.

CHAPTER EIGHT

Wednesday, January 1st: p.m.

I therefore come before you armed with the delusions of adequacy with which so many of us equip ourselves.

(AIR VICE-MARSHAL A. D. BUTTON)

LEWIS PULLED IN behind the two other police cars outside the Haworth Hotel, where a uniformed constable in a black-and-white chequered hat stood outside the main entrance, with one of his colleagues, similarly attired, guarding the front door of the adjacent property further down the Banbury Road.

'Who's in charge?' asked Morse, of the first constable, as he passed through into the foyer, stamping the snow from his shoes on the doormat.

'Inspector Morse, sir.'

'Know where he is?' asked Morse.

'Not sure, sir. I've only just got here.'

'Know him by sight, do you?'

'I don't know him at all.'

Morse went on in, but Lewis tapped the constable on the shoulder and whispered in his ear: 'When you meet this Morse fellow, he's a *chief* inspector – all right? – and a nasty one at that! So watch your step, lad!'

'Famous pair, we are!' murmured Morse as the two of them stood at Reception, where in a small room at the back of the desk Sergeant Phillips of the City CID (Morse recognized him) stood talking to a pale-faced, worried-looking man who was introduced as Mr John Binyon, the hotel proprietor. And very soon Morse and Lewis knew as much – or as little – as anyone about the tragedy so recently discovered in his own hotel by the proprietor himself.

The two Anderson children had been putting the finishing touches to their snowman just as it was getting dark that afternoon when they were joined by their father, Mr Gerald Anderson. And it had been he who had observed that one of the rear windows on the ground floor of the annexe was open; and who had been vaguely uneasy about this observation, since the weather was raw, with a cutting wind sweeping down from the north. He had finally walked closer and seen the half-drawn curtains flapping in the icy draught – although he had not gone all the way up to the window, under which (as he'd noticed) the snow was still completely undisturbed. He had mentioned this fact to his wife once he was back in the hotel, and it was at her instigation that he reported his disquiet to the pro- prietor himself – at about 5 p.m., that was; with the result that the pair of them, Anderson and Binyon, had walked across to the annexe and along the newly carpeted corridor to the second bedroom on the right, where over the doorknob was hooked a notice, written in English, French, and German, instructing potential intruders that the incumbent was not to be disturbed.

After repeated knockings, Binyon had opened the door with his master-key, and had immediately discovered why the man they found there had been incapable (for some considerable time, it seemed) of responding to any knocking from within or to any icy blast from without.

For the man on the bed was dead and the room was cold as the grave.

The news of the murder was known almost immediately to everyone in the hotel; and despite Binyon's frenetic protestations, some few of the guests (including, it appeared, *everyone* from the annexe) had taken the law into their own hands, packed their belongings, strapped up their cases (and in one case not paid any part of the bill), and disappeared from the Haworth Hotel before Sergeant Phillips from St Aldates had arrived at about 5.40 p.m.

'You *what?*' bellowed Morse as Phillips explained how he'd allowed four more of the guests to leave the hotel when full names and addresses had been checked.

'Well, it was a very difficult situation, sir, and I thought—'

'Christ man! Didn't someone ever tell you that if you've got a few suspicious circumstances you're expected to hold on to a few of the *suspects*? And what do *you* do, Sergeant? You tell 'em all to bugger off!'

'I got all the details—'

'Bloody marvellous!' snapped Morse.

Binyon, who had been standing by in some embarrassment as Morse (not, it must be admitted, without just cause) lashed the luckless Phillips, decided to come to the rescue.

'It really was a very difficult situation, Inspector, and we thought—'

'*Thought?*' Morse's instantaneous repetition of the monosyllable sounded like a whiplashed retaliation for such impertinence, and it was becoming abundantly clear that he had taken an instant dislike to the hotel proprietor. 'Mr Binyon! They don't pay you, do they, for having any thoughts about this case? No? But they *do* pay *me*! They even pay Sergeant Phillips here; and if I was angry with him just now it was only because I basically respect what *he* thought and what he tried to do. But I shall be obliged if *you* will kindly keep your thoughts out of things until I ask for them – all right?'

In the latter part of this little homily, Morse's voice was as cool and as level as the snow upon which Sarah Jonstone had looked out early that same morning; and she herself as she sat silently at Reception was more than a little alarmed by this new arrival; more than a little upset by his harsh words. But gossip had it that the corpse found in the room called Annexe 3 had been horridly mutilated about the face; and she was relieved that the police seemed at least to have matched the gravity of the crime by sending a man from the higher echelons of its detective branch. But he was disturbingly strange, this man with the hard-staring, startling eyes – eyes that had at first reminded her of the more fanatical politicians, like Benn or Joseph or Powell, as she'd watched them on TV; eyes that seemed uncommunicative and unseeing, eyes fixed, it seemed, upon some distanced, spiritual shore. And yet that wasn't true, and she knew it; for after his initial ill-temper he had looked so directly and so daringly into her eyes that for a second or two she could have sworn that he was about to wink at her.

A man she'd seen three times now in three days!

Another man had come in – the humpbacked man she'd seen earlier – and he, too, was in Sarah's eyes one of the more unusual specimens of humankind. With a cigarette hanging down at forty-five degrees from a thin-lipped, mournful mouth, and with the few remaining strands of his lank, black hair plastered in parallels across a yellowish dome of a skull, anyone could perhaps be forgiven for supposing his profession to be that of a moderately unsuccessful undertaker. (Oddly enough, over the fifteen years they had known – and respected – each other, Morse had invariably addressed this police surgeon by his Christian name, whilst the surgeon had never addressed Morse by anything other than his surname.)

'I was here an hour ago,' began the surgeon.

'You want me to give you a medal or something?' said Morse.

'You in charge?'

'Yes.'

'Well, go and have a look at things. I'll be ready when you want me.'

Following closely behind Binyon and Phillips and Lewis, Morse was walking over to the annexe when he stopped halfway and gazed up at the giant crane, its arm outstretched some hundred and twenty feet above the ground as if in benediction, or perhaps in bane, upon one or other of the two blocks of buildings between which it was positioned.

'Not a job they'd get me on, Lewis,' he said, as his eyes went up towards the precarious-looking box at the top of the structure, in which, presumably, some operator would normally sit.

'No need, sir. You can operate those things from the bottom.' Lewis pointed to a platform, only some six feet above the ground, on which a series of knobbed levers stuck up at various angles through the iron floor. Morse nodded; and averted his eyes from the crane's nest atop the criss-crossed iron girders that stood out black against the heavy, darkened sky.

Through the side door of the annexe they proceeded, where Morse looked along the newly carpeted passage that stretched some ten to twelve yards in front of him, its terminus marked by pieces of boarding, nailed (not too professionally) across an aperture which would, in due course, lead through to the front entrance hall of the annexe. Morse strode to the far end of the corridor and looked through the temporary slats to the foyer beyond, where rickety-looking planks, resting on pairs of red bricks, were set across the recently cemented floor. Dust from such activities had filtered through, and was now lying, albeit lightly, on the surfaces just a few feet inside the completed section of the ground-floor annexe, and it seemed clear that there had been no recent entrance, and no recent exit, from that particular point. Morse turned, and for a few seconds looked back up the short corridor down which they had walked; looked at the marks of many muddy shoes (including their own) on the purple carpeting – the latter seeming to Morse almost as distasteful as the reproduction of the late Renoir, 'Les nues dans l'herbe', which hung on the wall to his right.

As he stood there, still looking back up to the side entrance, he noted the simple geography of the annexe. Four doors led off the corridor: to his right were those numbered 2 and 1; immediately opposite 1 was 4; and then, set back behind a narrow, uncarpeted flight of stairs (temporarily blocked off but doubtless leading to the hitherto undeveloped first floor) a door numbered 3. From what he had already learned, Morse could see little hope of lifting any incriminatory finger-prints from the doorknob of this last room which had been twisted quite certainly by Binyon and probably by others. Yet he looked at the knob with some care, and at the trilingual notice that was still hooked over it.

'There should be an umlaut over the "o" in "Storen",' said Morse.

'*Ja! Das sagen mir alle,*' replied Binyon.

Morse, whose only knowledge of German stemmed from his addiction to the works of Richard Wagner and Richard Strauss, and who was therefore supremely unfitted to converse in the language, decided that it would be sensible to say no more on the point; decided, too, that Binyon was not perhaps quite the nonentity that his weak-chinned appearance might seem to signify.

Inside Annexe 3, a door immediately to the right

gave access to a small, rather cramped toilet area, with a washbasin, a WC, and a small bath with shower attachment. In the bedroom itself, the main items of furniture were twin beds, pulled close together, with matching white coverlets; a dressing table opposite them, a TV set in the corner; and just to the left of the main door a built-in wardrobe. Yet it was not the furniture which riveted the attention of Morse and Lewis as they stood momentarily in the doorway. Across the further of the two beds, the one that stood only some three or four feet from the opened window, lay the body of a dead man. Morse, as he invariably did, recoiled from an immediate inspection of the corpse; yet he knew that he had to look. And an extraordinary oddity it was upon which he looked: a man dressed in Rastafarian clothes lay on his side, his face towards them, his head lying in a great, coldly clotted pool of blood, like red wine poured across the snow. The dead man's left hand was trapped beneath the body; but the right hand was clearly visible below the long sleeve of a light blue shirt; and it was – without any doubt – the hand of a white man.

Morse, now averting his eyes from this scene of gory mutilation, looked long and hard at the window, then at the TV set, and finally put his head inside the small washroom.

'You've got a good fingerprint man coming?' he asked Phillips.

'He's on his way, sir.'

'Tell him to have a go at the radiator, the TV, and the lever on the WC.'

'Anything else, sir?'

Morse shrugged. 'Leave it to him. I've never had much faith in fingerprints myself.'

'Oh, I don't know, sir—' began Phillips.

But Morse lifted his hand like a priest about to pronounce a benediction, and cut off whatever Phillips had intended to say. 'I'm not here to argue, lad!' He looked around again, and seemed just on the point of leaving Annexe 3 when he stepped back inside the room and opened the one drawer, and then the other, of the chest below the TV set, peering carefully into the corners of each.

'Were you expecting to find something?' asked Lewis quietly as he and Morse walked back across to the Haworth Hotel.

Morse shook his head. 'Just habit, Lewis. I once found a ten-pound note in a hotel in Tenby, that's all.'

CHAPTER NINE

Wednesday, January 1st: p.m.

The great advantage of a hotel is that it's a refuge from
home life.

(G. B. SHAW)

ON THEIR RETURN to the main building, Morse
himself addressed the assembled guests in the ballroom
area (not, as Lewis saw things, particularly impres-
sively), telling everyone what had happened (they knew
anyway), and asking everyone to be sure to tell the
police if they had any information which might be of
use (as if they wouldn't!).

None of those still remaining in the hotel appeared at
all anxious to return home prematurely. Indeed, it soon
became apparent to Lewis that the 'Annexe Murder' was,
by several kilometres, the most exciting event of most
lives hitherto; and that far from wishing to distance themselves physically from the scene of the crime, the majority
of the folk left in the hotel were more than happy to stay
where they were, flattered as they had been to be told
that their own recollections of the previous evening's
events might possibly furnish a key clue in solving the
murder which had been committed. None of these guests

appeared worried about the possibility of an indiscrimi-
nate killer being abroad in Oxford's semi-civilized acres –
a worry which would, in fact, have been totally unfounded.

Whilst Lewis began the documentation of the hotel
guests, Morse was to be seen sitting at the receipt of cus-
tom, with Sarah Jonstone to his right, looking through
the correspondence concerned with those annexe guests
whom (the duly chastened) Sergeant Phillips had earlier
blessed or semi-blessed upon their homeward ways.

A pale Sarah Jonstone, a nerve visibly twitching at
her left nostril, lit a cigarette, drew upon it deeply, and
then exhaled the rarefied smoke. Morse, who the
previous day (for the thousandth time) had rid himself
of the odious habit, turned to her with distaste.

'Your breath must smell like an old ashtray,' he said.

'Yes?'

'Yes!'

'Who to?'

'"To whom?", do you mean?'

'Do you want me to help you or not?' said Sarah
Jonstone, the skin around her cheekbones burning.

'Room 1?' asked Morse.

Sarah handed over the two sheets of paper, stapled
together, the lower sheet reading as follows:

29A Chiswick Reach
London, W4
20 Dec

Dear Sir(s)

My wife and I would like to book a double room –
preferably with double bed – for the New Year Offer your

hotel is advertising. If a suitable room is available, we look
forward to hearing from you.

> Yours faithfully,
> F. Palmer

On top of this originating handwritten letter was the
typewritten reply (ref JB-SJ) to which Morse now briefly
turned his attention:

Dear Mr Palmer,

Thank you for your letter of 20 Dec. Our New Year
programme has been extremely popular, and we are now
fully booked as far as the main hotel is concerned. But you
may be interested in the Special Offer (please see last page
of current brochure) of accommodation in one of the
rooms of our newly equipped annexe at three-quarters of
the normal tariff. In spite of a few minor inconveniences,
these rooms are, we believe, wonderfully good value, and
we very much hope that you and your wife will be able to
take advantage of this offer.

Please be sure to let us know immediately – preferably
by phone. The Christmas post is not likely to be 100 per
cent reliable.

Yours sincerely,

There was no further correspondence; but across the
top letter was a large tick in blue biro, with 'Accepted
23rd Dec' written beneath it.

'You remember them?' asked Morse.

'Not very well, I'm afraid.' She recalled (she
thought) a darkly attractive woman of about thirty or

so, and a smartly dressed, prosperous-looking man about ten years her senior, perhaps. But little else. And soon she found herself wondering whether the people she was thinking of were, in fact, the Palmer pair at all.

'Room 2?'

Here the documentary evidence Sarah produced was at an irreducible minimum: one sheet of hotel paper recorded the bare facts that a Mr Smith – a 'Mr J. Smith' – had rung on December 23rd and been told that there had been a late cancellation in the annexe, that a double room would now be available, and that written confirmation should be put in the post immediately.

'There's no confirmation here,' complained Morse.

'No. It was probably held up in the Christmas post.'

'But they came?'

'Yes.' Again, Sarah thought she remembered them – certainly *him*, a rather distinguished-looking man, hair prematurely grey, perhaps, with a good-humoured, twinkling sort of look about him.

'You get quite a few "John Smiths"?'

'Quite a few.'

'The management's not worried?'

'No! Nor me. Or would you prefer "Nor I"?'

'"That'd be a little bit pedantic, wouldn't it, miss?'

Sarah felt the keen glance of his eyes upon her face, and again (maddeningly) she knew that her cheeks were a burning red.

'Room 3?'

Sarah, fully aware that Morse already knew far more about the situation in Room 3 than she did, handed over the correspondence without comment – this time a typewritten originating letter, stapled below a typewritten reply.

84 West Street
Chipping Norton
Oxon
30th Nov

Dear Proprietor,

Please book in my husband and myself for the Haworth Hotel's New Year Package as advertised. We would particularly wish to take advantage of the rates offered for the 'annexe rooms'. As I read your brochure, it seems that each of these rooms is on the ground floor and this is essential for our booking since my husband suffers from vertigo and is unable to climb stairs. We would prefer twin beds if possible but this is not essential. Please answer as a matter of urgency by return (s.a.e. enclosed) since we are most anxious to fix things up immediately and shall not be at our present address (see above) after the 7th December, since we shall be moving to Cheltenham.

Yours sincerely,
Ann Ballard (Mrs)

The prompt reply (dated 2nd December) was as follows:

Dear Mrs Ballard,

Thank you for your letter of 30th November. We are glad to be able to offer you a double room on the ground-floor annexe, with twin beds, for our New Year Package.

We look forward to your confirmation, either by letter or by phone.

We very much look forward to meeting you and your husband, and we are confident that you will both greatly enjoy your stay with us.

Yours sincerely,

In biro across this letter, too, the word 'Accepted' was written, with the date '3rd Dec'.

Morse looked down again at the letter from Mrs Ballard, and seemed (at least to Sarah Jonstone) to spend an inexplicably long time re-reading its meagre content. Finally he nodded very slowly to himself, put the two sheets of paper down, and looked up at her.

'What do you remember about that pair?'

It was the question Sarah had been afraid of, for her recollections were not so much vague as confused. She thought it had been *Mrs* Ballard who had collected the key from Reception; Mrs Ballard who had been nodded in the direction of the annexe at about 4 p.m. that New Year's afternoon; Mrs Ballard who had appeared in her Iranian outfit just before the evening festivities were due to begin and pointed out the distasteful graffito in the Ladies' loo. And it had been *Mr* Ballard, dressed in his distinctively Rastafarian outfit of light blue shirt, white trousers, baggy checked cap, and maroon knee-boots, who had emerged from the Gents' loo just before everyone was due to eat; Mr Ballard who in fact had eaten very little at all that evening (indeed Sarah herself had cleared away his first two courses virtually untouched); Mr Ballard who had kept very close to his wife throughout the evening, as if they were still in some lovey-dovey idyll of a recent infatuation; Mr Ballard who had asked her – Sarah! – to dance in the latter part of an evening which was becoming less and less of a distinct sequence of events the more she tried to call it back to mind . . .

All these things Sarah told a Morse intensely interested (it seemed) in the vaguest facts she was able to dredge up from the chaotic jumble of her memory.

'Was he drunk?'

'No. I don't think he drank much at all.'

'Did he try to kiss you?'

'No!' Sarah's face, she knew, was blushing again, and she cursed herself for such sensitivity, aware that Morse appeared amused by her discomfiture.

'No need to blush! Nobody'd blame a fellow for wanting to kiss someone like you after one of your boozy midnight parties, my love!'

'I'm not your "love"!' Her upper lip was trembling and she felt the tears beginning to brim behind her eyes.

But Morse was looking at her no more: he picked up the phone and dialled Directory Enquiries on 192.

'There's no Ballard at 84 West Street,' interrupted Sarah. 'Sergeant Phillips—'

'No, I know that,' said Morse quietly, 'but you don't mind if I just check up, do you?'

Sarah was silent as Morse spent a few minutes speaking to some supervisor somewhere, asking several questions about street names and street numbers. And whatever he'd learned, he registered no surprise, certainly no disappointment, as he put down the phone and grinned boyishly at her. 'Sergeant Phillips was right, Miss Jonstone. There isn't a Mr Ballard of 84 West Street, Chipping Norton. There isn't even a number 84! Which makes you think, doesn't it?' he asked, tapping the letter that Sarah herself had written to precisely that non-existent address.

'I'm past thinking!' said Sarah quietly.

'What about Room 4?'

Here, the initiating letter, addressed from 114 Worcester Road, Kidderminster, and dated 4th December, was a model of supremely economical, no-nonsense English, and written in a small, neat hand:

Dear Sir,

Single — cheapest available — room for your New Year Package. Confirm, please.

Yours,

Doris Arkwright

Such confirmation had been duly forthcoming in the form of an almost equally brief reply, this time signed by the proprietor himself, and dated 6th December. But across this letter was now pencilled 'Cancelled 31st Dec – snow.'

'Did she ring up?' asked Morse.

'Yes, she must have rung Mr Binyon, I think.'

'You don't ask for a deposit?'

She shook her head. 'Mr Binyon doesn't think it's good business practice.'

'You don't get many cancellations?'

'Very few.'

'Really? But you've had two out of the four rooms in the annexe!'

Yes, he was right. And he looked like the wretched sort of man who would *always* be right.

'Have you ever had this old biddy staying with you before?' continued Morse.

'What makes you think she's an "old biddy", Inspector?'

'With a name like Doris Arkwright? Straight out of the Lancashire mills, isn't it? Pushing a sprightly ninety, I shouldn't wonder, and drives an ancient Austin.'

Sarah opened her mouth, but closed it again. Morse (as she watched him) had perched a pair of NHS half-lenses on his Jewish-looking nose and looked again at the short letter from Doris Arkwright.

'Do you think she's got anything to do with the case?' asked Sarah.

'Do I think so?' He waited for a few pregnant seconds before taking off his spectacles and looking at her quizzically. 'No, I don't think she's got anything at all to do with the murder. Do *you*, Miss Jonstone?'

CHAPTER TEN

Wednesday, January 1st: p.m.

He was once a doctor but is now an undertaker; and
what he does as an undertaker he used to do as a doctor.

(MARTIAL)

FOR LEWIS, THE next two hours of the evening of
New Year's Day were hardly memorable. A good deal
of the earlier excitement had dissipated, with even the
novelty of murder worn thin; and the Haworth Hotel
now looked an uninviting place, its high-ceilinged
rooms harshly lit by neon strips, its guests standing or
sitting in small groups, quiet and unsmiling – and
waiting. Morse had asked him to check (factually) with
Phillips all the names and addresses of those staying in
the hotel, and briefly himself to interview as many vital
witnesses as he could find – with Phillips to take on the
rest; to try to form a picture (synoptically) of the scene
at the hotel on the previous evening; and to keep his
antennae attuned (almost metaphysically, it appeared)
for any signals from an unsuspected psychopath or any
posthumous transmissions from the newly dead. Festivities – all of them, including the pantomine – had been
cancelled, and the hotel was now grimly still, with not

even the quiet click of snooker balls from the games room to suggest that murder was anything but a deadly serious matter.

Lewis himself had never spent a Christmas or a New Year away from home since his marriage; and although he knew that family life was hardly prize-winning roses all along the way, he had never felt the urge to get away from his own modest semi-detached house up in Headington over such holiday periods. Yet now – most oddly, considering the circumstances – he began to see for the first time, some of the potential attractions: no frenetic last-minute purchases from supermarkets; no pre-feastday preparations of stuffings and sauces; no sticky saucepans to scour; no washing-up of plates and cutlery. Yes! Perhaps Lewis would mention the idea to the missus, for it seemed perfectly clear to him as he spoke to guest after guest that a wondrously good time was being had by all – until a man had been found murdered.

Exactly where Morse had been during the whole of this period, Lewis had little idea, although (Lewis had heard part of it) the chief inspector had interviewed the woman on Reception at some considerable length – a woman (as Lewis saw her) most pleasingly attractive, with a quiet, rather upper-class manner of speaking that contrasted favourably with the somewhat abrasive questioning she was being subjected to – with Morse obviously still in a tetchy frame of mind after his altercations with the luckless Phillips, and apparently quite unconcerned about venting his temporary ill-humour on anyone and everyone, including Sarah Jonstone.

It was just after 10 p.m. that the police surgeon came back into the main building again, the inevitable long-ashed cigarette dropping from his lips, his black bag in one hand, two sheets of A4 in the other.

'My God, you do pick 'em, Morse!' began the surgeon as the three of them, Max, Morse and Lewis, sat down together in the deserted games room.

'Get on with it, Max!' said Morse.

The surgeon looked quickly at his notes – then began.

'One – he's a wasp, Morse.'

'He's a *what?*'

'He's a WASP – a White Anglo-Saxon Protestant – though he could well be a Catholic, of course.'

'Of course.'

'Two – his age is about thirty to forty, though he could be twenty-nine or forty-one, for that matter.'

'Or forty-two,' said Morse.

The surgeon nodded. 'Or twenty-eight.'

'Get on with it!'

'Three – his height's five foot seven and a half inches. You want that in metres, Morse?'

'Not so long as it's accurate in inches.'

'Can't promise that.'

'Christ!'

'Four – he's dressed up as a Rastafarian.'

'Very perceptive!'

'Five – he's got a wig on: black, curlyish.'

'Something several of us could do with!'

'Six – he's got dreadlocks.'

'Which are?'

'Long, thin bits of hair, plaited into strands, with cylindrical beads at the end.'

'I saw them! It's just that I didn't know—'

'Seven – these strands of hair are stapled to the inside of the hat he's wearing.'

Morse nodded.

'Eight – this hat is a sort of baggy, felt "cap", with a big peak, a black-grey-white check pattern, filled out with folded toilet-paper. You want to know which brand?'

'No!'

'Nine – his face is darkened all over with what's known in theatrical circles as "stage-black".'

Again Morse nodded.

'Ten – this stage-black stretches down to the top of the shirt-level, just round his neck; the backs of the hands are similarly bedaubed, Morse, but not the palms.'

'Is that important?'

'Eleven' – the surgeon ignored the question – 'his light blue shirt has got six buttons down the front, all but the top one done up, long-sleeved, obviously very new and probably being worn for the first time.'

No comment from Morse.

'Twelve – his white trousers are made of some cheap summer-wear material, a bit worn here and there.'

'And nothing in the pockets,' said Morse; but it wasn't a question.

'Thirteen – he's got three longish chains round his neck: junk stuff that you'd find in a cheap second-hand shop.'

Morse was beginning to show the first signs of restlessness.

'Fourteen – there was a pair of sunglasses on the floor just between the two beds, the ear-hooks quite shallowly slanted.'

'As if they'd fall off his ears, you mean?'

'They *did* fall off his ears.'

'I see.'

'Fifteen – a false moustache, affixed with strong adhesive, still exactly in position across the upper lip.'

'Why do you say "affixed", instead of just plain "fixed"?'

'Sixteen – a pair of high-heeled, knee-level boots: highly polished, light maroon plastic.'

'You sure it's not a *woman* we've got there on the bed, Max?'

'Seventeen – time of death: difficult to judge.'

'As well we might have known!'

'About sixteen to twenty-four hours before the body was found – at a guess. But the room temperature is only just above freezing point – which could upset calculations either way.'

'So?'

For the first time, the surgeon seemed slightly less than happy with himself: 'As I say, Morse, it's very difficult.'

'But you *never* come up with a plain statement of when—'

'They pay me to report facts.'

'And they pay me to find out who killed the poor sod, Max.' But Morse, it seemed, was making little impression upon the mournful man who lit another cigarette before continuing.

'Eighteen – cause of death? A mighty whack, probably only one, across the front of the skull, with the bone smashed in from the top of the right eye across the nasal bridge to the left cheekbone.'

Morse was silent.

'Nineteen – he wasn't a navvie, judging from his fingernails.'

'Now you're getting down to things.'

'No I'm not, Morse. I've nearly finished.'

'You're going to tell me who he is, you mean?'

'Twenty – he had flat feet.'

'You mean he *has* flat feet?'

The surgeon permitted himself a bleak smile. 'Yes, Morse. When he was alive he had flat feet, and in death those feet were not unflattened.'

'What does that suggest, Max?'

'Perhaps he's a policeman, Morse.' The surgeon stood up, the cigarette ash dropping on to his black waistcoat. 'I'll let you have the written report as soon as I can. Not tonight though.' He looked at his watch. 'We've got half an hour if you want to nip up to the Gardeners'? I've got a car.'

For a moment or two, Lewis almost thought that Morse was going to resist the temptation.

CHAPTER ELEVEN

Wednesday, January 1st: p.m.

When I drink, I think; and when I think, I drink.

(RABELAIS)

'GIN AND CAMPARI for me, Morse, and buy yourself one as well. My GP keeps on telling me it's sensible to keep off the spirits.'

Soon the two old friends were seated facing each other in the lounge bar, the surgeon resting his heavy-looking dolichocephalic skull upon his left hand.

'Time of death!' said Morse. 'Come on!'

'Nice drink this, Morse.'

'The science of thanatology hasn't advanced a milli-metre in your time, has it?'

'Ah! Now you're taking advantage of my classical education.'

'But nowadays, Max, you can look down from one of those space-satellite things and see a house fly rubbing its hands over a slice of black pudding in a Harlem delicatessen – you know that? And yet *you* can't—'

'The room was as cold as a church, Morse. How do you expect—'

'You don't know anything about churches!'

'True enough.'

They sat silently for a while, Morse looking at the open fire where a log suddenly shifted on its foundations and sent a shower of red-glowing sparks against the back of the old grate, beside which was a stack of wood, chopped into quartered segments.

'Did you notice they'd chopped down a couple of trees at the back of the annexe, Max?'

'No.'

Morse sipped his gin. 'I could develop quite a taste for this.'

'You think it might have been the branch of a tree or something . . .? Could have been, I suppose. About two feet long, nice easy grip, couple of inches in diameter.'

'You didn't see any wood splinters?'

'No.'

'What about a bottle?'

'No broken glass on his face, either, as far as I could see.'

'Tough things, though. Some of these people who launch battleships have a hell of a job breaking champagne bottles.'

'We may find something, Morse.'

'When can you let me have a report?'

'Not tonight.'

'Much blood, would there have been?'

'Enough. No spurting though.'

'No good asking the guests if they saw a fellow walking around with blood all over his best shirt?'

'What about a *woman*, Morse? With blood all over her liberty bodice?'

'Perhaps, I suppose.'

The surgeon nodded non-committally and looked into the fire: 'Poor sod . . . Do *you* ever think of death? *Mors, mortis,* feminine – remember that?'

'Not likely to forget a word like that, am I? Just add on "e" to the end and . . .'

The surgeon smiled a sour acknowledgement of the point and drained his glass. 'We'll just have the other half. Then we'll get back, and show you round the scene of the crime again.'

'When the body's out of the way?'

'You don't like the sight of blood much, do you?'

'No. I should never have been a policeman.'

'Always turned me on, blood did – even as a boy.'

'Unnatural!'

'Same again?'

'Why not?'

'What turns *you* on?' asked the surgeon as he picked up the two glasses.

'Somebody from the *Oxford Times* asked me that last week, Max. Difficult, you know – just being asked out of the blue like that.'

'What did you say?'

'I said I was always turned on by the word "unbuttoning".'

'Clever!'

'Not really. It comes in one of Larkin's poems somewhere. It's just that you know nothing about the finer things in life . . .'

But the surgeon, apparently unhearing, was already standing at the bar and rattling an empty glass imperiously on the counter.

80

CHAPTER TWELVE

Wednesday, January 1st: p.m.

Close up the casement, draw the blind,
Shut out that stealing moon.

(THOMAS HARDY)

UNDER THE SURGEON'S supervision, the frozen-
footed ambulancemen had finally stretchered away the
white-sheeted corpse to the morgue at the Old Radcliffe
at 11.30 p.m., and Lewis was glad that the preliminaries
of the case were now almost over. The two fingerprint
men had departed just after eleven, followed ten minutes later by the spiky-haired young photographer,
clutching the neck of his flash-bulb camera as if it were
some poisonous serpent. The surgeon himself had
driven off in his old black Ford at a quarter to midnight,
and the hotel seemed strangely still as Lewis followed
Morse across the slush and blackened snow to the room
called Annexe 3, where the two men stood for the
second time that evening, and where, each in his own
way, they now took a more detailed mental inventory of
what they saw.

Immediately to the left in the spacious room (about
twenty feet by fourteen feet) stood a built-in wardrobe

of white wood, in which nine plastic coat-hangers hung from the cross-rail; beyond it stood a dressing table, its drawers (as we have seen) quite empty, with a brochure of the hotel lying on its top, next to a card with the handwritten message: 'Welcome – your room has been personally prepared by Mandy'; a colour TV set stood in the corner; and, between it and the dressing table, a ledge some four feet from the floor held a kettle, a small teapot, two cups and two saucers, and a rectangular plastic tray, on which, in separate compartments, were small cellophaned packets of biscuits, sachets of Nescafé, sachets of sugar, teabags, and little squat tubs of Eden Vale milk.

Along the far wall was a long low radiator, and just above its top the sill of an equally long window, the latter a triptych of panes, the centre one fixed, but the left and right panes still opened outwards to the elements at an angle of forty-five degrees, and the darkish-green curtains drawn only half across. Liberally sprinkled fingerprint powder was observable all round the window, where a few daubs of unpromising-looking blotches had been circled with a black felt pen.

'Perhaps,' said Morse, a shiver running down his vertebrae, 'we should take our first positive moves in this case, Lewis, eh? Let's close those bloody windows! And turn on the radiator!'

'You're not worried about the prints, sir?'

'It's not going to help us to arrest anybody if we land up in some intensive-care unit with bronchial pneumonia.'

(Lewis, at that moment, felt quite unconscionably happy.)

The twin beds occupied most of the area in the rest of the room, their tops close against the wall to the right, beneath a long headboard panel of beige plastic, set into which were the controls for TV and radio, loud-speakers, various light switches, and an early-morning-alarm unit with what seemed to Lewis instructions that were completely incomprehensible. On a small table between the beds was a white digital telephone; and on a shelf beneath that, the Holy Bible, as placed by the ever-persevering Gideons. The walls and ceiling were painted in a very pale shade of apple green, and the floor was carpeted wall to wall in a grey-green chequered pattern.

All very neat, very clean, and very tidy – apart from the obscene blotch of dried blood across the further bed.

Completing the circuit of this accommodation, the two men came to the tiny bathroom, only some seven feet by five feet, whose door stood a few feet inside and to the right of the main entrance to Annexe 3. Immediately facing was the WC, a unit of the usual white enamel, the bowl a sparkling tribute to the ministrations of the conscientious Mandy; on the left was a washbasin by which stood two tumblers and a diminutive bar of soap (unopened) in a pink paper wrapping bearing the name 'Haworth'; to the right was a bath, fairly small, with shower attachment, and a ledge let into the wall containing a second bar of soap (also unopened); finally, on the wall opposite, to the left of the WC, were racks for a whole assortment of fluffy white towels (all seemingly unused), and fixtures for toilet paper and Kleenex tissues. The walls were tiled in a light olive-green, with the vinyl flooring of a slightly darker, matching green.

'They don't look, whoever they were, as if they made much use of the facilities, sir.'

'No-o.' Morse walked back into the main part of the room and stood there nodding to himself. 'Good point! I wonder if . . .' He fiddled with some of the buttons and switches which appeared to determine the reception of a TV programme; but with no effect.

'Shall I plug it in, sir?'

'You mean . . .?' Again Morse appeared deep in thought as an indeterminate blur dramatically developed into a clearly delineated picture, and a late-night newsreader announced that in Beirut the Shi'ite and the Christian Militias had begun the new year with exactly the same implacable hatred as they had finished the old one.

'Funny, you know, Lewis – turn that thing off! – you'd have thought they would have made *some* use of the facilities, wouldn't you?' Morse carefully drew back the coverings on the bed nearer the window; but the sheets appeared quite virgin, apart from the indentations caused by the superimposition of a corpse. With the other bed, too, the evidence seemed very much the same: someone might well have sat on the side, perhaps, but it seemed reasonably clear that neither bed had been the scene of any frolicsome coition.

It was Lewis, emerging from the bathroom, who had found the only tangible trace of the room's most recent tenants: a screwed-up brown-stained Kleenex tissue, which had been the only item in the waste-bin.

'Looks like this is the only thing they left behind, sir.'

'Not blood is it?'

'It's the stage-black for the make-up, I think.'

'Well, at least we've got *one* clue, Lewis!'

Before leaving, Morse once more slid open the door of the wardrobe along its smooth runners and took another look inside.

'Doesn't look as if your fingerprint lads did much dusting here.'

Lewis looked at the powder marks that covered several points on the white outer-door: 'I wouldn't say that, sir. It looks as if—'

'I meant *inside*,' said Morse quietly.

It was midnight before Sarah Jonstone got to bed that night, and way into the early hours before she finally dropped off into a restless slumber. Her mind was reverting continually to the strangely disturbing chief inspector – a man she was growing to dislike intensely – and to what he had asked, and asked, and asked her. Occasionally, as he had listened to her answers, he had seemed to promote a simple, honest confession of ignorance or forgetfulness on her part to the status of an almost unforgivable sin. And above all her mind reverted to his repeated insistence that she must try to recall anything unusual: anything *unusual, anything unusual* ... The words had re-echoed round the walls of her brain – being all the more disturbing precisely because there *had*, she thought, been something unusual ... Yet this 'something' continued to elude her: almost, on several occasions, she had it in her grasp – and then it had slithered away like a slippery bar of soap along the bottom of the bath.

Chapter Thirteen

Thursday, January 2nd: a.m.

Snow is all right while it is snowing: it is like inebriation, because it is very pleasing when it is coming, but very unpleasing when it is going.

(OGDEN NASH)

MORSE HAD DECIDED that it was needful, at least for a couple of days, to set up a temporary Murder HQ *in situ*; and from the comparatively early hours of the next morning, the room at the rear of the annexe building, a broad-windowed area that looked as if it would make an excellent classroom, was taken over by Lewis and Morse as an official 'Operations Room'.

An innocently deep night's sleep, an early-morning shower and a fried breakfast of high cholesterol risk had launched a zestful Lewis on his way to the Haworth Hotel at 6.30 a.m., where an ill-rested, unshowered, unbreakfasted Morse had joined him twenty minutes later.

At half-past seven it was John Binyon, the hotel proprietor, who was the first of many that day to sit opposite the two detectives at a rickety trestle table.

'It's a terrible thing,' said Binyon. 'Terrible! Just when we'd started getting things going nicely, too.'

'Never mind, sir,' said Morse, calling upon all his powers of self-control to force the last of these three words through the barrier of his teeth. 'Perhaps you'll have a long queue of people waiting to sleep in the famous room.'

'Would you queue for it, Inspector?'

'Certainly not!' said Morse.

The talk turned to the subject of guests in general, and Binyon admitted that things had changed a good deal, even during his own limited experience. 'They don't even pretend these days, some of them – don't even put a ring on, some of the women. Mind you, we turn one or two away – well, you know, make out we're full up.'

'Do you think you could always spot them – if they weren't married?'

Binyon gave the question serious thought. 'No! No – I wouldn't say that. But I think I'd know if they were staying together for the first time.'

'How so?'

'Lots of things. The way they act, I suppose – and they always pay by cash – and they often get addresses wrong. For example, we had a fellow last month who came with his girlfriend, and he put down his address as Slough, *Berks*!'

'What did you do?' asked Morse, frowning.

'Nothing. I wasn't on the desk when he signed in; but I was when he booked out, and I told him straight that the next hotel he went to it might be valuable to know that Slough was in Bucks.'

'What did *he* say?' asked Morse, frowning more than ever.

'He just grinned – as if he hadn't heard me.'

'But Slough *is* in Berks!' said Morse.

The proprietor's general grasp of hotel procedures was clearly considerably in advance of his knowledge of geography, and Morse found himself not unfavourably impressed by his succinct account of current practice at the Haworth Hotel. Normally, between 80 per cent and 90 per cent of the guests contacted the hotel, in the first instance, by phone. Often, there would be insufficient time to seek or to obtain confirmation by letter. Most usually, a credit-card number was sufficient warranty from the hotel's point of view to establish a *bona fides*; but for something so specifically pre-planned and widely advertised as a Christmas or a New Year function, obviously the great majority of guests had *some* correspondence with the hotel. As far as actual registration was concerned, the pattern was (the two detectives learned) exactly what any seasoned traveller would expect at any established hostelry: 'Name?' would be the first question; and, when this was checked against the booking list, a card would be handed over which asked for surname, forename(s), company, company address, home address, method of settling account, nationality, car registration, passport number, and finally signature. Such a fairly straightforward task completed, the guest (or guests) would be given a card showing details of room number, tariff, type of break-fast, type of room, and the like. With a room key handed over from one of the hooks behind Reception, 'registration' was now appropriately effected, with only a final negotiation remaining about the choice of a morning newspaper. And that was that. In such a comparatively small hotel, no porter was employed to carry cases, although the management was of course always on the lookout to ensure suitable assistance for any ageing couples who appeared at risk from cardiac arrest at the prospect of lugging their belongings to the first-floor landing.

At eight fifteen, confirmation was received from Chipping Norton that none of the five Ballard couples on the local Electoral Register had a wifely component answering to the name Ann; and that the town's official archivist, after delving as far back towards Domesday as local records allowed, was prepared to state quite categorically that there was not, nor ever had been, a number 84 along the thoroughfare now known, and always known, as West Street, Chipping Norton.

At eight forty-five, Superintendent Bell rang through from St Aldates to ask if Morse required any further men to help him. But Morse declined the offer; for the moment he could think of nothing he could profitably effect with a posse of policemen, except perhaps to conduct some inevitably futile house-to-house inquiries in and around Chipping Norton to ascertain whether anyone had knowledge of a man of indeterminate age, partner to a pseudonymous Ann Ballard, with neither a club-foot, nor a withered arm, nor a swastika tattooed on his forehead to assist any possible identification. Further, it became quite clear from the guests interviewed later that morning that none of them would with any certitude be able to recognize Mr Ballard again. Such diffidence (as Morse saw things) was hardly surprising: the only time the other guests had met Ballard was during that one evening; up until then he had been a complete stranger to them; and he had spent most of the evening closely shielded and chaperoned by what others had taken to be a jealously possessive wife. Indeed the only reason that many could recall him at all was the extremely obvious one: he had won first prize in the men's fancy-dress competition, dressed in the consummately skilful disguise of a West Indian reggae musician. The only new fact of any substance to emerge was that he had, certainly in the later part of the evening, drunk more than one glass of whisky – Bell's, according to Mandy, the stand-in barmaid. But there was also general agreement, fully corroborating Sarah Jonstone's earlier evidence, that Ballard had eaten very little indeed. Several witnesses had a clear recollection of him dancing with his yashmak'd companion (lover? mistress? wife?), and only with her, for most of the evening; but Mr Dods ('With t'one "d"') was almost prepared to swear on Geoffrey Boycott's batting average that Ballard had also danced, towards midnight, with an animated youngish woman named Mrs Palmer – 'Philippa' or 'Pippa' Palmer, as he recalled – as well as with the hotel receptionist ('A little tipsy, Inspector, if ah mair sair sor!'). And that was about that. And towards the end of the morning it was becoming increasingly obvious to both Morse and Lewis that the only firm and valuable testimony they were going to get was that given the previous evening by Sarah (tipsy or not!) Jonstone, who had claimed in her statement to Lewis that she had peeped out of her window at about 1 a.m. and seen at that late, flake-falling, whitely covered hour, the prize-winning Rastafarian walking back across to the annexe with an arm around each of the women on either side of him. It seemed good to Morse, therefore, to summon the fair Miss Jonstone once again.

She sat there, her legs crossed, looking tired, every few moments pushing her spectacles up to the top of her nose with the middle finger of her ringless left hand – and thereby irritating Morse to a quite disproportionate extent – as he himself hooked his half-lenses behind his ears and trusted that he projected an appropriate degree of investigative acumen.

'After the annexe lot left the party, the others finished too – is that right?'

'I think so.'

'You don't *know* so?'

'No.'

'You say Ballard had his arms round these two women?'

'No, he had one arm round one woman and one—'

'Which two women?'

'Mrs Palmer was one – I'm fairly sure of that.'

'And the other one?'

'I think it was . . . Mrs Smith.'

'You'd had quite a lot to drink, hadn't you!'

Sarah Jonstone's pale face coloured deeply; and yet perhaps it was, that morning, more from anger than from shame. 'Oh yes!' she said, in a firm, quiet voice. 'I don't think you'll find a single person in the hotel who would disagree with that.'

'But you saw the women fairly clearly?' (Morse was beginning to appreciate Miss Jonstone more and more.)

'I saw them clearly from the back, yes.'

'It was snowing, wasn't it?'

'Yes.'

'So they had their coats on?'

'Yes. Both of them had light-coloured winter macs on.'

'And you say' – Morse referred to her statement – 'that the other three members of the annexe sextet were just behind them?'

Sarah nodded.

'So, if you're right about the first three, that leaves us with Mrs Ballard, Mr Palmer and Mr . . . Smith – yes?'

Sarah hesitated – and then said 'Yes!' – then pushed her spectacles up once more towards her luminous eyes.

'And behind them all came Mr Binyon?'

'Yes – I think he was going to make sure that the side door to the annexe was locked up after them.'

'That's what *he* says, too.'

'So it might be true, Inspector.'

But Morse appeared not to have heard her. 'After Mr Binyon had locked up the annexe, no one else could have got *in* there?'

'Not unless he had a key.'

'Or *she* had a key!'

'Or she had a key, yes.'

'But anyone could have got *out* of the annexe later on?'

Again Sarah hesitated before answering. 'Yes, I suppose so. I hadn't really thought of it, but – yes. The lock's an ordinary Yale one, and any of the guests could have got out, if they'd wanted to.'

It was Lewis who, at this point, made an unexpected intervention.

'Are you absolutely *sure* it was snowing then, Miss Jonstone?'

Sarah turned towards the sergeant, feeling relieved to look into a pair of friendly eyes and to hear a friendly voice. And she *wasn't* quite sure, now she came to think of it. The wind had been blowing and lifting up the settled snow in a drifting whirl around her window; and whether it *had* been snowing, at that particular moment, she wasn't really prepared to assert with any dogmatism.

'No,' she said simply. 'I'm *not* absolutely sure.'

'It's just,' continued Lewis, 'that according to the weatherman on Radio Oxford the snow in this area had virtually stopped falling just about midnight. There may have been the odd flurry or two; but it had pretty well finished by then – so they say.'

'What are you trying to get at, Sergeant? I'm not . . . quite sure . . .'

'It's just that if it *had* stopped snowing, and if someone had left the annexe that night, there would have been some footprints, wouldn't there? Wouldn't such a person have to make his way across to the main road?'

Sarah was thinking back, thinking back so very hard. There had been *no* prints the next morning leading from the annexe across to the Banbury Road. None! She could almost swear to that. But *had* it been snowing when she looked out that fateful evening? Yes, it had!

Thus it was that she answered Lewis simply and quietly. 'No, there were no footprints from the annexe to be seen that morning – yesterday morning. But yes, it *was* snowing when I looked out – I'm sure of it.'

'You mean that the weatherman at Radio Oxford has got things all wrong, miss?'

'Yes, I do, Sergeant.'

Lewis felt a little taken aback by such strong, and such conflicting evidence, and he turned to Morse for some kind of arbitration. But as he did so, he noticed (as he had so often in the past) that the chief inspector's eyes were growing brighter and brighter by the second, in some sort of slow incandescence, as though a low-powered filament had been switched on somewhere at the back of his brain. But Morse said nothing for the moment, and Lewis tried to rediscover his bearings.

'So from what you say, you think that Mr Ballard

must have been murdered by one of those five other people there?'

'Well, yes! Don't you? I think he was murdered by Mr or Mrs Palmer, or by Mr or Mrs Smith, or by Mrs Ballard – whoever *she* is!'

'I see.'

During these exchanges, Morse himself had been watching the unshadowed, unrouged, unlipsticked blonde with considerable interest; but no longer. He stood up and thanked her, and then seemed relieved that she had left them.

'Some shrewd questioning there, Lewis!'

'You really think so, sir?'

But Morse made no direct answer. 'It's time we had some refreshment,' he said.

Lewis, who was well aware that Morse invariably took his lunchtime calories in liquid form, was himself perfectly ready for a pint and a sandwich; but he was a little displeased about Morse's apparently total lack of interest in the weather conditions at the time of the murder.

'About the snow, sir—' he began.

'The snow? The snow, my old friend, is a complete white herring,' said Morse, already pulling on his greatcoat.

In the back bar of the Eagle and Child in St Giles', the two men sat and drank their beer, and Lewis found himself reading and reading again the writing on the wooden plaque fixed to the wall behind Morse's head:

C.S. LEWIS, his brother, W.H. Lewis, J.R.R. Tolkien, Charles Williams, and other friends met every Tuesday morning, between the years 1939–1962 in the back room of this their favourite pub. These men, popularly known as the 'Inklings', met here to drink beer and to discuss, among other things, the books they were writing.

And strangely enough it was Sergeant Lewis's mind, after (for him) a rather liberal intake of alcohol, which was waxing the more imaginative as he pictured a series of fundamental emendations to this received text; 'CHIEF INSPECTOR MORSE, with his friend and colleague Sergeant Lewis, sat in this back room one Thursday, in order to solve . . .'

CHAPTER FOURTEEN

Thursday, January 2nd: p.m.

'Is there anybody there?' he said.
(WALTER DE LA MARE, *The Listeners*)

IF, AS NOW seemed most probable, the Haworth Hotel
murderer was to be sought amongst the fellow guests
who had been housed in the annexe on New Year's
Eve, it was high time to look more carefully into the
details of the Palmers and the Smiths, the guests (now
vanished) who had been staying in Annexe 1 and
Annexe 2 respectively; and Lewis looked at the registration forms he had in front of him, each of them fully
filled in; each of them, on the face of it, innocent
enough.

The Palmers' address, the same on the registration
form as on the earlier correspondence, was given as
29A Chiswick Reach; and the telephone operator confirmed that there was indeed such a property, and that
it did indeed have a subscriber by the name of Palmer,
P. (sex not stated) listed in the London Telephone
Directory. Lewis saw Morse's eyebrows lift a little, as if
he were more than a fraction surprised at this intelligence; but for his own part he refused to assume that

everyone who had congregated quite fortuitously in the Haworth annexe was therefore an automatic criminal. He dialled the number and waited, letting the phone at the other end ring for about a minute before putting down the receiver.

'We could get someone round there, perhaps?'

'Not yet, Lewis. Give it a go every half-hour or so.'

Lewis nodded, and looked down at the Smiths' card.

'What's their address?' asked Morse.

'Posh sort of place, by the look of it, "*Aldbrickham*, 22 Spring Street, Gloucester".'

This time Lewis saw Morse's eyebrows lift a lot. 'Here! Let me look at that!' said Morse.

And as he did so, Lewis saw him shake his head slowly, a smile forming at the corners of his mouth.

'I'm prepared to bet you my bank-balance that there's no such address as that!'

'I'm not betting anything!'

'I know the place, Lewis. And so should you! It's the street where Jude and Sue Fawley lived!'

'Should I know them?'

'In *Jude the Obscure*, Lewis! And "Aldbrickham" is Hardy's name for Reading, as you'll remember.'

'Yes, I'd forgotten for the moment,' said Lewis.

'Clever!' Morse nodded again as though in approbation of the literary tastes of Mr and Mrs John Smith. 'There's no real point in trying but . . .' Lewis heard an audible sigh from the girl on 192 as she heard that Lewis wanted Smith, J.; and it took her a little while to discover there was no subscriber of that name with a

Spring Street address in Gloucester. A further call to the Gloucester Police established, too, that there was not a Spring Street in the city.

Lewis tried Chiswick again: no reply.

'Do you reckon we ought to try old Doris – Doris Arkwright?' asked Morse. 'Perhaps she's another crook.'

But before any such attempt could be made, a messenger from the pathology lab came in with the police surgeon's preliminary findings. The amateurishly typewritten report added little to what had already been known, or assumed, from the previous evening's examination: age thirty-five to forty-five; height five foot eight and a half ('He's grown an inch overnight!' said Morse); no fragments of wood or glass or steel in the considerable facial injury, caused likely enough by a single powerful blow; teeth – in exceptionally good condition for a male in the age group, with only three minor fillings in the left-hand side of the jaw, one of them very recent; stomach – a few mixed vegetables, but little recent intake by the look of things.

That, in essence, was all the report said. No further information about such key issues as the time of death; an array of medical terms, though, such as 'supra-orbital foramen' and 'infra-orbital fissure', which Morse was perfectly happy to ignore. But there was a personal note from the surgeon written in a spidery scrawl at the foot of this report. 'Morse: A major drawback to any immediate identification is going to be the very extensive laceration and contusion across the inferior nasal concha – this doesn't give us any easily recognizable lineaments for a photograph – and it makes the look of the face harrowing for relatives. In any case, people always look different when they're dead. As for the time of death, I've nothing to add to my definitive statement of yesterday. In short, your guess is as good as mine, although it would come as a profound shock to me if it was any better. Max.'

Morse glanced through the report as rapidly as he could, which was, to be truthful, not very rapidly at all. He had always been a slow reader, ever envying those of his colleagues whose eyes appeared to have the facility to descend swiftly through the centre of a page of writing, taking in as they went the landscape both to the left and to the right. But two points – two simple, major points – were firmly and disappointingly apparent: and Morse put them into words.

'They don't know who he is, Lewis; and they don't know when he died. Bloody typical!'

Lewis grinned: 'He's not a bad old boy, though.'

'He should be pensioned off! He's too old! He drinks too much! No – he's not a bad old boy, as you say; but he's on the downward slope, I'm afraid.'

'You once told me *you* were on the downward slope, sir!'

'We're *all* on the downward slope!'

'Shall we go and have a look at the other bedrooms?' Lewis spoke briskly, and stood up as if anxious to prod a lethargic-looking Morse into some more purposive line of inquiry.

'You mean they may have left their Barclaycards behind?'

'You never know, sir.' Lewis fingered the great bunch of keys that Binyon had given him, but Morse appeared reluctant to get moving.

'Shall I do it myself, sir?'

Morse got up at last. 'No! Let's go and have a look round the rooms – you're quite right. You take the Palmers' room.'

In the Smiths' room, Annexe 2, Morse looked around him with little enthusiasm (wouldn't the maid have tidied Annexe 1 and Annexe 2 during the day?), finally turning back the sheets on each of the twin beds, then opening the drawers of the dressing table, then looking inside the wardrobe. Nothing. In the bathroom, it was clear that one or both of the Smiths had taken a shower or a bath fairly recently, for the two large white towels were still slightly damp and the soap in the wall-niche had been used – as had the two squat tumblers that stood on the surface behind the washbasin. But there was nothing to learn here, Morse felt sure of that. No items left behind; no torn letters thrown into the waste-paper basket; only a few marks over the carpet, mostly just inside the door, left by shoes and boots that had tramped across the slush and snow. In any case, Morse felt fairly sure that the Smiths, whoever they were, had nothing at all to do with the crime, because he thought he knew just how and why the pair of them had come to the Haworth Hotel, booking *in* at the last possible moment, and getting *out* at the earliest possible moment after the murder of Ballard had been discovered.

'Smith, J.' (there was little doubt in Morse's mind) was an ageing rogue in middle management, drooling with lust over a new young secretary, who'd told his long-suffering spouse that he had to go to a business conference in the Midlands over the New Year. Such conduct was commonplace, Morse knew that; and perhaps there was little point in pursuing the matter further. Yet he would like to meet her, for she was, according to the other guests, a pleasingly attractive woman. He sat on one of the beds, and picked up the phone.

'Can I help you?' It was Sarah Jonstone.

'Do you know what's the first thing they tell you if you go on a course for receptionists?'

'Oh! It's you.'

'They tell you never to say "Can I help you?"'

'Can I hinder you, Inspector?'

'Did the Smiths make any telephone calls while they were here?'

'Not from the bedroom.'

'You'd have a record of it – on their bill, I mean – if they'd phoned anyone?'

'Ye-es. Yes we would.' Her voice sounded oddly hesitant, and Morse waited for her to continue. 'Any phone call gets recorded automatically.'

'That's it then.'

'Er – Inspector! We've – we've just been going through accounts and we shall have to check again but – we're almost sure that Mr and Mrs Smith didn't square up their account before they left.'

'Why the hell didn't you tell me before?' snapped Morse.

'Because – I – didn't – know,' Sarah replied, spacing the four words deliberately and quietly and only just resisting the impulse to slam the receiver down on him.

'How much did they owe?'

Again, there was a marked hesitation at the end of the line. 'They had some champagne taken to their room – expensive stuff—'

'Nobody's ever had a *cheap* bottle of champagne – in a hotel – have they?'

'And they had four bottles—'

'*Four?*' Morse whistled softly to himself. 'What exactly was this irresistible vintage?'

'It was Veuve Clicquot Ponsardin 1972.'

'It it good stuff?'

'As I say, it's expensive.'

'How expensive?'

'£29.75 a bottle.'

'It's *what?*' Again Morse whistled to himself, and his interest in the Smiths was obviously renascent. 'Four twenty-nines are . . . Phew!'

'Do you think it's important?' she asked.

'Who'd pick up the empties?'

'Mandy would – the girl who did the rooms.'

'And where would she put them?'

'We've got some crates at the back of the kitchen.'

'Did anyone else raid the champagne cellar?'

'I don't think so.'

'So you ought to have four empty bottles of '72 whatever-it-is out there?'

'Yes, I suppose so.'

'No "suppose" about it, is there?'

'No.'

'Well, check up – straight away, will you?'

'All right.'

Morse walked back into the bathroom, and without picking up the tumblers leaned over and sniffed them one by one. But he wasn't at all sure if either smelled of champagne, though one pretty certainly smelled of some peppermint-flavoured toothpaste. Back in the bedroom, he sat down once more on the bed, wondering if there was something *in* the room, or something *about* the room, that he had missed. Yet he could find nothing – not even the vaguest reason for his suspicions; and he was about to go when there was a soft knocking on the door and Sarah Jonstone came in.

'Inspector, I—' Her upper lip was shaking and it was immediately clear that she was on the verge of tears.

'I'm sorry I was a bit short with you—' began Morse.

'It's not that. It's just . . .'

He stood up and put his arm lightly round her shoulders. 'No need to tell me. It's that penny-pinching Binyon, isn't it? He's not only lost the Smiths' New Year contributions, he's an extra one hundred and nineteen pounds short – yes?'

She nodded, and as the eyes behind the large round lenses brimmed with glistening tears Morse lightly lifted off her spectacles and she leaned against his shoulder, the tears coursing freely down her cheeks. And finally, when she lifted her head and smiled feebly, and rubbed the backs of her hands against her tear-stained face, he took out his only handkerchief, originally white and now a dirty grey, and pushed it into her grateful hands. She was about to say something, but Morse spoke first.

'Now don't you worry, my girl, about Binyon, all right? Or about these Smiths, either! I'll make sure we catch up with 'em sooner or later.'

Sarah nodded. 'I'm sorry I was so silly.'

'Forget it!'

'You know the champagne bottles? Well, there are only *three* of them in the crate. They must have taken one away with them – it's not here.'

'Perhaps they didn't quite finish it.'

'It's not very easy to carry a half-full bottle of bubbly around.'

'No. You can't get the cork back in, can you?'

She smiled, feeling very much happier now, and found herself looking at Morse and wondering if he had a wife or a series of women-friends or whether he just wasn't interested: it was difficult to tell. She was conscious, too, that his mind hadn't seemed to be on her at all for the last few minutes. And indeed this was true.

'You feeling better?' she heard him say; but he appeared no longer to have any interest in her well-being, and he said no more as she turned and left him in the bedroom.

A few minutes later he poked his head round the door of Annexe 1 and found Lewis on his hands and knees beside the dressing table.

'Found anything?' he asked.

'Not yet, sir.'

*

Back in the temporary Operations Room, Morse rang the pathology lab and found the police surgeon there.

'Could it have been a bottle, Max?'

'Perhaps,' admitted that morose man. 'But if it was it didn't break.'

'You mean even you would have found a few lumps of glass sticking in the fellow's face?'

'Even me!'

'Do you think with a blow like that a bottle *would* have smashed?'

'*If* it was a bottle, you mean?'

'Yes, *if* it was a bottle.'

'Don't know.'

'Well, bloody guess, then!'

'Depends on the bottle.'

'A champagne bottle?'

'Many a day since I saw one, Morse!'

'Do you think whoever murdered Ballard was left-handed or right-handed?'

'If he was a right-handed tennis player it must have been a sort of backhand shot: if he was left-handed, it must have been a sort of smash.'

'You're not very often as forthcoming as that!'

'I try to help.'

'Do you think our tennis player was right-handed or left-handed?'

'Don't know,' said the surgeon.

Lewis came in a quarter of an hour later to report to his rather sour-looking superior that his exhaustive search of the Palmer suite had yielded absolutely nothing.

'Never mind, Lewis! Let's try the Palmer number again.'

But Morse could hear the repeated 'Brr-brrs' from where he sat, and sensed somehow that for the moment at least there would be no answer to the call. 'We're not having a great afternoon, one way or another, are we?' he said.

'Plenty of time yet, sir.'

'What about old Doris? Shall we give her a ring? We know *she's* at home – warming her corns on the radiator, like as not.'

'You want me to try?'

'Yes, I do!'

But there was no Arkwright of any initial listed in the Kidderminster area at 114 Worcester Road. But there *was* a subscriber at that address; and after some reassurance from Lewis about the nature of the inquiry the supervisor gave him the telephone number. Which he rang.

'Could I speak to Miss Doris Arkwright, please?'

'I think you've got the wrong number.'

'That *is* 114 Worcester Road?'

'Yes.'

'And you haven't got a Miss or a Mrs Arkwright there?'

'We've got a butcher's shop 'ere, mate.'

'Oh, I see. Sorry to have troubled you.'

'You're welcome.'

'I just don't believe it!' said Morse quietly.

Chapter Fifteen

Thursday, January 2nd: p.m.

Even in civilized mankind, faint traces of a monogamic
instinct can sometimes be perceived.

(BERTRAND RUSSELL)

HELEN SMITH'S HUSBAND, John, had told her he
would be back at about one o'clock, and Helen had the
ingredients for a mushroom omelette all ready.
Nothing for herself, though. She would have found it
very difficult to swallow anything that lunchtime, for
she was sick with worry.

The headlines on 'The World at One' had just
finished when she heard the crunch of the BMW's
wheels on the gravel outside – the same BMW which
had spent the New Year anonymously enough in the
large multi-storey car park in the Westgate shopping
centre at Oxford. She didn't turn as she felt his light
kiss on the back of her hair, busying herself with
excessive fussiness over the bowl as she whisked the
eggs, and looking down at the nails of her broad, rather
stumpy fingers, now so beautifully manicured . . . and
so very different from the time, five years ago, when
she had first met John, and when he had mildly

criticized her irritating habit of biting them down to the quicks ... Yes, he had smartened her up in more than one way in their years of marriage together. That was certain.

'Helen! I've got to go up to London this afternoon. I may be back later tonight; but if I'm not, don't worry. I've got a key.'

'Um!' For the moment, she hardly dared risk a more fully articulated utterance.

'Is the water hot?'

'Mm!'

'Will you leave the omelette till I've had a quick bath?'

She waited until he had gone into the bathroom; waited until she heard the splash of water; even then gave things a couple of minutes more, just in case ... before stepping out lightly and quietly across the drive and trying the front passenger door of the dark-blue BMW – almost whimpering with anticipation.

It was open.

Two hours after Mr John Smith had stretched himself out in his bath at Reading, Philippa Palmer lay looking up at the ceiling of her own bedroom in her tastefully furnished, recently redecorated, first-floor flat in Chiswick. The man who lay beside her she had spotted at 12.30 p.m. in the Cocktail Lounge of the Executive Hotel just off Park Lane – a tall, dark-suited, prematurely balding man, perhaps in his early forties. To Philippa, he looked like a man not short of a few pounds, although it was always difficult to be certain. The exorbitant tariffs at the Executive (her favourite hunting-ground) were almost invariably settled on business expense accounts, and bore no necessary correlation with the apparent affluence of the hotel's (largely male) clientèle. She'd been sitting at the bar, nylon-stockinged, legs crossed, split skirt falling above the knee; he'd said 'Hullo', pleasantly; she'd accepted his offer of a drink – gin and tonic; she'd asked him, wasting no time at all, whether he wanted to be 'naughty' – an epithet which, in her wide experience, was wonderfully efficacious in beguiling the vast majority of men; he had demurred, slightly; she had moved a little closer and shot a sensual thrill throughout his body as momentarily she splayed a carmine-fingered hand along his thigh. The 'How much?' and the 'When?' and the 'Where?' had been settled with a speed unknown in any other professional negotiating body; and now here she lay – a familiar occurrence! – in her own room, in her own bed, waiting with ineffable boredom for the two-hour contract (at £60 per hour) to run its seemingly interminable course. She'd gauged him pretty well correctly from the start: a man of rather passive, voyeuristic tendencies rather than one of the more thrusting operatives in the fornication field. Indeed, the aggregate time of his two (hitherto) perfunctory penetrations could hardly have exceeded a couple of minutes; and of that Philippa had been duly glad. He might, of course, 'after a few minutes' rest' as the man had put it, rise to more sustained feats of copulatory stamina; but blessedly (from Philippa's point of view) the few minutes' rest had extended itself to a prolonged period of stertorous slumber.

The phone had first rung at about 2.30 p.m., the importunate burring making the man quite disproportionately nervous as he'd undressed. But she had told him that it would only be her sister; and he had appeared to believe her, and to relax. And as she herself had begun unzipping her skirt, he had asked if she would wear a pair of pyjamas while they were in bed together – a request with which she was not unfamiliar, knowing as she did that more than a few of her clients were less obsessed with nudity than with *semi*-nudity, and that the slow unbuttoning of a blouse-type top, with its tantalizing lateral revelations, was a far more erotic experience for almost all men than the vertically functional hitch of a nightdress up and over the thighs.

It was 3.15 p.m. when the phone rang again, and Philippa felt the man's eyes feasting on her body as she leaned forward and picked up the receiver.

'Mrs Palmer? Mrs Philippa Palmer?' The voice was loud and clear, and she knew that the man at her side would be able to hear every word.

'Ye-es?'

'This is Sergeant Lewis here, Thames Valley Police. I'd like to have a word with you about—'

'Look, Sergeant. Can you ring me back in ten minutes? I'm just having a shower and—'

'All right. You'll make sure you're there, Mrs Palmer?'

'Of course! Why shouldn't I be?'

The man had been sitting on the edge of the bed pulling on his socks with precipitate haste from the words 'Sergeant Lewis' onwards, and Philippa was relieved that (as always) pecuniary matters had been fully settled before the start of the performance. Seldom had Philippa seen a man dress himself so quickly; and his hurried goodbye and immediate departure were a relief to her, although she knew he was probably quite a nice sort of man, really. She admitted to herself that his underclothes had been the cleanest she had seen in weeks; and he hadn't mentioned his wife, if he had one, once.

It was a different voice at the end of the line when the telephone rang again ten minutes later: an interesting, educated sort of voice that she told herself she rather liked the sound of, announcing itself as Chief Inspector Morse.

Morse insisted that it would be far more sensible for himself (not Lewis) to go to interview the woman finally found at the other end of a telephone line in Chiswick. He fully appreciated Lewis's offer to go, but he also emphasized the importance of someone (Lewis) staying at the hotel and continuing to 'sniff around'. Lewis, who had heard this sort of stuff many times, was smiling to himself as he drove Morse down to Oxford station to catch the 4.34 train to Paddington that afternoon.

CHAPTER SIXTEEN

Thursday, January 2nd: p.m.

And he that seeketh findeth.

(MATTHEW vii, 8)

ON HIS RETURN from Oxford railway station, Lewis was tempted to call it a day and get off home. He had been up since 5 a.m., and it was now just after 5 p.m. A long enough stretch for anybody. But he didn't call it a day; and in retrospect his decision was to prove a crucial one in solving the mystery surrounding Annexe 3.

He decided to have a last look round the rooms in the annexe before he went home, and for this purpose he left the Operations Room by the front door (the partition between the main annexe entrance and the four rooms in use had not been dismantled) and walked round the front of the building to the familiar side-entrance, where a uniformed constable still stood on duty.

'It's open, Sarge,' Lewis heard as he fumbled with his embarrassment of keys.

'Give it till seven, I reckon. Then you can get off,' said Lewis. 'I'll just have a last look round.'

First, Lewis had a quick look round the one room that no one had as yet bothered about, Annexe 4; and here he made one small find – alas, completely insignificant. On the top shelf of the built-in wardrobe he found a glossy magazine illustrated with lewdly pornographic photographs, and filled out with a minimum of text which (judging from a prevalence of ø-looking letters) Lewis took to be written in some Scandinavian tongue. If Morse had been there (Lewis knew it so well) he would have sat down on the bed forthwith and given the magazine his undivided attention; and it often puzzled Lewis a little to understand how an otherwise reasonably sensitive person such as Morse could simultaneously behave in so unworthily crude a fashion. Yet he knew that nothing was ever likely to change the melancholy, uncommitted Morse; and he put the magazine back on the shelf, deciding that his superior should know nothing of it.

In Annexe 3 itself, there were so many chalked marks, so many biro'd circles, so many dusted surfaces, so much shifted furniture, that it was impossible to believe any clue would now be found there that had not been found already; and Lewis turned off the light and closed the door, making sure it was locked behind him.

In Annexe 1, the Palmers' room, Lewis could find nothing that he had missed in his earlier examination, and he paused only for a moment before the window, seeing his own shadow in the oblong of yellow light that was thrown across the snow, before turning the light off there too, and closing the door behind him.

He would have a quick look at the last room, the Smiths' room, and then he really would call an end to his long, long day.

In this room, Annexe 2, he could find nothing of any import; and Morse (Lewis knew) would have looked over it with adequate, if less than exhaustive, care. In any case, Morse had a creative imagination that he himself could never hope to match, and often in the past there had been things – those oddly intangible things – which the careful Lewis himself had missed and which Morse had almost carelessly discovered. Yet it would do no harm to have one final eleventh-hour check before permission was given to Binyon (as soon it must be) for the rooms to be freed for hotel use once more.

It was five minutes later that Lewis made his exciting discovery.

Sarah Jonstone saw Lewis leave just before 6 p.m., his car headlights, as he turned in front of the annexe, sending revolving patches of yellow light across the walls and ceiling of her unlit room. Then the winter darkness was complete once more. She had never minded the dark, even as a little girl, when she'd always preferred the door of her bedroom shut and the light on the landing switched off; and now as she looked out she was again content to leave the light turned off. She was developing a slight headache and she had dropped two soluble Disprin into a glass of water and was slowly swishing the disintegrating tablets round. Mr Binyon had asked her to stay on another night, and in the circumstances it would have been unkind for her to refuse. But it was an oddly unsatisfactory, anticlimactic sort of time: the night was now still after so many comings and goings; the lights in the annexe all switched off, including the light in the large back room which Morse and Lewis had been using; the press, the police, the public – almost everyone seemed to have gone; gone, too, were all the New Year revellers, all of them gone back home again – all except one, of course, the one who would never see his home again. The only signs left of all the excitement were the beribboned ropes that still cordoned off the annexe area, and the single policeman in the flat, black-and-white checked hat who still stood at the side entrance of the annexe, his breath steaming in the cold air, stamping his feet occasionally, and pulling his greatcoat ever more closely around him. She was wondering if she ought to offer him something – when she heard Mandy, from just below her window, call across and ask him if he wanted a cup of tea.

She herself drank the cloudy, bitter-tasting mixture from the glass, switched on the light, washed the glass, smoothed the wrinkled coverlet on which she had earlier been lying, turned on the TV, and listened to the main items of the six o'clock news. The world that day, that second day of the brand-new year, was familiarly full of crashes, hijackings, riots and terrorism; yet somehow such cataclysmic, collective disasters seemed far less disturbing to her than the murder of that one man, only some twenty-odd yards from where she stood. She turned off the TV, and went over to the window to pull the curtains across; she would smarten herself up a bit before going down to have her evening meal with the Binyons.

Odd!

A light was on again in the annexe, and she wondered who it could be. Probably the constable, for he was no longer standing by the side door. It was almost certainly in Annexe 2 that the light was on, she thought, judging from the yellow square of snow in front of the building. Then the light was switched off; and standing there at her window, arms outspread, Sarah was just about to pull the curtains across when she saw a figure, just inside the annexe doorway, pressed against the left-hand wall. Her heart seemed to miss a beat, and she felt a constriction somewhere at the back of her throat as she stood there for a few seconds completely motionless, mesmerized by what she had seen. Then she acted. She threw open the door, scampered down the stairs, rushed through to the main entrance and then along to the side door of the main building, where the constable stood talking with Mandy over a cup of steaming tea.

'There's someone across there!' Sarah whispered hoarsely as she pointed over to the annexe block.

'Pardon, miss?'

'I just saw someone in the doorway!'

The man hurried across to the annexe, with Sarah and Mandy walking nervously a few steps behind. They saw him open the side door (it hadn't been locked, that much was clear) and then watched as the light flicked on in the corridor, and then flicked off.

'There's no one there now,' said the worried-looking constable, clearly conscious of some potentially disastrous dereliction of duty.

'There *was* someone,' persisted Sarah quietly. 'It was in Annexe 2 – I'm sure of it. I saw the light on the snow.'

'But the rooms are all locked up, miss.'

Sarah said nothing. There were only two sets of master-keys, and Binyon (Sarah knew) had given one of those sets to Sergeant Lewis. But Sergeant Lewis had gone. Had Binyon used the other set *himself?* Had the slim figure she had seen in the doorway been Binyon's? And if so, what on earth—?

It was Binyon himself, wearing a raincoat but no hat, who had startlingly materialized from somewhere, and who now stood behind them, insisting (once he had asked about the nature of the incident) that they should check up on the situation forthwith.

Sarah followed him and the constable into the annexe corridor, and it was immediately apparent that someone *had* stood – and that within the last few minutes or so – in front of the door to Annexe 2. The carpet just below the handle was muddied with the marks of slushy footwear, and little slivers of yet unmelted snow winked under the neon lighting of the corridor.

*

Back in her room, Sarah thought hard about what had just happened. The constable had refused to let the door of Annexe 2 be touched or opened, and had immediately tried to contact Lewis at the number he had been instructed to ring should anything untoward occur. But Lewis had not yet arrived home; and this fact tended to bolster the belief, expressed by both Binyon and the constable, that it had probably been Lewis who had called back for some unexpected though probably quite simple reason. But Sarah had kept her counsel. She knew quite certainly that the figure she had glimpsed in the annexe doorway could never have been the heavily built Sergeant Lewis. *Could* it have been Mr Binyon, though? Whilst not impossible, that too, thought Sarah, was wildly improbable. And, as it happened, her view of the matter was of considerably greater value than anyone else's. Not only was she the sole witness to the furtive figure seen in the doorway; she was also the only person, at least for the present, who knew a most significant fact: the fact that although there were only two sets of master-keys to the annexe rooms, it was perfectly possible for *someone else* to have entered the room that evening without forcing a door or breaking a window. *Two other people*, in fact. On the key-board behind Reception, the hook was still empty on which should have been hanging the black-plastic oblong tab, with 'Haworth' printed over it in white, and the room key to Annexe 2 attached to it. For Mr and Mrs John Smith had left behind their unsettled account, but their room key they had taken with them.

CHAPTER SEVENTEEN

Thursday, January 2nd: p.m.

Aspern Williams wanted to touch the skin of the
daughter, thinking her beautiful, by which I mean
separate and to be joined.

(PETER CHAMPKIN, *The Waking Life of Aspern Williams*)

MORSE WALKED THROUGH the carpeted lounge of
the Great Western Hotel where several couples, seemingly with little any longer to say to each other, were
desultorily engaged in reading paperbacks, consulting
timetables or turning over the pages of the London
Standard. Time, apparently, was the chief item of
importance here, where a video-screen gave travellers
up-to-the-minute information about arrivals and depar-
tures, and where frequent glances were thrown towards
the large clock above the Porters' Desk, at which stood
two slightly supercilious-looking men in gold-braided
green uniforms. It was 5.45 p.m.

Immediately in front of him, through the revolving
door that gave access to Praed Street, Morse could see
the white lettering of PADDINGTON on the blue
Underground sign as he turned right and made his way
towards the Brunel Bar. At its entrance, a board

announced that 5.30 p.m. to 6.30 p.m. encompassed 'The Happy Hour', with any drink available at half-price – a prospect doubtless accounting for the throng of dark-suited black-briefcased businessmen who stood around the bar, anxious to get in as many drinks as possible before departing homewards to Slough or Reading or Didcot or Swindon or Oxford. Wall-seats, all in a deep maroon shade of velveteen nylon, lined the rectangular bar; and after finally managing to purchase his half-priced pint of beer, Morse sat down near the main entrance behind one of the free-standing, mahogany-veneered tables. The tripartite glass dish in front of him offered nuts, crisps, and cheese biscuits, into which he found himself dipping more and more nervously as the hands of the clock crept towards 6 p.m. Almost (he knew it!) he felt as excited as if he were a callow youth once more. It was exactly 6 p.m. when Philippa Palmer walked into the bar. For purposes of recognition, it had been agreed that she should carry her handbag in her left hand and a copy of the London *Standard* in her right. But the fact that she had got things the wrong way round was of little consequence to Morse; he himself was quite incapable of any instant and instinctive knowledge of east and west, and he would have spotted her immediately. Or so he told himself.

He stood up, and she walked over to him.

'Chief Inspector Morse?' Her face betrayed no emotion whatsoever: no signs of nervousness, embarrassment, co-operation, affability, humour – nothing.

'Let me get you a drink,' said Morse.

She took off her raincoat, and as Morse waited his turn again at the crowded bar he watched her from the corner of his eye: five foot five or six, or thereabouts, wearing a roll-necked turquoise-blue woollen dress which gently emphasized the rounded contours of her bottom but hardly did the rest of her figure much justice, perhaps. When he set the glass of red wine in front of her, she had crossed her nyloned legs, her slim-style high-heeled shoes accentuating the slightly excessive muscularity of her calves; and across the back of her right ankle Morse noticed a piece of Elastoplast, as though her expensive shoes probably combined the ultimate in elegance with a sorry degree of discomfiture.

'I tried to run a half-marathon – for charity,' she said, following his eyes, and his thoughts.

'For the Police Welfare Fund, I trust!' said Morse lightly.

Her eyes were on the brink of the faintest smile, and Morse looked closely at her face. It was undeniably an attractive face, framed by a head of luxuriant dark-brown hair glinting overall with hints of auburn; but it was the eyes above the high cheekbones – eyes of a deep brown – that were undoubtedly the woman's most striking feature. When she had spoken (with a slight Cockney accent) she had shown rather small regular teeth behind a mouth coated with only the thinnest smear of dark-red lipstick, and a great many men (Morse knew it) would find her a very attractive woman; and more than a few would find her necessary, too.

She had quite a lot to tell, but it took no great time
to tell it. She was (she admitted) a high-class call-girl,
who regularly encountered her clients in the cocktail
bars of the expensive hotels along Park Lane and
Mayfair. Occasionally, especially in recent years with
wealthy Arabian gentlemen, she would dispense her
favours on the site, as it were, in the luxury apartments
and penthouse suites on the higher floors of the hotels
themselves. But with the majority, the more usual
routine was a trip back to Chiswick in a taxi, where her
own discreet flat, on the eighth (and top) floor of a
private, modern block, was ideal, served as it was by a
very superior lift, and where no children, pets or
hawkers (in that order) were allowed. This flat she
shared with a happy-souled, feckless, mightily bosomed,
blonde dancer who performed in the Striporama Revue
Club off Great Windmill Street; but the two of them
had agreed from the start that no men visitors should
ever be invited to stay overnight, and the agreement
had as yet remained unbreached. So that was her CV –
not much else to say, really. 'Mr Palmer', a stockbroker
from Gerrards Cross, she had met several times previously; and when the prospect cropped up of a New
Year conference in Oxford – well, that's how this
business had all started. They needed an address for
correspondence, and she, Philippa, had written and
booked the room from her Chiswick flat – perfectly
above board. (An address *was* needed, she insisted; and
Morse refrained from arguing the dubious point.) She
herself had completed the documentation for both of
them at lunchtime on the 31st, though not filling in the

registration number of the Porsche which they had left in the British Rail car park. He'd had a good time, her client – she was quite sure of that until . . . And then, of course, there was every chance of him being found out – 'Just like being caught by the police in a raid on a Soho sex-joint!' – and he'd asked her to settle up immediately in cash, and then he'd got the pair of them out of there in double quick time, taking her with him to the station in a taxi and leaving her on the platform. From what he'd told her, he was going to book in at the Moat Hotel (at the top of the Woodstock Road) for the rest of the conference, and keep as big a distance as he possibly could between himself and the ill-fated annexe at the Haworth. Did the inspector *really* have to have his name? And in any case she hadn't the faintest idea of his address in Gerrards Cross. Quite certainly, in her view, he could have had nothing whatsoever to do with the killing of Ballard, because when she'd gone back to her room after the party she'd actually walked across to the annexe *with Ballard*, and then gone immediately into her own room with her, well, her sleeping companion, and she could vouch for the fact that he hadn't left the room that night – or left the bed for that matter! Assuredly not!

Morse nodded, a little enviously, perhaps. 'He was a pretty rich man, then?'

'Rich enough.'

'But not rich enough to afford a room in the main hotel?'

'There weren't any rooms left. We had to take what was going.'

125

'I know, yes. I'm glad you're telling me the truth, Miss Palmer. I've seen your correspondence with the hotel.'

For a few seconds her dark eyes held his – eyes that seemed momentarily to have grown hard and calculating – and she continued in a somewhat casual tone: 'He gave me the cash – in £20 notes. He was happy for me to make all the arrangements.'

'You made a bit on the side, then?'

'Christ!' It seemed as if she were about to explode at such a banal accusation, and her eyes flashed darkly with anger. 'You think that I have to rely on fiddling a few quid like that to make a living?'

But Morse couldn't answer. He was furious with himself for his stupid, naïve, condescending question; and he was relieved when she agreed to a second glass of red wine.

The Happy Hour was over.

The New Year party itself? It had been good fun, really – and the food had been surprisingly good. She herself had dressed up – maybe the inspector preferred 'dressed down'? – as a Turkish belly-dancer; with her companion, to her surprise, entering into the party spirit with considerable zest and ingenuity, and fashioning for himself from the rag-bag provided by the hotel an outfit not unworthy of an Arabian sheik. Quite a success, too! Not half as good as Ballard's, of course; but then some people took these things too seriously, as *he* had done – coming along all prepared with the necessary gear and grease and everything. As far as Philippa could remember, the Ballards had come in a few minutes later than all the rest; but she wasn't really very clear about the point, or about a lot of other things that went on during that evening. There had been eating and drinking and dancing and no doubt a little bit of semi-licit smooching (yes! on her part, too – just a little) in the candle-lit ballroom, and perhaps later on still a bit of . . . Philippa appeared to have difficulty in finding the right words for what Morse took to be some incidence of *sub mensa* gropings. Ballard, she thought, hadn't really come to life until after the judging of the fancy dress, spending much of the earlier part of the evening looking into the eyes (about the only feature he could look into!) of his yashmak'd wife – or whatever was another word for 'wife'. For it had seemed pretty clear to Philippa that she was not the only one involved that evening in extra-conjugal infidelity.

Anything else? She didn't think so. She'd already mentioned that Ballard had walked back to the annexe with her? Yes, of course she had. One arm round her, and one arm round Helen Smith: yes, she remembered Helen Smith; *and* liked her. Liked her husband, John, too, if he *was* her – augh! What was the point? She didn't know what their relationship was, and she wasn't in the slightest degree concerned! The next day? New Year's Day? She'd had a terrible head – which only served her right; had nothing but coffee at breakfast; had missed the Treasure Hunt; had spent the hour pre-lunch in bed; had enjoyed the roast beef; had spent the hour post-lunch in bed; and had only begun to take any interest in hotel activities during the late afternoon when she'd played ping-pong with one of the young lads. Oddly enough, she had been looking forward a good deal to going to the pantomime until . . . No, she hadn't seen anything at all of Mrs Ballard all that day, not so far as she could remember; and, of course, quite certainly nothing of Mr Ballard, either . . .

Morse got another drink for each of them, conscious that he was beginning to make up questions just for the sake of things. But why not? She couldn't tell him anything of importance, he was *almost* sure of that; but she was a lovely girl to be with – he was *absolutely* sure of that! They were sitting close together now, and gently she moved her left leg against the roughish tweed of his trousers. And, just as gently, he responded, saying nothing and yet saying everything.

'Would you like to treat me to a night in the Great Western Hotel?' She asked the question confidently; and yet there had been (had Morse but known it) a vibrancy and gentleness in her voice that had seldom been heard by any other man. Morse semi-shook his head, but she knew from the slow, sad smile that played about his lips that such an immediate reaction was more the mark of sad bewilderment than of considered refusal.

'I don't snore!' said Philippa softly against his ear.

'I don't know whether I do or not,' replied Morse. He was suddenly desperately aware that the time for a decision had come; but he was conscious, too, of the need (he had drunk four pints of beer already) to relieve himself, and he left her for a while.

On his return from the ground-floor Gents', he

walked over to Reception and asked the girl there whether there was a room available for the night.

'Just for yourself, is it, sir?'

'Er, no. A double room – for myself and my wife.'

'Just a second . . . No, I'm awfully sorry, sir, we've no rooms left at all this evening. But we may get a cancellation – we often get one or two about this time. Will you be in the hotel for a while, sir?'

'Yes – just for a while. I'll be in the bar.'

'Well, I'll let you know if I hear of anything. Your name, sir?'

'Er, Palmer. Mr Palmer.'

'All right, Mr Palmer.'

It was ten minutes later that the Muzak was switched off and a pleasantly clear female voice made the announcement to everyone in the Great Western Hotel, in the lounge, in the restaurant, and in the bar: 'Would Chief Inspector Morse please come to Reception immediately. Chief Inspector Morse, to Reception, please.'

He helped her on with her mackintosh, an off-white expensive creation that would have made almost any woman look adequately glamorous; and he watched her as she pulled the belt tight and evened out the folds around her slim waist.

'Been nice meeting you, Inspector.'

Morse nodded. 'We shall probably need some sort of statement.'

'I'd rather not – if you can arrange it.'

'I'll see.'

As she turned to leave, Morse noticed the grubby brown stain on the left shoulder of her otherwise immaculate raincoat: 'Were you wearing that when you left the party?' he asked.

'Yes.' She squinted down at the offending mark. 'You can't walk around semi-nude in the snow, can you?'

'I suppose not.'

'Pity, though. Cost a fiver at least to get it cleaned, that will. You'd 'a'thought, wouldn't you, if you dress up as a wog you might keep your 'ands off . . .'

The voice had slipped, and the mask had slipped; and Morse felt a saddened man. She could have been a lovely girl, but somehow, somewhere, she was flawed. A man had been savagely murdered – a man (who knows? with maybe just a little gentleness in his heart) who after a party one night had put his left hand, sweatily stained with dark-brown stage make-up, on to a woman's shoulder; and she was angry because it would possibly cost a few pounds to get rid of a stain that might detract from her appearance. They said farewell, and Morse sought to hide his two-fold disappointment behind the mask that he, too, invariably wore for most occasions before his fellow men. Perhaps – the thought suddenly struck him – it was the masks that were the reality, and the faces beneath them that were the pretence. So many of the people in the Haworth that fatal evening had been wearing some sort of disguise –

a change of dress, a change of make-up, a change of attitude, a change of partner, a change of life almost; and the man who had died had been the most consummate artist of them all.

After she had left, Morse walked back through the lounge to Reception (it *must* be Lewis who had rung for him – Lewis was the only person who had any idea where he was) and prayed that it would be a different young girl on duty. But it wasn't. Furthermore she was a girl who obviously possessed a fairly retentive memory.

'I'm afraid we haven't had any cancellations yet, Mr Palmer.'

'Oh, Christ!' muttered Morse under his breath.

CHAPTER EIGHTEEN

Thursday, January 2nd: p.m.

> Men seldom make passes
> At girls who wear glasses.
>
> (DOROTHY PARKER)

MR JOHN SMITH returned home that evening, unexpectedly early, to find his wife Helen in a state of tear-stained distraction; and once he had persuaded her to start talking, it was impossible to stop her . . .

Helen had caught the 3.45 train from Reading that afternoon, and arrived in Oxford at 4.20. Apart from the key to Annexe 2 which she clasped tight in the pocket of her duffel coat, she carried little else: no handbag, no wallet, no umbrella – only the return ticket to Reading, two pound coins, and a few shillings in smaller change. A taxi from Oxford station might have been sensible, but it certainly wasn't necessary; and in any case she knew that the twenty-minute walk would do her no harm. As she began to make her way to the Haworth Hotel her heart was beating as nervously as when she had opened the front passenger door of the BMW, and had frantically felt all over the floor of the car, splayed her hands across and under

and down and round the sides of seats and everywhere
– *everywhere*! And found nothing: nothing except a two-
pence piece, a white indigestion tablet, and a button
from a lady's coat (not one of her own) . . .

She walked quickly past the vast glass-fronted Black-
wells' building in Hythe Bridge Street, through
Gloucester Green, and then along Beaumont Street
into St Giles', where at the Martyrs' Memorial she
crossed over to the right-hand side of the thoroughfare
and, now more slowly, made her way northwards along
the Banbury Road.

Opposite the Haworth Hotel she could see the two
front windows of the annexe clearly – and so very near!
There seemed to be some sort of light on at the back
of the building somewhere; but each of the two rooms
facing the street – and especially one of them, the one
on the left as she watched and waited – was dark and
almost certainly empty. A glass-sided bus shelter almost
directly opposite the annexe protected her from the
drizzle, if not from the wind, and gave her an ideal
vantage point from which to keep watch without arous-
ing suspicion. A bus came and picked up the two
people waiting there, a very fat West Indian woman and
a wiry little English woman, both about sixty, both (as
Helen gathered) cleaners in a nearby hospice, who
chatted together on such easy and intimate terms that
it was tempting to be optimistic about future prospects
for racial harmony. Helen stood aside – and continued
to watch. Soon another bus was coming towards her, its

headlights illuminating the silvery sleet; but she stood back inside the shelter, and the bus passed on without stopping. Then she saw something – something which seemed to make her heart lurch towards her mouth. A light had been turned on in the room on the right, Annexe 1: the window, its curtains undrawn, glared brightly in the darkness, and a figure was moving around inside. Then the light was switched off, and the light in the next room – *her* room – was switched on. A bus had stopped, the doors, folding inwards, inviting her to climb aboard; and she found herself apologizing and seeing the look on the driver's face as he tossed his head in contempt before leaning forward over the great steering-wheel and driving away. The light was still on in Annexe 2, and she saw a figure silhouetted against the window for a few seconds; and then that light too was switched off. A man came out of the side door, walked round to the front of the annexe, immediately opposite to her, and disappeared inside; and the two rooms facing the street were dark and empty once more. *But the policeman was still there at the side entrance.* He had been there all along, his black-and-white checkered cap conspicuous under the light that illuminated the path between the Haworth Hotel and the cordoned area of the annexe – the red, yellow, and white tabs on the ropes tilting back and forth in the keen wind.

If Helen Smith had ever been likely to despair, she would have done so at this point. And yet somehow she knew that she would *not* despair. It may have been the cold, the hopelessness, the futility of it all; it may have been her awareness that there could be nothing more for her to lose. She didn't know. She didn't want to know. But she sensed within herself a feeling of wild determination that she had never known before. Her whole being seemed polarized between the black-and-white hat across the road and the key still clutched so tightly and warmly in her right hand. There had to be *some* way of diverting the man's attention, so that she would have the chance to slip swiftly and silently through the side door. But it had been so much easier than that! He had just walked across to the main hotel, where he now stood drinking a cup of something from a white plastic beaker, and happily engrossed in conversation with a young woman from the hotel.

Helen was in the corridor almost before her courage had been called upon.

No problem! With shaking hand she inserted the key in the lock of Annexe 2, closed the door behind her, and stood stock-still for a moment or two in the dark. Then she felt her way across to the bed nearer the window, and ran her hands along the smooth sheets, and beneath and around the pillow, and along the headboard, and finally over the floor. They *had* been there: they *had* been underneath her pillow – she *knew* it. And an embryo sob escaped her lips as again her hands frantically, but fruitlessly, searched around. There were two switches on the headboard, and she turned on the one above the bed she had slept in: she *had* to make sure! For half a minute she searched again desperately in the lighted room; but to no avail. And now, for the first time, it was fear that clutched her heart as she switched off the light, left the room and edged her way noiselessly through the side door. Then she froze where she stood against the wall. Immediately opposite, at one of the windows on the first floor of the main hotel, a woman stood watching her – and then was gone. Helen felt quite certain that the woman had seen her, and an icy panic seized her. She could remember little of how she left the hotel; but fear had given its own winged sandals to her feet.

The next thing she knew, she was walking along the Banbury Road, a good way down from the Haworth Hotel, her heart thumping like a trip-hammer in an ironmaster's yard. She walked without looking back for a single second; she walked and walked like some revenant zombie, oblivious to her surroundings, still panic-stricken and trembling – yet safe, blessedly safe! At the railway station, with only ten minutes to wait, she bought herself a Scotch, and felt fractionally better. But as she sat in a deserted compartment in the slow train back to Reading, she knew that each of the wearisome stops, like the stations of the cross, was bringing her nearer and nearer to a final reckoning.

Morse had made no secret of the fact that he would be meeting Philippa Palmer at the Great Western Hotel, and had agreed that should Lewis think it necessary he might be reached there. The news *could* wait until the morning of course – Lewis knew that; and it probably wasn't crucially important in any case. Yet everyone is anxious to parade a success, and for Lewis it had been a successful evening. In Annexe 2, the room in which

Mr and Mrs John Smith had spent the night of December 31st, he had found, beneath the pillow of the bed nearer the window, in a brown imitation-leather case, a pair of spectacles: small, feminine, rather fussy little things. At first he had been disappointed, since the case bore no optician's name, no address, no signification of town or county – nothing. But inside the case, squashed down at the very bottom, he had found a small oblong of yellow material for use (as Lewis knew) in the cleaning of lenses; and printed on this material were the words 'G.W. Lloyd, Opticians, High Street, Reading'. Fortunately Mr Lloyd, a garrulous Welshman hailing from Mountain Ash, had still been on the premises when Lewis rang him, and had willingly agreed to remain so until Lewis arrived. If it had taken Lewis only forty minutes to reach Reading, it had taken Lloyd only four or five to discover the owner of the lost spectacles. In his neat records the resourceful Lloyd kept full information about all his clients: this defect, that defect; long sight, short sight; degrees of astigmatism; type of spectacle frames; private or NHS. And tracing the spectacles had been almost childishly easy. Quite an able fellow, Lewis decided, this little Welshman who had opted for ophthalmology.

'I found them under the pillow, sir,' said Lewis when he finally got through to Morse at Paddington.

'Did you?'

'I thought it wouldn't perhaps do any harm just to check up on things a bit.'

'Check up on me, you mean!'

'Well, we can all miss things.'

'You mean to say they were there when I looked over that room? Come off it, Lewis! You don't honestly think I'd have missed something like that, do you?'

The thought that the spectacles had been planted in Annexe 2 by some person or other *after* Morse had searched the room had not previously occurred to Lewis, and he was beginning to wonder about the implications of such a strange notion when Morse spoke again.

'I'm sorry.'

'Pardon, sir?'

'I said I'm sorry, that's all. I must have missed the bloody things! And there's something else I want to say. Well done! No wonder I sometimes find it useful having you around, my old friend.'

Lewis was looking very happy when, after giving Morse the Smiths' address, he put down the phone, thanked the optician, and drove straight back to Oxford. He and Morse had agreed not to try to see either of the mysterious Smith couple until the following day. And Lewis was glad of that since he was feeling very tired indeed.

Mrs Lewis could see that her husband was happy when he finally returned home just before 9 p.m. She cooked him egg and chips and once again marvelled at the way in which Chief Inspector Morse could, on occasions, have such a beneficent effect upon the man she'd married. But she was very happy herself, too; she was always happy when he was.

Deciding, after he had finished his telephone conversation with Lewis, that he might just as well stay on in London and then stop off at Reading the following morning on his return to Oxford, Morse approached the receptionist (the same one) for the third time, and asked her sweetly whether she could offer him a single room for the night. Which she could, for there had been a cancellation. The card which she gave him Morse completed in the name of Mr Philip Palmer, of Irish nationality, and handed it back to her. As she gave him his room key, the girl looked at him with puzzlement in her eyes, and Morse leaned over and spoke quietly to her. 'Just one little t'ing, miss. If Chief Inspector Morse happens to call, please send him up to see me immediately, will you?'

The receptionist, now utterly bewildered, looked at him with eyes that suggested that either he was quite mad, or she was. And when he walked off towards the main staircase, she wondered whether she should ring the duty manager and acquaint him with her growing suspicion that she might have just booked an IRA terrorist into the hotel. But she decided against it. If he had a bomb with him, it was quite certainly not in his suitcase, for he had no suitcase; had no luggage at all, in fact – not even a toothbrush by the look of things.

CHAPTER NINETEEN

January 2nd/3rd

Love is strong as death; jealousy is cruel as the grave.
(SONG OF SOLOMON viii, 6)

THE WHOLE DESPERATE business had acquired a gathering momentum born of its own progress. It was, for Margaret Bowman, like driving a car whose brakes had failed down an ever more steeply inclined gradient – where the only thing to do was to try to steer the accelerating vehicle with the split-second reactions of a racing driver and to pray that it would reach the bottom without a fatal collision. To stop was utterly impossible.

It had been about a year ago when she had first become aware that her husband was showing unmistakable signs of becoming a semi-drunkard. There would be days when he would not touch a drop of alcohol; but there were other periods when two or three times a week she would return from work to find him in a sort of slow-thinking half-daze after what must clearly have been fairly prolonged bouts of drinking, about which her own occasional criticism had served merely to trigger off an underlying crude and cruel streak in his nature which had greatly frightened her. Had it been because of his drinking that (for the first time in their marriage) she had been unfaithful to him? She wasn't sure. Possibly – probably, even – she might in any case have drifted into some sort of illicit liaison with one or two of the men she had recently got to know at work. Everyone changed as the years went by, she knew that. But Tom, her husband, seemed to have undergone a fundamental change of character, and she had become increasingly terrified of him finding out about her affair, and deeply worried about what dreadful things he would do to her; and to *him*, and perhaps to himself, if he ever did find out. Her infidelity had spanned the late summer and most of the autumn before she began to realize that any affair was just as fraught with risk as marriage was. For the first few weeks, a single afternoon a week had sufficed: he, by regulating his varied weekend workings, was able to take a day off every week, and this was easily synchronized with her own afternoon off (on Thursdays) when the pair of them made love in the bedroom of an erstwhile council house in North Oxford which he now owned himself. That had been the early pattern; and for the first two or three months he had been interesting to be with, considerate, anxious to please. But as time went on, he too (just like her husband) had appeared to change: he became somewhat crude in one or two respects, more demanding, less talkative, with (quite clearly to Margaret Bowman) his own craving for sexual gratification dominating their post-meridian copulations. Progressively he'd wished to see her more often, ever badgering her to fabricate for her employers a series of visits to dentists, doctors, and terminally ill relatives; or to take home to her husband tales of overtime workings necessitated by imaginary backlogs. And while she despised the man to some degree for so obviously allowing all his professed love for her to degenerate into an undisguised lust, yet there was a physical side to her own nature, at once as crude and selfish and demanding as his, which welded them into an almost perfect partnership between the sheets. The simple truth was that the more he used and abused her, the more sexual satisfaction he managed to wring from her, and the more she was conscious of her pride in being the physical object of his apparently insatiable appetite for her body. Indeed, as the year moved into its last quarter, she began to suspect that she needed him almost as much as he needed her, although for a long time she refused to countenance, even to herself, the full implications of such a suspicion. But then she was forced to face them. He was soon making *too* many demands upon her, begging her to be with him even for an odd half-hour at lunchtimes when (truth to tell) she would more often than not have preferred a glass of red wine and a ham sandwich with her friend and colleague Gladys Taylor in the Dew Drop. And then had come the show-down, as perhaps she'd known would be inevitable. He'd asked her to leave her husband and come to live with him: it was about time, surely, that she left the man she didn't love and moved in with the one she did. And although coming within an ace of saying 'yes', she'd finally said 'no'.

Why Margaret Bowman had thus refused, she would

herself have found difficult to explain. Perhaps it was because (for the present at least) it was all far too much *bother*. The rather dull, the slightly overweight, the only semi-successful man who was her husband, was the man with whom she had shared so much for so many years now. And there were far too many other shared things to think of packing everything up just like that: payments on the car, life insurances, the house mortgage, family friends and relations, neighbours – even the disappointments and the quarrels and the boredoms, which all seemed to form a strangely binding sort of tie between them. Yet there was perhaps, too, one quite specific reason why she had refused. Gladys (Margaret had come to work in the same section as Gladys in the spring) had become a genuine friend; and one day in the Dew Drop she had told Margaret how she had been temporarily jilted by her husband, and how for many months after that she had felt so hurt and so belittled that she'd wondered whether she would ever be able to lift up her head in life again. 'Having had it done to me' (she'd confided) 'I couldn't ever think of doing it to anyone else.' It had been a simple little thing to say, and it had not been said with any great moral fervour; yet it had made its point with memorable effect . . .

That particular Thursday afternoon when she had finally said 'no' they'd had their first blazing row, and she had been alarmed by the look of potential violence in his eyes. Although he had finally calmed down, she found herself making excuses for the whole of the next week, including the hitherto sacrosanct p.m. period on Thursday. It had been a sad mistake, though, since the following fortnight had been a nightmare. He had rung her at work, where she had taken the message in front of all the other women in the section, their eyes glued on her as (nonchalantly, she hoped) she promised to get in touch. Which she *had* done, asking him sensibly, soberly, just to let things ride for a few weeks and see if they would sort themselves out. Then there had been the first letter, addressed to her at work – pleasantly, lovingly, imploring her to go back to the old pattern of their former meetings. And then, when she did not reply to the first letter, a second one, which was addressed to her home and which she'd picked up from the front-hall mat at eight o'clock on a wet and miserable November morning *when she was going to a funeral.* Tom was still in bed, and she'd hurriedly torn the envelope open and looked through the letter – the cruel, vindictive, frightening letter which she'd quickly stuck into the bottom of her handbag as she heard the creak at the top of the stairs.

When, that same morning, her husband sat opposite her at the kitchen table, she seemed engrossed in the half-dozen brochures she had picked up the previous lunchtime in Summertown Travel, giving details of trips ranging from gentle strolls round the hill-forts of Western England to lung-racking rambles in the Himalayan foothills. *Yet how fervently at that moment did she wish her lover dead!*

Tom Bowman had not told his wife about his discovery of the letter until the following Wednesday evening. It had been a harrowing occasion for her, but Tom had not flown into a rage or threatened her with physical violence. In retrospect, she almost wished he had done so; for far more frightening, and something that sent the four guardians scurrying from the portals of her sanity, was the change that seemed to have come over him: there was a hardness in his voice and in his eyes; an unsuspected deviousness about his thinking; a firmness of purpose about his frightening suggestions; and, underlying all (she suspected), a terrifyingly vicious and unforgiving jealousy against the man who had tried to rob him of his wife. What he said that evening was so fatuous really, so fanciful, so silly, that his words had not registered with her as forming any plausible or practicable plan of revenge. Yet slowly and inexorably the ideas which he had outlined to her that evening had set in motion a self-accelerating series of events which had culminated in murder.

Even now, right at the end of things, she was aware of the ambivalence of all her thoughts, her motives, her hopes – and her mind would give her no rest. After watching the late-night news on BBC2 she took four aspirin tablets and went to bed, where (wonderfully!) she fell easily enough into sleep. But by a quarter past one she was awake once more, and for the next four hours her darting eyes could not remain still for a second in their burning sockets as the whirligig of her brain sped round and round without any hint of slowing down, as if the fairground operator had pushed the lever forward on to 'Fast' and then fallen into an insensate stupor over the controls.

*

That same night, the night of January 2nd, Morse himself had a pleasantly refreshing sleep, with a mildly erotic dream (about a woman with a large Elastoplast over one ankle) thrown in for good measure. He told himself, on waking at 6.30 a.m., that if only there had been a double room available the night before . . . But he had never been a man to be unduly perturbed by the 'if onlys' of life, and he possessed a wholly enviable capacity for discounting most disappointments. Remembering a programme he had heard the previous week on cholesterol (a programme which the Lewis family had obviously missed), Morse decided to forgo the huge and rare treat of a fried breakfast in the restaurant, and caught the 9.10 train to Reading from platform 2. In the second-class compartment in which he made the journey were two other persons: in one corner, an (equally unshaven) Irishman who said nothing whatsoever after a polite 'Good morning, sorr!' but who thereafter smiled perpetually as though the day had dawned exceedingly bright; and in the other corner, a pretty young girl wearing (as Morse recognized it) a Lady Margaret Hall scarf, who scowled unceasingly as she studied a thick volume of anthropological essays, as though the world had soured and worsened overnight.

It seemed, to Morse, a metaphor.

Chapter Twenty

Friday, January 3rd: a.m.

There's a kind of release
And a kind of torment in every goodbye for every man.

(C. DAY LEWIS)

FOR MANY HOURS before Morse had woken, Helen Smith had been lying wide awake in bed, anticipating the worries that would doubtless beset her during the coming day. After her dreadful ordeal of the previous day, it had been wonderfully supportive of John to show such understanding and forgiveness; indeed, he had almost persuaded her that, even if she *had* left anything potentially incriminating behind, police resources were so overstretched in coping with major felonies that it was very doubtful whether anyone would find the time to pursue their own comparatively minor misdemeanours. And at that point, she had felt all the old love for him which she had known five years previously when they had met in Yugoslavia, her native country; and when after only two weeks' courtship she had agreed to marry him and go to live in England. He had given her the impression then – very much so! – of being a reasonably affluent businessman; and in any case she was more than glad to get away from a country in which her family lived under the shadow of a curiously equivocal incident from the past, in which her paternal grandfather, for some mysterious reason, had been shot by the Titoists outside Trieste. But from the earliest days in England she had become aware of her husband's strange lifestyle, of his dubious background, of his shady present, and of his far from glittering prospects for the future. Yet in her own quiet, gentle way, she had learned to love him, and to perform (without overmuch reluctance) the rôle that she was called upon to play.

At 7.30 a.m. they sat opposite each other over the pine-wood table in the small kitchen of their rented property, having a breakfast of grapefruit juice, toast and marmalade, and coffee. When they had finished, John Smith looked across at his wife and put his hand over hers. In his eyes she was still a most attractive woman – that at least was a point on which he had no need to lie. Her legs, for the purist, were perhaps a little too slim; and likewise her bust was considerably less bulging than the amply bosomed models who unfailingly featured on one of the earlier pages of their daily newspaper; her face had a pale, Slavonic cast, with a slightly pitted, rather muddy-looking skin; but the same face, albeit somewhat sullen in repose, was ever irradiated when she smiled, the intense, greenish eyes flashing into life, and the lips curling back over her regular teeth. She was smiling, though a little sadly, even now.

'Thank you!' she said.

*

At 8 a.m. John Smith told his wife that he wanted her to go up to the January sales in Oxford Street and buy herself a new winter coat. He gave her five £20 notes, and would countenance no refusal. He took her down to the station in the car, and waited on the platform with her until the 8.40 '125' pulled in to carry her off to the West End.

As her train drew into Paddington's platform 5 at 9.10 a.m., another '125' was just pulling out of platform 2 and soon gliding along the rails at a high, smooth speed towards Reading. In a second-class compartment (as we have already seen), rather towards the rear of this train, and with only two wholly uncommunicative fellow-passengers for company, sat Morse, reading the *Sun*. At home he invariably took *The Times*, though not because he much enjoyed it, or even read it (apart from the letters page and the crossword); much more because the lady local councillor who ran the newsagent's shop down in Summertown was fully aware of Morse's status, and had (to Morse's knowledge) more than once referred to him as 'a really civilized gentleman'; and he had no wish prematurely to destroy such a flattering illusion.

If the serious-minded undergraduette from Lady Margaret Hall had bothered to lift her eyes from her reading, she would have seen a man of medium height who had filled out into a somewhat barrel-shaped figure, with his waist and stomach measurements little altered from his earlier days and yet with his shirt now stretching tight around his chest. His unshaven jowls (the young student might have thought) suggested an age of nearer sixty than fifty (in fact, the man was fifty-four), and his face seemed cast in a slightly melancholy mould, not at all brightened that morning by the insistence of the young ticket-collector that he was obliged to pay a surcharge on the day-return ticket he had paid for the previous evening.

The taxi carrying its fare from Reading railway station to the Smiths' newly discovered address was told to pull up fifty yards into Eddleston Road, where Morse told the driver to wait as he walked across the road and rang the bell on the door of number 45.

When John Smith turned into the street, he immediately saw the taxi opposite his house, and stopped dead in his tracks at the corner shop where he appeared to take an inordinate interest in the hundred-and-one rectangular white notices which announced a multitude of wonderful bargains, from a pair of training shoes (hardly ever worn) to a collection of Elvis Presley records (hardly ever played). The taxi's exhaust was still running, sending a horizontal stream of vapour across the lean, cold air; and reflected in the corner-shop window Smith could see a man in an expensive-looking dark grey overcoat seemingly reluctant to believe that neither of the occupants of the house could be at home. Finally, slowly, the importunate caller walked away from the house, stood back to take a last look at the property, and then got back into the taxi, which was off immediately in a spurt of dirty slush.

*

John Smith entered the shop, purchased a packet of twenty Silk Cut, and stood for three or four minutes at the magazine rack leafing through *Wireless Weekly, Amateur Photographer,* and the *Angling Times.* But apparently he had decided that none of these periodicals was exactly indispensable, and he walked out empty-handed into the street. He had always prided himself on being able to sniff out danger a mile away. But he sensed there was none now; and he strolled down the street with exaggerated unconcern, and let himself into number 45.

He had a fastidiously tidy mind, and even now was tempted to wash up the few breakfast things that stood in the kitchen sink, particularly the two knives that looked almost obscenely sticky from the polyunsaturated Flora and Cooper's Thick Cut Oxford Marmalade. But the walls were closing in, he knew it. The BMW would have been the riskiest thing; and half an hour ago he had sold the three-year-old beauty at Reading Motors for a ridiculously low-pitched £6,000 in cash. Then he had gone along to the town-centre branch of Lloyds Bank, where he had withdrawn (again in cash) the £1,200 which stood in the joint account of John and Helen Smith.

Helen had spent a brief but successful time in Selfridges (she had bought herself a new white mackintosh) and was back in the house just after noon, when she immediately saw the note beside the telephone.

Helen, my love!

They are on to us, and there's little option for me but to get away. I never told you quite everything about myself but please believe that if they catch up with me now I shall be sent to prison for a few years – I can't face that. I thought they might perhaps confiscate the little savings we managed to put together, and so I cashed the lot and you'll find thirty £20 notes in your favourite little hiding place – that's a precaution just in case the police get here before you find this! If I ever loved anyone in the world, I loved you. Remember that! I'm sorry it's got to be like this.

Ever yours,
John

She read the brief letter without any sense of shock – almost with a sense of resigned relief. It couldn't have gone on for ever, that strange life she'd led with the oddly maverick confidence-man who had married her, and who had almost persuaded her at times that he loved her. Yes, that was the only really deep regret: if he had *stayed* – stayed with her and faced the music whatever tune they played – then life would indeed have been an undoubted triumph for the dark young lady from Yugoslavia.

She was upstairs in the front bedroom, changing her clothes, when she heard the front-door bell.

CHAPTER TWENTY-ONE

Friday, January 3rd: mostly a.m.

As when heaved anew
Old ocean rolls a lengthened wave to shore
Down whose green back the short-lived foam, all hoar
Burst gradual, with a wayward indolence.

(JOHN KEATS)

MORSE HAD FELT tempted to ring Lewis to tell him not to bother with their original plan of meeting in Eddleston Road at 11 a.m. But he didn't so do. The prospect of more trains and more taxis was an intolerable one; and in any case he was now almost completely out of ready cash. At 10.50 he was again knocking on the door of the Smiths' house; once again without getting any reply. The road was part of a reasonably elegant residential quarter. But heading off from it, on the southern side, were smaller, meaner streets of Victorian two-storey red-brick terraced houses; and as Morse strolled through this area he began to feel pleasantly satisfied with life, a state of mind that may not have been unconnected with the fact that he was in unfamiliar circumstances, with nothing immediately or profitably to be performed, with a small public house on the next corner facing him and with his wrist-watch showing only a minute or so short of opening time.

The Peep of Dawn (as engagingly named a pub as Morse could remember) boasted only one bar, with wooden wall-seats, and after finding out from the landlord which bitter the locals drank he sat with his pint in the window alcove and supped contentedly. He wasn't quite sure whether his own oft-repeated insistence that he could always think more lucidly after an extra ration of alcohol was wholly true. He certainly *believed* it to be true, though; and quite certainly many a breakthrough in previous investigations had been made under such attendant circumstances. It was only in recent months that he had found himself querying his earlier assumption about such a *post hoc, ergo propter hoc* proposition; and it had occasionally occurred to him that fallacious logic was not infrequently the offspring of wishful thinking. Yet for Morse (and he quite simply accepted the fact) the world *did* invariably seem a much warmer, more manageable place after a few pints of beer; and quite certainly he knew that (for himself, at any rate) it was on such occasions that the imaginative processes usually *started*. It may have been something to do with the very *liquidity* of alcohol, for he had often seen these processes in terms of just such a metaphor. It was as if he were lulled and sitting idly on the sea-front, and watching, almost entranced, as some great Master of the Tides drew in the foam-fringed curtains of the waters towards his feet and then pulled them back in slow retreat to the creative sea.

But whatever the truth of the matter, he knew he would have to do some serious thinking very soon, and for the moment the problem that was uppermost in his mind was how a letter which had been written from a non-existent address had also been received at the very same non-existent address. It was easy of course to write anything *from* anywhere in the world – say from 'Buckingham Palace, Kidlington'; but how on earth, in turn, was it possible for a letter to be delivered *to* such improbably registered premises? Yet that is what *had* happened, or so it seemed. The man who had been murdered was, on the face of things, the husband of a woman who had booked a room from an address which did not exist; had booked the room by letter; and had received confirmation of the booking, also by letter – with the pair of them duly arriving on December 31st, taking part in the evening's festivities (incidentally, with outstanding success), and finally, after joining their fellow guests in wishing themselves, one and all, a happily prosperous new year, walking back to their room in the annexe. And then . . .

'You'd not forgotten me, had you?' said a voice above him.

'Lewis! You're a bit late aren't you?'

'We agreed to meet at the house, if you remember, sir!'

'I went there. There's no one at home.'

'I *know* that. Where do you think *I've* been?'

'What's the time now?'

'Twenty past eleven.'

'Oh dear! I am sorry! Get yourself a drink, Lewis – and a refill for me, please. I'm a bit short of cash, I'm afraid.'

'Bitter, was it?'

Morse nodded. 'How did you find me?'

'I'm a detective. Had you forgotten that, too?'

But it would have taken more than Morse's meanness with money, and more than Morse's cavalier notions of punctuality, to have dashed Lewis's good spirits that morning. He told Morse all about his encounter with the Welsh optician; and Morse, in turn, told Lewis (almost) all about his encounter with the fair Philippa at Paddington. At a quarter to twelve Lewis made another fruitless visit to Eddleston Road. But half an hour later, this time with Morse, it was immediately clear that someone had returned to number 45. It was the only house in the row whose occupants had dispensed with the need for keeping its front garden in any neat trim by the simple (albeit fairly drastic) expedient of covering the whole area with small beige pebbles, which crunched noisily as the two men walked up the sinking shingle to the door.

CHAPTER TWENTY-TWO

Friday, January 3rd: p.m.

You can fool too many of the people too much of the time.

(JAMES THURBER)

THROUGHOUT THE WHOLE of the last five years (admitted Helen Smith) the two of them had successfully contrived to defraud dozens of honourable institutions of their legitimate income. But neither her husband John nor herself had the means whereby to make any reparation even fractionally commensurate with such deceit. She, Helen, fully understood why society at large should expect some expiation for her sins; but (she stressed the point) if such compensation were to be index-linked to its £ s. d. equivalents, there was no prospect whatsoever of any settlement of the overdue account. She showed Lewis the note she had found on her return from London; and would be happy to show him, too, the little hidey-hole beneath the second floorboard from the left in the spare bedroom where she had duly found the £600 referred to – that is if Lewis wanted to see it. (Lewis didn't.) Unshakably, however, she refused to hazard any information about where her husband might have made for; and indeed her refusal was genuinely founded in total ignorance, both of his present whereabouts and of his future plans.

The pattern had seldom varied: ringing round half a dozen hotels at holiday periods; taking advantage of late cancellations (an almost inevitable occurrence); there and then accepting, by phone, any vacancy which so lately had arisen; promising a.s.a.p. a confirmatory letter (with both parties appreciating the unreliability of holiday-time postal services); staying only two nights where 'The Businessman's Break' was scheduled for three; or staying just the one night where it was scheduled for two. And that was about it. Easy enough. There were of course always a few little secrets about such professional deception: for example, it was advisable *always* to carry as little baggage as was consistent with reasonably civilized standards of hygiene; again, it was advisable *never* to park a car on the hotel premises, or to fill in the section on the registration form asking for car-licence numbers. Yet there was one principle above all that had to be understood, namely, that the more demands you made upon the establishment, the more enhanced would be your status *vis-à-vis* the management and staff of all hotels. Thus it was that the Smiths had learned *always* to select their meals from the higher echelons of the *à la carte* specialities of the chef, and wines and liqueurs from any over-valued vintage; to demand room-service facilities at the most improbable periods of day or night; and, finally, *never* to exchange too many friendly words with anyone in sight – from the manager down, through receptionist to waitress, porter or cleaner. Such (Helen testified) were the basic principles she and her husband had observed in their remarkably successful bid to extract courtesy and respect from some of the finest hotels across the length and breadth of the United Kingdom. The only thing then left to be staged was their disappearance, which was best effected during that period when no one normally booked out of hotels – midafternoon. And that had usually been the time when the Smiths had decided to take leave of their erstwhile benefactors – sans warning, sans farewell, sans payment, sans everything.

When Helen Smith came to court (inevitably so, as Lewis saw things) it seemed wholly probable that this darkly attractive, innocent-looking defendant would plead guilty to the charges brought against her, and would pretty certainly ask, too, for one-hundred-and-one other offences to be taken into consideration. But she hardly looked or sounded like a criminal, and her account of the time she had spent at the Haworth Hotel appeared honest and clear. Four (yes!) bottles of champagne had been ordered – they both liked the lovely stuff! – two on New Year's Eve and two on New Year's Day, with the last of the four still in the larder if Lewis wanted to see it. (Lewis did.) Yes, she remembered a few things about the Ballards, *and* about the Palmers; but her recollections of specific times and specific details were even hazier than Philippa Palmer's had been the previous evening. Like Philippa, though, she thought that the evening had been well organized – and great fun; and that the food and drink had been very good indeed. The Smiths, both of them, enjoyed fancy-dress parties; and that New Year's Eve they had appeared – an oddly uncomplementary pair! – as a seductive Cleopatra and as a swordless Samurai. Would Lewis like to see the costumes? (Lewis would.) Whether Ballard had eaten much or drunk much that evening, she couldn't remember with any certainty. But she did remember, most clearly, Ballard walking back with her through the snow (Oh yes! it had been snowing heavily then) to the hotel annexe, and ruining the right shoulder-lapel of her mackintosh, where his right hand had left a dirty dark-brown stain – which of course Lewis could see if he so desired. (As Lewis did.)

During the last part of this interview Morse had seemed only minimally interested in Lewis's interrogation, and had been leafing through an outsize volume entitled *The Landscape of Thomas Hardy*. But now, suddenly, he asked a question.

'Would you recognize *Mrs* Ballard if you saw her again?'

'I – I don't really know. She was in fancy dress and—'

'In a yashmak, wasn't she?'

Helen nodded, somewhat abashed by the brusqueness of his question.

'Didn't she *eat* anything?'

'Of course, yes.'

'But you can't eat anything in a yashmak!'

'No.'

'You must have *seen* her face, then?'

Helen knew that he was right; and suddenly, out of the blue, she *did* remember something. 'Yes,' she began slowly. 'Yes, I did see her face. Her top lip was a bit red, and there were red sort of pin-pricks – you know, sort of little red spots . . .'

But even as Helen spoke these words, her own upper lip was trembling uncontrollably, and it was clear that the hour of questioning had left her spirits very low indeed. The tears were suddenly springing copiously and she turned her head sharply away from the two policemen in total discomfiture.

In the car, Lewis ventured to ask whether it might not have been wiser to take Helen Smith back to Oxford there and then for further questioning. But Morse appeared unenthusiastic about any such immediate move, asserting that, compared with the likes of Marcinkus & Co. in the Vatican Bank, John and Helen Smith were sainted folk in white array.

It was just after they had turned on to the A34 that Morse mentioned the strange affair of the yashmak'd lady's upper lip.

'How did you guess, Lewis?' he asked.

'It's being married, sir – so I don't suppose you ought to blame yourself too much for missing it. You see, most women like to look their best when they go away, let's say for a holiday or a trip abroad or something similar; and the missus has a bit of trouble like that – you know, a few unsightly hairs growing just under the chin or a little fringe of hairs on the top lip. A lot of women have the same trouble especially if they've got darkish sort of hair—'

'But your missus has got *fair* hair!'

'All right; but it happens to everybody a bit as they get older. You get rather self-conscious and embarrassed about it if you're a woman, so you often go to one of the hair clinics like the *Tao* or something and they give you electrolysis and they put a needle sort of thing into the roots of the hairs and – well, sort of get rid of them. Costs a bit though, sir!'

'But being a rich man you can just about afford to let the missus go along to one of these beauty parlours?'

'Just about!'

Lewis suddenly put down his foot with a joyous thrust, turned on his right-hand flasher, took the police car up to 95 m.p.h., veered in a great swoop across the outside lane, and netted a dozen lorries and cars which had thoughtfully decelerated to the statutory speed limit as they'd noticed the white car looming up in their rear mirrors.

'The treatment they give you,' continued Lewis, 'makes the skin go a bit pinkish all over and they say if it's on the top lip it's very sensitive and you often get a histamine reaction – and a sort of tingling sensation . . .'

But Morse was no longer listening. His own body was tingling too; and there crossed his face a beatific smile as Lewis accelerated the police car faster still towards the City of Oxford.

*

Back in Kidlington HQ, Morse decided that they had spent quite long enough in the miserably cold and badly equipped room at the back of the Haworth annexe, and that they should now transfer things back home, as it were.

'Shall I go and get a few new box-files from the stores?' asked Lewis. Morse picked up two files which were heavily bulging with excess paper, and looked cursorily through their contents. 'These'll be OK. They're both OBE.'

'OBE, sir?'

Morse nodded: 'Overtaken By Events.'

The phone rang half an hour later and Morse heard Sarah Jonstone's voice at the other end. She'd remembered a little detail about Mrs Ballard; it might be silly of her to bother Morse with it, but she could almost swear that there had been a little red circular sticker – an RSPCA badge, she thought – on Mrs Ballard's coat when she had booked in at registration on New Year's Eve.

'Well,' said Morse, 'we've not done a bad job between us, Lewis. We've managed to find two of the three women we were after – and it's beginning to look as if it's not going to be very difficult to find the last one! Not tonight, though. I'm tired out – and I could do with a bath, and a good night's sleep.'

'*And* a shave, sir!'

CHAPTER TWENTY-THREE

Saturday, January 4th

Arithmetic is where the answer is right and everything is
nice and you can look out of the window and see the blue
sky — or the answer is wrong and you have to start all
over and try again and see how it comes out this time.

(CARL SANDBURG, *Complete Poems*)

THE THAW CONTINUED overnight, and lawns that
had been totally subnivean the day before were now
resurfacing in patches of irregular green under a blue
sky. The bad weather was breaking; the case, it seemed,
was breaking too.

At Kidlington HQ Morse was going to be occupied
(he'd said) with other matters for most of the morning;
and Lewis, left to his own devices, was getting progressively more and more bogged down in a problem which
at the outset had looked comparatively simple. The
Yellow Pages had been his starting point, and under
'Beauty Salons and Consultants' he found seven or
eight addresses in Oxford which advertised specialist
treatment in what was variously called Waxing, Facials,
or Electrolysis; with another five in Banbury; three
more (a gloomier Lewis noticed) in Bicester; and a

good many other establishments in individual places that could be reached without too much travelling by a woman living in Chipping Norton – if (and in Lewis's mind it was a biggish 'if') 'Mrs Ballard' *was* in fact a citizen of Chipping Norton.

But there were *two* quadratic equations, as it were, from which to work out the unknown 'x': and it was the second of these – the cross-check with the charity flag days – to which Lewis now directed his thinking. In recent years, the most usual sort of badge received from shakers of collection tins had come in the form of a little circular sticker that was pressed on to the lapel of the contributor's coat; and Lewis's experience was that such a sticker often fell off after a few minutes rather than stuck on for several days. And so Morse's view, Lewis agreed, was probably right: if Mrs Ballard was still wearing a sticker on New Year's Eve, she'd probably bought it the same day, or the day before at the very outside. But Lewis had considerable doubts about Morse's further confidently stated conviction that there must have been an RSPCA flag day in Oxford on the 30th or 31st, and that Mrs Ballard had bought a flag as she went into a beauty salon in the city centre. 'Beautifully simple!' Morse had said. 'We've got the time, we've got the place – and we've almost got the woman, agreed? Just a little phoning around and . . .'

But Lewis had got off to a bad start. His first call elicited the disappointing information that the last street-collection in Oxford for the RSPCA had been the previous July; and he had no option but to start making another list, and a very long list at that. First came the

well-known medical charities, those dealing with mul-
tiple sclerosis, rheumatoid arthritis, heart diseases,
cancer research, blindness, deafness, et cetera; then the
major social charities, ranging from Christian Aid and
Oxfam to War on Want and the Save the Children
Fund, et cetera; next came specific societies that looked
after ambulancemen, lifeboatmen and ex-servicemen,
et cetera; finally were listed the local charities which
funded hospices for the terminally ill, hostels for the
criminally sick or the mentally unbalanced, et cetera.
Lewis could have added scores of others – and he knew
he was getting into an awful mess. He could even have
added the National Association for the Care and Reset-
tlement of Criminal Offenders. But he didn't.

Clearly some sort of selection was required, and he
would have been more than glad to have Morse at his
side at that moment. It was like being faced with
a difficult maths problem at school: if you weren't
careful, you got more and more ensnared in some
increasingly complex equations – until the master
showed you a beautifully economic short-cut that
reduced the problem to a few simple little sums and
produced a glittering (and correct) solution at the foot
of the page. But his present master, Morse, was still
apparently otherwise engaged, and so he decided to
begin in earnest: on the second of the two equations.

Yet an hour later he had advanced his knowledge of
charity collections in Oxford not one whit; and he was
becoming increasingly irritated with telephone numbers which didn't answer when called, or which (if they
did answer) appeared manned by voluntary envelope-

lickers, decorators, caretakers or idiots – or (worst of all!) by intimidating answering machines telling Lewis to start speaking 'now'. And after a further hour of telephoning, he hadn't found a single charitable organization which had held a flag day in Oxford – or anywhere else in the vicinity, for that matter – in the last few days of December.

He was getting, ridiculously, nowhere; and he said as much when Morse finally put in another appearance at 11 a.m. with a cup of coffee and a digestive biscuit, both of which (mistakenly) Lewis thought his superior officer had brought in for him.

'We need some of those men we've been promised, sir.'

'No, no, Lewis! We don't want to start explaining everything to a load of squaddies. Just have a go at the clinic angle if the other's no good. I'll come and give you a hand when I get the chance.'

So Lewis made another start – this time on those Oxford hair clinics which had bothered to take a few centimetres of advertising space in the Yellow Pages: only four of them, thank goodness! But once again the problem soon began to take on unexpectedly formidable dimensions – once he began to consider the sort of questions he could ask a clinic manageress – *if* she was on the premises. For what *could* he ask? He wanted to find out if a woman whose name he didn't know, whose appearance he could only very imperfectly describe, and of whose address he hadn't the faintest notion, except perhaps that it might just be in Chipping Norton – whether such a woman had been in for some unspecified treatment, but probably upper-lip depilation, at some unspecified time, though most probably on the morning of, let him say, any of the last few days of December. What a farce, thought Lewis; and what a fruitless farce it did in fact become. The first of the clinics firmly refused to answer questions, even to the police, about such 'strictly confidential' matters; the second was quite happy to inform him that it had no customers whatsoever on its books with an address in Chipping Norton; a recorded message informed him that the third would re-open after the New Year break on January 6th; and the fourth suggested, politely enough, that he must have misread the advertisement: that whilst it cut, trimmed, singed and dyed, the actual *removal* of hair was not included amongst its splendid services.

Lewis put down the phone – and capitulated. He went over to the canteen and found Morse – the only one there – drinking another cup of coffee and just completing *The Times* crossword puzzle.

'Ah, Lewis. Get yourself a coffee! Any luck yet?'

'No, I bloody haven't,' snapped Lewis – a man who swore, at the very outside, about once a fortnight. 'As I said, sir, I need some help: half a dozen DCs – that's what I need.'

'I don't think it's necessary, you know.'

'Well, I *do*!' said Lewis, looking as angry as Morse had ever seen him, and about to use up a whole month's ration of blasphemies. 'We're not even sure the bloody woman *does* come from Chipping Norton. She might just as well come from Chiswick – like the tart you met in Paddington!'

'Lew-is! Lew-is! Take it *easy*! I'm sure that neither the "Palmers" nor the Smiths had anything at all to do with the murder. And when I said just now it wasn't necessary to bring any more people in on the case, I didn't mean that you couldn't have as many as you like – if you really need them. But not for this particular job, Lewis, I don't think. I didn't want to disturb you, so I've been doing a bit of phoning from here; and I'm waiting for a call that ought to come through any minute. And if it tells me what I think it will, I reckon we know exactly who this "Mrs Ballard" is, and exactly where we should be able to find her. Her name's Mrs Bowman – Mrs Margaret Bowman. And do you know where she lives?'

'Chipping Norton?' suggested Lewis, in a rather wearily defeated tone.

CHAPTER TWENTY-FOUR

Sunday, January 5th

A man is in general better pleased when he has a good
dinner upon his table than when his wife talks Greek.

(SAMUEL JOHNSON)

MORSE HAD BEEN glad to accept Mrs Lewis's invitation
to her traditional Sunday lunch of slightly undercooked
beef, horseradish sauce, velvety-flat Yorkshire pudding,
and roast potatoes; and the meal had been a success. In
deference to the great man's presence, Lewis had
bought a bottle of Beaujolais Nouveau; and as Morse
leaned back in a deep-cushioned armchair and drank
his coffee, he felt very much at his ease.

'I sometimes wish I'd taken a gentle little job in the
Egyptian Civil Service, Lewis.'

'Fancy a drop of brandy, sir?'

'Why not?'

From the rattle and clatter coming from the kitchen,
it was clear that Mrs Lewis had launched herself into
the washing-up, but Morse kept his voice down as he
spoke again. 'I know that a dirty weekend away with
some wonderful woman sounds just like the thing for
some jaded fellow getting on in age a bit – like you,

Lewis – but you'd be an idiot to leave that lovely cook you married—'

'I've never given it a thought, sir.'

'There are one or two people in this case, though, aren't there, who seem to have been doing a bit of double-dealing one way or another?'

Lewis nodded as he, too, leaned back in his armchair sipping his coffee, and letting his mind go back to the previous day's startling new development, and to Morse's explanation of how it had occurred . . .

'. . . If you ever decide to kick over the traces' (Morse had said) 'you've *got* to have an accommodation address – that's the vital point to bear in mind. All right, there are a few people, like the Smiths, who can get away without one; but don't forget they're professional swindlers and they know all the rules of the game backwards. In the normal course of events, though, you've got to get involved in some sort of correspondence. Now, if the princess you're going away with isn't married or if she's a divorcee or if she is just living on her own anyway, then there's no problem, is there? She can be your mistress *and* your missus for the weekend and *she* can deal with all the booking – just like Philippa Palmer did. She can use – she *must* use – her own address and, as I say, there are no problems. Now let's just recap for a minute about where we are with the third woman in this case, the woman who wrote to the hotel as "Mrs Ann Ballard" and who booked in as "Mrs Ann Ballard" from an address in Chipping Norton. Obviously, if we can find her, and find out from her what went on in Annexe 3 on New Year's Eve – or New Year's morning – well, we shall be home and dry, shan't we? And in fact we know a good deal about her. The key thing – or what I *thought* was the key thing – was that she'd probably gone to a hair clinic a day or so before turning up at the Haworth Hotel. I'm sorry, Lewis, that you've had such a disappointing time with that side of things. But there was this *other* side which I kept on thinking about – the address she wrote *from* and the address the hotel wrote *to*. Now you can't exchange correspondence with a phoney address – obviously you can't! And yet, you know, you *can*! You *must* be able to – because it *happened*, Lewis! And when you think about it you can do it pretty easily if you've got one particular advantage in life – just the one. And you know what that advantage is? *It's being a postman.* Now let's just take an example. Let's take the Banbury Road. The house numbers go up a long, long way, don't they? I'm not sure, but certainly to about four hundred and eighty or so. Now if the last house is, say, number 478, what exactly happens to a letter addressed to a non-existent 480? The sorters in the main post office are not going to be much concerned, are they? It's only *just* above the last house-number; and as likely as not – even if someone did spot it – he'd probably think a new house was being built there. But if it were addressed, say, to 580, then obviously a sorter is going to think that something's gone askew, and he probably won't put that letter into the appropriate pigeon-hole. In cases like that, Lewis, there's a tray for problem letters, and one of the higher-echelon post-

office staff will try to sort them all out later. But whichever way things go, whether the letter would get into
the postman's bag, or whether it would get put into the
problem tray – it wouldn't matter! You see, the postman
himself would be there on the premises while all this
sorting was taking place! I know! I've had a long talk on
the phone with the Chief Postmaster from Chipping
Norton – splendid fellow! – and he said that the letter
we saw from the Haworth Hotel, the one addressed to
84 West Street, would pretty certainly have gone straight
into the West Street pigeon-hole, because it's only a
couple over the last street-number; and even if it had
been put in the problem tray, the postman waiting to
get his sack over his shoulder would have every opportunity of seeing it, and taking it. And there were only
two postmen who delivered to West Street in December:
one was a youngish fellow who's spending the New Year
with his girlfriend in the Canary Islands; and the other
is this fellow called Tom Bowman, who lives at Charlbury Drive in Chipping Norton. But there's nobody
there – neither him nor his wife – and none of the
neighbours knows where they've gone, although Margaret Bowman was at her work in Summertown on
Thursday and Friday last week: I've checked that.
Anyway there's not much more we can do this weekend.
Max says he'll have the body all sewn up and presentable
again by Monday, and so we ought to know who he is
pretty soon.'

It had been after Morse had finished that Lewis
ventured the most important question of all: 'Do you
think the murdered man is Tom Bowman, sir?' And

Morse had hesitated before replying. 'Do you know, Lewis, I've got a strange sort of feeling that *it isn't* . . .'

Morse had nodded off in his chair, and Lewis quietly left the room to help with the drying-up.

That same Sunday afternoon Sarah Jonstone at last got back to her flat. She knew that she would almost certainly never have such an amazing experience again in her life, and she had been reluctant to leave the hotel whilst police activity was continuously centred upon it. But even the ropes that had cordoned off the area were gone, and no policeman now stood by the side door of the annexe block. Mrs Binyon (who had not originally intended to stay at the Haworth for the New Year anyway, but who had been pressed into reluctant service because of the illnesses of so many staff) had at last, that morning, set off on her trip north to visit her parents in Leeds. Only half a dozen people were booked into the hotel that Sunday evening, although (perversely!) the staff who had been so ill were now almost fully recovered. Sarah was putting on her coat at 3.30 p.m. when the phone went in Reception and a young woman's voice, a quietly attractive one, asked if she could please speak to Mr Binyon if he was there. But when Sarah asked for the woman's name, the line went suddenly dead.

Sarah found herself recalling this little incident later in the evening as she sat watching TV. But it wasn't important, she told herself; probably just a line cut off by some technical trouble or other. *Could* it be important though? Chief Inspector Morse had begged her to dredge her memory to salvage *anything* that she could recall; and there *had* been that business about the sticker on Mrs Ballard's coat ... But there was something else, she knew, if only her mind could get hold of it.

But, for the moment, it couldn't.

Chapter Twenty-five

Monday, January 6th: a.m.

By working faithfully eight hours a day, you may eventually get to be a boss and work twelve hours a day.

(ROBERT FROST)

GLADYS TAYLOR WOULD be very sorry to leave 'The University of Oxford Delegacy of Local Examinations'. It was all a bit of a mouthful when people asked her where she worked; but the Examination Board's premises, a large, beige-bricked, flat-roofed building in Summertown, had been her happy second home for nineteen and a half years now – and some neat streak within her wished it could have been the full twenty. But the 'Locals', as the Board was affectionately known, insisted that those women like herself – 'supernumeraries', they were called – had their contracts terminated in the session following their sixtieth birthday. These 'sessions', four or five of them every academic year, varied in duration from three or four weeks to nine or ten weeks; and the work involved in each session was almost as varied as its duration. For example, the current short session (and Gladys's last – for she had been sixty the previous November) involved three weeks of concentrated arithmetical checking of scripts – additions, scalings, transfers of marks – from the autumn GCE retake examinations. The entry was very much smaller than the massive summer one, comprising those candidates who had failed adequately to impress the examiners on the earlier occasion. But such young men and women (the 'returned empties', as some called them) were rather nearer Gladys Taylor's heart than many of the precious summer thoroughbreds (she knew a few of them!) who seemed to romp around the academic racecourses with almost arrogant facility. For, in her own eyes, Gladys had been a bit of a failure herself, leaving her secondary-modern school at the beginning of the war, at the age of fifteen, with nothing to show any prospective employer except a lukewarm testimonial to her perseverance and punctuality. Then, at the age of forty-one, following the premature death of a lorry-driver husband who, besides faltering in fidelity, had failed to father any offspring, she had applied to work at the Locals – and she had been accepted. During those first few months she had brought to her duties a care over detail that was almost pathological in its intensity, and she had often found herself waking up in the early hours and wondering if she had perpetrated some unforgivable error. But she had settled down; and thoroughly enjoyed the work. Her conscientiousness had been recognized by her supervisors and acknowledged by her fellow 'Supers'; and finally, over the last few years, she had been rewarded by a belated promotion to a post of some small responsibility, part of which involved working with inexperienced women who came to join the various teams; and for the past six months Gladys had been training a very much younger woman in the mysteries of the whole complex apparatus. This younger woman's name was Margaret Bowman.

For the past three sessions, the two of them had worked together, becoming firm friends in the process, and learning (as women sometimes do) a good many things about each other. At the start, Margaret had seemed almost as diffident and insecure as she herself, Gladys, had been; and it was – what was the word? – yes, such vulnerability that had endeared the younger woman to Gladys, and very soon made the older woman come to look upon Margaret more as a daughter than a colleague. Not that Margaret was ever *too* forthcoming about the more intimate details of her life with Tom, her husband; or (during the autumn) about the clandestine affair she was so obviously having with someone else (Gladys had never learned his name). How could anyone *not* have guessed? For the affair was engendering the sort of bloom on the cheek which (unbeknown to Gladys) Aristotle himself had once used in seeking to define his notion of pure happiness. Then, in the weeks of late autumn, there had occurred a change in Margaret: there were now moments of (hitherto) unsuspected irritability, of (hitherto) uncharacteristic carelessness, and (perhaps most disturbing of all) a sort of coarseness and selfishness. Yet the strangely close relationship between them had survived, and on two occasions Gladys had tried to ask, tried to help, tried to offer more than just a natural friendliness; but nothing had resulted from these overtures. And when on a Friday in mid-December the last session of the calendar year had finally come to its close, that was the last Gladys had seen of her colleague until the new-year resumption – on January 2nd, a day on which it hardly required the talents of a clairvoyant to see that there was something quite desperately wrong.

Smoking was banned from the room in which the Supers worked; but several of the women were moderately addicted to the weed, and each day they greatly looked forward to the morning coffee-breaks and afternoon tea-breaks, both taken in the Delegacy canteen, in which smoking *was* allowed. Hitherto – and invariably – during the time Gladys had known her, Margaret would sit patiently puffing her way through a single cigarette a.m.; a single cigarette p.m. But on that January 2nd, and again on the 3rd, Margaret had been getting through three cigarettes in each of the twenty-minute breaks, inhaling deeply and dramatically on each one.

Margaret's work, too, during the whole of her first day back, had been quite unprecedentedly slack: ten marks missed at one point in a simple addition; a wrong scaling, and a very obvious one at that, not spotted; and then (an error which would have made Gladys herself blanch with shame and mortification) an addition of 104 and 111 entered as 115 – a total which, but for Gladys's own rechecking, would probably have given some luckless candidate an 'E' grade instead of an 'A' grade.

At lunchtime on Friday, January 3rd, Gladys had

invited Margaret for a meal at the Chinese restaurant just across the Banbury Road from the Delegacy; and over the sweet-and-sour pork and the Lotus House Special chop suey, Margaret had confided to Gladys that her husband was away on a course over the New Year and that she herself had been feeling a bit low. And how enormously it had pleased Gladys when Margaret had accepted the invitation to spend the weekend with her – in Gladys's home on the Cutteslowe housing estate in North Oxford.

Mrs Mary Webster, the senior administrative assistant who kept a very firm (if not unfriendly) eye upon the forty or so women who sat each day in the large first-storey room overlooking the playing fields of Summerfields Preparatory School, had not returned to her accustomed chair after the coffee-break on the morning of January 6th. Most unusual! But it was the intelligence gleaned by Mrs Bannister (a woman some-what handicapped in life by a bladder of minimal capacity, but whose regular trips to the downstairs toilet afforded, by way of compensation, a fascinating window on the world) that set the whole room a-buzzing.

'A police car!' she whispered (audibly) to half the assembled ladies.

'Two men! They're in the Secretary's room!'

'You mean the police are down there talking to *Mrs Webster*?' asked one of Mrs Bannister's incredulous colleagues.

But further commentary and interpretation was

immediately forestalled by Mrs Webster herself, who now suddenly entered the door at the top of the long room, and who began to walk down the central gangway between the desks and tables. The whole room was immediately still, and silent as a Trappist's cell. It was not until she reached Gladys's table, almost at the very bottom of the room, that she stopped.

'Mrs Bowman, can you come with me for a few minutes, please?'

Margaret Bowman said nothing as she walked down the wooden stairs, one step behind Mrs Webster, and then into the main corridor downstairs and directly to the room whose door of Swedish oak bore the formidable nameplate of 'The Secretary'.

CHAPTER TWENTY-SIX

Monday, January 6th: a.m.

The cruellest lies are often told in silence.

(ROBERT LOUIS STEVENSON)

'THE SECRETARY' WAS one of those endearingly archaic titles in which the University of Oxford abounded. On the face of it, such a title seemed to point to a personage with Supreme (upper-case, as it were) Stenographic Skills. In fact, however, the Secretary of the Locals, Miss Gibson, was a poor typist, her distinction arising from her outstanding academic and administrative abilities which had led, ten years previously, to her appointment as the boss of the whole outfit. Grey-haired, tight-lipped, pale-faced, Miss Gibson sat behind her desk, in an upright red leather chair, awaiting the arrival of Mrs Margaret Bowman. Arranged in front of her desk were three further red leather chairs, of the same design: in the one to the Secretary's left sat a man of somewhat melancholy mien, the well-manicured fingers of his left hand occasionally stroking his thinning hair and who was at that moment (although Miss Gibson would never have guessed the fact) thinking what a very attractive woman the Secretary must have been in her earlier years; in the middle sat a slightly younger man – another police-man, and one also in plain clothes – but a man both thicker set, and kindlier faced. Miss Gibson introduced the two police officers after Margaret Bowman had knocked and entered and been bidden to the empty chair.

'You live in Chipping Norton?' asked Lewis.

'Yes.'

'At 6 Charlbury Drive, I think?'

'Yes.' Even with the two monosyllabic answers, Margaret knew that her tremulous upper lip was betraying signs of her nervousness, and she felt uncomfortably aware of the fierce blue-grey eyes of the other man upon her.

'And you work here?' continued Lewis.

'I've been here seven months.'

'You had quite a bit of time off over Christmas, I understand?'

'We had from Christmas Eve to last Thursday.'

'Last Thursday, let's see – that was January the second?'

'Yes.'

'The day after New Year's Day.'

Margaret Bowman said nothing, although clearly the man had expected – hoped? – that she would make some comment.

'You had plenty of things to occupy you, I suppose,' continued Lewis. 'Christmas shopping, cooking the mince pies, all that sort of thing?'

'Plenty of shopping, yes.'

'Summertown's getting a very good shopping centre, I hear.'

'Very good, yes.'

'And the Westgate down in the centre – they say that's very good, too.'

'Yes, it is.'

'Did you shop in Summertown here – or down in Oxford?'

'I did all my shopping at home.'

'You didn't come into Oxford at all, then?'

Why was she hesitating? Was she lying? Or was she just thinking back over things to make sure?

'No – I didn't.'

'You didn't go to the hairdressers'?'

Margaret Bowman's right hand went up to the top of her head, gently lifting a few strands of her not-so-recently-dyed-blonde hair, and she permitted herself a vague and tired-looking smile: 'Does it look like it?'

No, it doesn't, thought Lewis. 'Do you go to any beauty salons, beauty clinics, you know the sort of thing I mean?'

'No. Do you think I ought to?' Miraculously almost, she was feeling very much more at ease now, and she took a paper handkerchief from her black leather handbag and held it under her nose as she snuffled away some of the residual phlegm from a recent cold.

For his own part, Lewis was conscious that his questioning was not yet making much progress. 'Does your husband work in Oxford?'

'Look! Can you please give me some idea of why

you're asking me all these things? Am I supposed to have done something wrong?'

'We'll explain later, Mrs Bowman. We're trying to make all sorts of important inquiries all over the place, and we're very glad of your co-operation. So, please, if you don't mind, just answer the questions for the minute, will you?'

'He works in Chipping Norton.'

'What work does he do?'

'He's a postman.'

'Did he have the same time off as you over Christmas?'

'No. He was back at work on Boxing Day.'

'You spent Christmas Day together?'

'Yes.'

'And you celebrated the New Year together?'

The question had been put, and there was silence in the Secretary's office. Even Morse who had been watching a spider up in the far corner of the ceiling stopped tapping his lower teeth with a yellow pencil he had picked up, its point needle-sharp. *How long was the well-nigh unbearable silence going to last?*

It was the Secretary herself who suddenly spoke, in a quiet but firm voice: 'You must tell the police the truth, Margaret – it's far better that way. You didn't tell the truth just now – about being in Oxford, did you? We saw each other in the Westgate Car Park on New Year's Eve, you'll remember. We wished each other a Happy New Year.'

Margaret Bowman nodded. 'Oh yes! Yes, I do

remember now.' She turned to Lewis. 'I'm sorry, I'd forgotten. I did come in that Tuesday – I went to Sainsbury's.'

'And then you went back and you spent the New Year at home with your husband?'

'No!'

Morse, whose eyes had still been following the little spider as it seemed to practise its eight-finger exercises, suddenly shifted in his chair and turned round fully to face the woman.

'Where is your husband, Mrs Bowman?' They were the first six words he had spoken to her, and (as events were to work themselves out) they were to be the last six. But Margaret Bowman made no direct answer. Instead, she unfastened her bag, drew out a folded sheet of paper and handed it over to Lewis. It read as follows:

31st December

Dear Maggie

You've gone into Oxford and I'm here sitting at home. You will be upset and disappointed I know but please try and understand. I met another woman two months ago and I knew straightaway that I liked her a lot. I've just got to work things out that's all. Please give me that chance and don't think badly of me. I've decided that if we can go away for a few days or so we can sort things out. You are going to want to know if I love this woman and I don't know yet and she doesn't know either. She is not married and she is thirty one. We are going in her car up to Scotland if the roads are all right. Nobody else need know

anything. I got a week off work quite officially though I
didn't tell you. I know what you will feel like but it will be
better for me to sort things out.

Tom

Lewis read through the letter quickly – and then
looked at Mrs Bowman. Was there – did he notice –
just a brief flash of triumph in her eyes? Or could it
have been a glint of fear? He couldn't be sure, but the
interview had obviously taken a totally unexpected turn,
and he would have welcomed at that point a guiding
hand from Morse. But the latter still appeared to be
perusing the letter with inordinate interest.

'You found this note when you got back home?'
asked Lewis.

She nodded. 'On the kitchen table.'

'Do you know this woman he mentions?'

'No.'

'You've not heard from your husband?'

'No.'

'He's taking a long time to, er "sort things out".'

'Has – has my husband had an accident – a car
accident? Is that why—'

'Not so far as we know, Mrs Bowman.'

'Is that – is that all you want me for?'

'For the minute, perhaps. We shall have to keep the
letter – I'm sure you'll understand why.'

'No, I *don't* understand why!'

'Well, it might not be from your husband at all –
have you thought of that?' asked Lewis slowly.

'Course it's from him!' As she spoke these few words,

she sounded suddenly sharp and almost crude after her earlier quietly civilized manner, and Lewis found himself wondering several things about her.

'Can you be sure about that, Mrs Bowman?'

'I'd know his writing anywhere.'

'Have you got any more of his writing with you?'

'I've got the very first letter he wrote me – years ago.'

'Can you show it to us, please?'

From her handbag she brought out an envelope, much soiled, drew from it a letter, much creased, and handed it to Lewis, who cursorily compared the two samples of handwriting, and pushed them along the desk to Morse – the latter nodding slowly after a few moments: it seemed to him that by amateur and professional experts alike, the writing would pretty certainly be adjudged identical.

'Can I please go now?'

Lewis wasn't at all sure whether or not this oddly unsatisfactory interview should be temporarily terminated, and he turned to Morse – receiving only a non-committal shrug.

So it was that Margaret Bowman left the office, exhorted in a kindly way by the Secretary to get herself another cup of coffee from the canteen, and to be ready to come down again if the police needed her for further questioning.

'We're sorry to have taken so much of your time, Miss Gibson,' said Morse after Mrs Bowman had left. 'And if we could have a room for an hour or so we'd be most grateful.'

'You can stay here if you like, Inspector. There are a good many things I've got to see to round the office.'

'What do you make of all that, sir?' asked Lewis when they were alone.

'We haven't got a thing to charge her with, have we? We can't take her in just for forgetting she bought a pound of sausages from Sainsbury's.'

'We're not getting far, are we, sir? It's all a bit disappointing.'

'What? Disappointing? Far from it! We've just been looking at things from the wrong end, Lewis, that's all.'

'Really?'

'Oh yes. And we owe a lot to Mrs Bowman – it was about time somebody put me on the right track!'

'You think she was telling the truth?'

'Truth?' Morse shook his head. 'I didn't believe a word of her story, did you?'

'I don't know, sir. I feel very confused.'

'Confused? Surely not!' He turned to Lewis and put the yellow pencil down on the Secretary's desk. 'Do you want to know what happened in Annexe 3 on New Year's Eve?'

CHAPTER TWENTY-SEVEN

Monday, January 6th: a.m.

It is a bad plan that admits of no modification.

(PUBLILIUS SYRUS)

'LET ME EXPLAIN one thing from the start. I just said we've been looking at things from the wrong end and I mean just that. Max gave us a big enough margin for the time of death, and instead of listening to him I kept trying to pin him down. Even now it's taken a woman's pack of lies to put me on the right track, because the most important thing about Mrs Bowman is that she was forced to show us the letter, supposedly from her husband, to give herself a reasonable alibi. It was the last shot in her locker; and she had no option but to use it, because we were getting – we *are* getting! – dangerously close to the truth. And I just said "supposedly from her husband" – but that's not the case: it *was* from her husband, you can be certain of that. Everything fits, you see, *once you turn the pattern upside down*. The man in Annexe 3 wasn't murdered after the party: he was murdered *before the party*. Let's just assume that Margaret Bowman has been unfaithful, and let's assume that she gets deeply involved with this lover of hers, and that he threatens to blackmail her in some way if she doesn't agree to see him again – threatens to tell her husband – to cut his own throat – to cut *her* throat – anything you like. Let's say, too, that the husband, Tom Bowman, deliverer of Her Majesty's mail at Chipping Norton, finds out about all this – let's say that he intercepts a letter; or, more likely, I think, she's desperate enough to tell him all about it – because there must have been some sort of reconciliation between them. Together, they decide that something has got to be done to get rid of the threat that now affects *both* of them; and at that point, as I see it, the plot was hatched. They book a double room for a New Year break at a hotel, using a non-existent accommodation address so that later on no one will be able to trace them; and Tom Bowman is exactly the person to cope with that problem – none better. So things really start moving. Margaret Bowman tells this dangerous and persistent lover of hers – let's call him Mr X – that *she can spend the New Year with him.* He's a single man; he's head over heels about her; and now he's over the moon, too! He thought she'd ditched him. But here she is offering to spend a couple of whole days with him. *She's* taken the initiative; *she's* fixed it all up; *she's* booked the hotel; *she* wants *him*! She's even told him – and she must have expected he'd agree – that *she'll* provide the fancy-dress costumes they're going to wear at the New Year party. She tells him to be ready, let's say, from four o'clock on the 31st. She herself probably books in under her false name and a false address an hour or so earlier, but a bit later than most of the other guests. She wants to be

seen by as few of the others as possible, but she's still
got to give herself plenty of time. She finds herself
alone at the reception desk, she turns up her coat and
pulls her scarf around her face, she signs the form, she
takes the room key, she takes her suitcase over to
Annexe 3 – and all is ready. She rings up X from the
public phone-box just outside the hotel, tells him what
their room number is, and he's on his way like a shot.
And while the rest of the guests are playing Cluedo,
he's spending the rest of that late afternoon and early
evening with his bottom on the top sheet, as they say.
Then, when most of the passion's spent itself, she tells
him that they'd better start dressing up for the party;
she shows him what she's brought for the pair of them
to wear; and about 7 p.m. the pair of them are ready:
she rubs a final bit of stage-black on his hands – makes
some excuse about leaving her purse or her umbrella
at Reception – says she'll be back in a minute – takes
the key with her – pulls her mackintosh over her
costume – and goes out bang on the stroke of seven.
Tom Bowman, *himself dressed in exactly the same sort of
outfit as X,* has been waiting for her, somewhere in the
immediate vicinity of the hotel; and while Margaret
Bowman spends the most nerve-racking few minutes of
her life, probably in the bus shelter just across from the
hotel, *Tom Bowman lets himself into Annexe 3.*

'Exactly what happened then, we don't know – and
we may never know. But very soon the Bowmans are
playing out the rest of the evening as best they can –
pretending to eat, pretending to be lovey-dovey with
each other, pretending to enjoy the festivities. There's

little enough chance of them being recognized, anyway: she's hiding behind her yashmak, and he's hiding behind a coat of dark greasepaint. But they both want to be seen going into the annexe after the party's over, and in fact Tom Bowman performs his role with a bit of panache. He waits for the two other women he knows are lodged in the annexe, throws an arm across their shoulders – incidentally ruining their coats with his greasy hands – and gives the impression to all and sundry that he's about to hit the hay. As it happens, Binyon was bringing up the rear – pretty close behind them. But the lock on the side door is only a Yale; and after Binyon had made sure all was well, the Bowmans slipped out quietly into the winter's night. They went down and got their car from the Westgate – or wherever it was parked – and Tom Bowman dropped Margaret back to Charlbury Drive, where she'd left the lights on anyway so that the neighbours would assume she was celebrating the New Year. And then Bowman himself took off into the night somewhere so that if ever the need arose he could establish an alibi for himself up in Inverness or wherever he found himself the next morning, leaving Margaret the pre-planned note about his fictitious girlfriend. And that's about it, Lewis! That's about what happened, as far as I can make out.'

Lewis himself had listened with great interest, and without interruption, to what Morse had said. And although, apart from the *time* of the murder, it wasn't a particularly startling analysis, it was just the sort of self-consistent hypothesis that Lewis had come to expect from the chief inspector, bringing together, as it did, into one coherent scheme all the apparently inconsistent clues and puzzling testimony. But there were one or two weaknesses in Morse's argument: at least as Lewis saw things.

'You said they spent the afternoon in bed, sir. But we didn't, to be honest, find much sign of anything like that, did we?'

'Perhaps they performed on the floor – I don't know. I was just telling you what probably happened.'

'What about the maid, sir – Mandy, wasn't it? Doesn't someone usually come along about seven o'clock or so and turn down the counterpane—'

'Counterpane? Lewis! You're still living in the nineteenth century. And this wasn't the Waldorf Astoria, you know.'

'Bit of a risk, though, sir – somebody coming in and finding—'

'They were short-staffed, Lewis – you know that.'

'But the *Bowmans* didn't know that!'

Morse nodded. 'No-o. But they could have hung one of those "Do Not Disturb" signs on the door. In fact, they *did*.'

'Bit risky, though, hanging out a sign like that if you're supposed to be at a party.'

'Lewis! Don't you understand? They were taking risks the whole bloody time.'

As always when Morse blustered on in such fashion, Lewis knew that it was best not to push things overmuch. Obviously, what Morse had said was true; but Lewis felt that some of the explanations he was receiving were far from satisfactory.

'If, as you say, sir, Bowman was dressed up, all ready to go, in exactly the same sort of clothes as the other fellow, where was he—?'

'*Where?* I dunno. But I'm sure all he had to do was put a few finishing touches to things.'

'Do you think he did that in Annexe 3?'

'Possibly. Or he could have used the Gents' just off Reception.'

'Wouldn't Miss Jonstone have seen him?'

'How am I supposed to know? Shall we *ask* her, Lewis? Shall *I* ask her? Or what about *you* asking her – you're asking *me* enough bloody questions.'

'It's only because I can't quite understand things, that's all, sir.'

'You think I've got it all wrong, don't you?' said Morse quietly.

'No! I'm pretty sure you're on the right lines, sir, but it doesn't all *quite* hang together, does it?'

CHAPTER TWENTY-EIGHT

Monday, January 6th: a.m.

What is the use of running when we are not on the right road?

(GERMAN PROVERB)

THERE WAS A knock on the door and Judith, the slimly attractive personal assistant to the Secretary, entered with a tray of coffee and biscuits.

'Miss Gibson thought you might like some refreshment.' She put the tray on the desk. 'If you want her, she's with the Deputy – the internal number's 208.'

'We don't get such VIP treatment up at HQ,' commented Lewis after she'd left.

'Well, they're a more civilized lot here, aren't they? Nice sort of people. Wouldn't harm a fly, most of them.'

'Perhaps *one* of them would!'

'I see what you mean,' said Morse, munching a ginger biscuit.

'Don't you think,' said Lewis, as they drank their coffee, 'that we're getting a bit too complex, sir?'

'Complex? Life *is* complex, Lewis. Not for *you*, perhaps. But for most of us it's a struggle to get through from breakfast to coffee-time, and then from coffee-time—'

There was a knock on the door and Miss Gibson herself re-entered. 'I saw Mrs Webster just now and she said that Mrs Bowman hadn't got back to her work yet. I thought perhaps she might be back here . . .'

The two detectives looked at each other.

'She's not in the canteen?' asked Morse.

'No.'

'She's not in the Ladies'?'

'No.'

'How many exits are there here, Miss Gibson?'

'Just the one. We've all been so worried about security recently—'

But Morse was already pulling on his greatcoat. He thanked the Secretary and with Lewis in his wake walked quickly along the wooden-floored corridor towards the exit. At the reception desk sat the Security Officer. Mr Prior, a thick-set, former prison officer, whose broad, intelligent face looked up from the Court Circular of the *Daily Telegraph* as Morse fired a salvo of questions at him.

'You know Mrs Bowman?'

'Yessir.'

'How long ago did she leave?'

'Three – four minutes.'

'By car?'

'Yessir. Maroon Metro – 1300 – A reg.'

'You don't know the number?'

'Not offhand.'

'Did she turn left or right at the Banbury Road?'

'Can't see from here.'

'She was wearing a coat?'

'Yessir. Black, fur-collared coat. But she hadn't changed her shoes.'

'What do you mean?'

'Most of 'em come in boots this weather – and then change into something lighter when they're here. She still had a pair of high heels on – black; black leather, I should think.'

Morse was impressed by Prior's powers of observation, said as much, and asked if he'd noticed anything else that was at all odd.

'Don't think so. Except perhaps when she said "Goodbye!"'

'Don't most people say "Goodbye" when they leave?'

Prior thought for a second before replying: 'No, they don't! They usually say "See you!" or "Cheers!" or something like that.'

Morse walked from the Locals, his eyes downcast, a deep frown on his forehead. The snow had been brushed away from the shallow steps that led down to the car park, and a watery-looking sun had almost dried the concrete. The forecast was for continued improvement in the weather, although in places there were still patches of hazardous ice.

'Where to?' asked Lewis as Morse got into the passenger seat of the police car.

'I'm – not – quite – sure,' replied Morse as they drove up to the black-and-yellow striped barrier that regulated the progress of unauthorized vehicles into Ewert Place, the narrow street that led down to the

Delegacy's private car park. Bob King, the courteous, blue-uniformed attendant, touched his peaked cap to them as he pressed the button to raise the barrier; but before going through, Morse beckoned him round to his window and asked him if he remembered a maroon Metro leaving a few minutes earlier; and if so whether it had turned left or right into the Banbury Road. But whilst the answer to the first question had been 'yes', the answer to the second question had been 'no'. And for the minute Morse asked Lewis to stop the car where it was: the Straw Hat Bakery ('Everything baked on the Premises') on the left; and, to the right (its immediate neighbour across the narrow road), the giant Allied Carpets shop, whose vast areas of glass frontage were perpetually plastered over with notices informing the inhabitants of Summertown that the current sale must undoubtedly rank as the biggest bargain in the annals of carpetry. Betwixt and between – there the car stood: left, down into Oxford; right, up and out of the city and, if need be, thence to Chipping Norton.

'Chipping Norton,' said Morse suddenly – 'quick as you can!'

Blue rooflight flashing, siren wailing, the white Ford raced up to the Banbury Road roundabout then across to the Woodstock Road roundabout, and was soon out on the A34, a happy-looking Lewis behind the wheel.

'Think she'll go back home straight away?'

'My God, I hope so!' said Morse with unwonted vehemence.

It was when the car had passed the Black Prince and was climbing the hill out of Woodstock that Morse spoke again. 'Going back to what you were saying about Annexe 3, Lewis, you *did* have a look at the bed-linen, didn't you?'

'Yes, sir. In both beds.'

'You don't think you missed anything?'

'Don't think so. Wouldn't matter much if I did, though. We've still got all the bedclothes – I sent everything along to the path lab.'

'You did?'

Lewis nodded. 'But if you want my opinion, nobody'd been sleeping in either of those two beds, sir.'

'Well, you couldn't tell with the one, could you? It was all soaked in blood.'

'No, it wasn't, sir. The blood had seeped through the counterpane or whatever you call it, and a bit through the blankets; but the sheets weren't marked at all.'

'And you don't think that they'd been having sex that afternoon or evening – in either of the beds.'

Lewis was an old hand in murder investigations, and some of the things he'd found in rooms, in cupboards, in wardrobes, in beds, under beds – he'd have been more than happy to be able to forget. But he knew what Morse was referring to, and he was more than confident of his answer. 'No. There were no marks of sexual emissions or anything like that.'

'You have an admirably delicate turn of phrase,' said Morse, as Lewis sped past an obligingly docile convoy of Long Vehicles. 'But it's a good point you made earlier, you know. If the old charpoy *wasn't* creaking all that afternoon . . .'

'As you said, though, sir – they might have made love on the carpet.'

'Have you ever made love on the carpet in mid-winter?'

'Well, no. But—'

'Central heating's one thing. But you get things like draughts under doors, don't you?'

'I haven't got much experience of that sort of thing myself.'

The car turned off left at the Chipping Norton/Moreton-in-Marsh/Evesham sign; and a few minutes later Lewis brought it to a gentle stop outside 6 Charlbury Drive. He noticed the twitch of a lace curtain in the front window of number 5; but no one seemed to be about at all, and the little road lay quiet and still. No maroon Metro stood outside number 6, or in the steep drive that led down to the white-painted doors of the single garage.

'Go and have a look!' said Morse.

But there was no car in the garage, either; and the front-door bell seemed to Lewis to re-echo through a house that sounded ominously empty.

CHAPTER TWENTY-NINE

Monday, January 6th: a.m.

The last pleasure in life is the sense of discharging our duty.

(WILLIAM HAZLITT)

WHERE MORSE DECIDED to turn right past Allied Carpets, Margaret Bowman, some five minutes earlier, had decided to turn left past the Straw Hat, and had thence proceeded south towards the centre of the city. In St Giles', the stiff penalty recently introduced for any motorists outstaying their two-hour maximum (even by a minute or so) had resulted in the unprecedented sight of a few free rectangles of parking space almost invariably being available at any one time; and Margaret pulled into the one she spotted just in front of the Eagle and Child, and walked slowly across to the ticket machine, some twenty-odd yards away. For the whole of the time from when she had sat down in the Secretary's office until now, her mind had been numbed to the reality of her underlying situation, and far-distanced, in some strange way, from what (she knew) would be the disastrous inevitability of her fate. Her voice and her manner, as she had answered the policemen, had been much more controlled than she could have dared to hope. Not *quite* all the time; but anyone, even someone who was wholly innocent, would always be nervous in those circumstances. Had they believed her? But she knew now that the answer even to such a crucial question was perhaps no longer of any great importance. (She prodded her fingers into the corner of her handbag for the necessary change.) But to say that at that very moment Margaret Bowman had finally come to any conclusion about ending her life would be untrue. Such a possibility had certainly occurred to her – oh, so many times! – over the past few days of despair and the past few nights of hell. Academically, she had not been a successful pupil at the Chipping Norton Comprehensive School, and in O-level *Greek Literature in Translation* (Margaret had not been considered for the high fliers' Latin course) she had been 'Unclassified'. Yet she remembered something (in one of the books they were supposed to read) about Socrates, just before he took the hemlock: when he'd said that he would positively welcome death if it turned out to be just one long and dreamless sleep. And that's what Margaret longed for now – a long, a wakeless and a dreamless sleep. (She could not find the exact number of coins which the notice on the ticket machine so inexorably demanded.) And then she remembered her mother, dying of cancer in her early forties, when Margaret was only fourteen: and before dying saying how desperately tired she was and how she just wanted to be free from pain and never wake again . . .

Margaret had found five 10p coins – still one short –

and she looked around her with a childlike pleading in her eyes, as though she almost expected her very helplessness to work its own deliverance. A hundred or so yards away, just passing the Taylorian, and coming towards her, she saw a yellow-banded traffic warden, and suddenly a completely new and quite extraordinary thought came to her mind. Would it matter if she *were* caught? Didn't she *want* to be caught? Wasn't there, after all hope had been cruelly cancelled, a point when even total despair could hold no further terrors? A notice ('No Change Given') outside the Eagle and Child informed Margaret that she could expect little help from that establishment; but she walked in and ordered a glass of orange juice.

'Ice?'

'Pardon?'

'You want ice in it?'

'Oh – yes. Er – no. I'm sorry, I didn't quite hear . . .'

She felt the hard eyes of the well-coiffeured bar-lady on her as she handed over a £1 coin and received 60p in exchange: one 50p piece, and one 10p. Somehow she felt almost childishly pleased as she put her six 10p pieces together and held the little stack of coins in her left hand. She had no idea how long she stayed there, seated at a table just in front of the window. But when she noticed that the glass in front of her was empty, and when she felt the coins so warmly snug inside her palm, she walked out slowly into St Giles'. It occurred to her – so suddenly! – that there she was, in St Giles'; that she had just come down the Banbury Road; that she must have passed directly in front of the Haworth Hotel; and that *she hadn't even noticed it*. Was she beginning to lose control of her mind? Or had she got *two* minds now? The one which had pushed itself into auto-pilot in the driving seat of the Metro; and the other, logical and sober, which even now, as she walked towards the ticket machine, was seeking to keep her shoes (the ones she had bought for the funeral) out of the worst of crunching slush. She saw the celluloid-covered document under the near-side windscreen-wiper; and caught sight of the traffic warden, two cars further up, leaning back slightly to read a number plate before completing another incriminating ticket.

Margaret walked up to her, pointing to the maroon Metro.

'Have I committed an offence?'

'Is that your car?'

'Yes.'

'You were parked without a ticket.'

'Yes, I know. I've just been to get the right change.' Almost pathetically she opened her left palm and held the six warm coins to view as if they might just serve as some propitiatory offering.

'I'm sorry, madam. It tells you on the sign, doesn't it? If you haven't got the right change, you shouldn't park.'

For a moment or two the two women, so little different in age, eyed each other in potential hostility. But when Margaret Bowman spoke, her voice sounded flat, indifferent almost.

'Do you enjoy your work?'

'Not the point, is it?' replied the other. 'There's nothing *personal* in it. It's a job that's got to be done.'

Margaret Bowman turned and the traffic warden looked after her with a marked expression of puzzlement on her face. It was her experience that on finding a parking ticket virtually all of them got into their cars and drove angrily away. But not this tall, good-looking woman who was now walking away from her car, down past the Martyrs' Memorial; and then, almost out of sight now, but with the warden's last words still echoing in her mind, across into Cornmarket and up towards Carfax.

CHAPTER THIRTY

Monday, January 6th: noon

Then the devil taketh him up into the holy city, and setteth him on a pinnacle of the temple.

(MATTHEW iv, 5)

MARGARET BOWMAN STOOD beneath Carfax Tower, a great, solid pile of pale-yellowish stone that stands on the corner of Queen Street and Cornmarket, and which looks down, at its east side, on to the High. White lettering on a background of Oxford blue told her that a splendid view of the city and the surrounding district was available from the top of the tower: admission 50p, Mondays to Saturdays, 10 a.m. to 6 p.m.; and her heart pounded as she stood there, her eyes ascending to the crenellated balustrade built four-square around the top. Not a high balustrade either; and often in the past she'd noticed people standing there, almost half their bodies visible as they gazed out over Oxford or waved to friends who stood a hundred feet below. She was not one of those acrophobes (as, for example, Morse was) who burst into a clammy sweat of vertiginous panic when forced to stand on the third or the fourth rung of a household ladder. But she was always terrified of being *pushed* – had been ever since one of the boys on a school party to Snowdon had *pretended* to push her, and when for a split second she had experienced a sense of imminent terror of falling over the precipitous drop that yawned almost immediately below her feet. People said you always thought of your childhood before you died, and she was conscious that twice already – no, three times – her mind had reverted to early memories. And now she was conscious of a fourth – of the words her father had so often used when she tried to put off writing a letter, or starting her homework: 'The longer you put things off, the harder they become, my girl!' Should she put things off now? Defer any fateful decision? No! She pushed the door to the tower. But it was clear that the tower was shut; and it was with a sense of despairing disappointment that she noticed the bottom line of the notice: '20th March – 31st October'.

The spire of St Mary the Virgin pointed promisingly skywards in front of her as she walked down the High, and into the Mitre.

'Large Scotch – Bell's, please – if you have it.' (How often had she heard her husband use those selfsame words!)

A young barmaid pushed a tumbler up against the bottom of an inverted bottle, and then pushed again.

'Ice?'

'Pardon?'

'Do you want ice?'

'Er – no. Er – yes – yes please! I'm sorry. I didn't quite hear . . .'

As she sipped the whisky, a hitherto dormant nerve

throbbing insistently along her left temple, the world seemed to her perhaps fractionally more bearable than it had done when she'd left the Delegacy. Like some half-remembered medicine – foul-tasting yet efficacious – the whisky seemed to do her good; and she bought another.

A few minutes later she was standing in Radcliffe Square; and as she looked up at the north side of St Mary's Church, a strange and fatal fascination seemed to grip her soul. Halfway up the soaring edifice, his head and shoulders visible over the tricuspid ornamentation that marked the intersection of tower and spire, Margaret could see a duffel-coated young man, binoculars to his eyes, gazing out across the northern parts of Oxford. The tower must be open, surely! She walked down the steps towards the main porch of the church and then, for a moment, turned round and gazed up at the dome of the Radcliffe Camera behind her; and noticed the inscription on the top step: *Dominus custodiat introitum tuum et exitum tuum.* But since she had no Latin, the potential irony of the words escaped her. TOWER OPEN was printed in large capitals on a noticeboard beside the entrance; and just inside, seated behind a table covered with postcards, guidebooks and assorted Christian literature, was a middle-aged woman who had already assumed that Margaret Bowman wished to ascend, for she held out a maroon-coloured ticket and asked for 60p. A few flights of wide wooden stairs led up to the first main landing, where a notice on a locked door to the left advised visitors that here was the Old Library – the very first one belonging to the University – where the few books amassed by the earliest scholars were so precious that they were chained to the walls. Margaret had seldom been interested in old churches, or old anythings for that matter; but she now found herself looking down at the leaflet the woman below had given her:

> when Mary became Queen and England reverted to Roman Catholicism, Archbishop Cranmer and two of his fellow bishops, Latimer and Ridley, were tried in St Mary's for heresy. Latimer and Ridley were burned at the stake. Cranmer himself, after officially recanting, was brought back to St Mary's and condemned to death. He was burned at the stake in the town ditch, outside Balliol College, holding his right hand (which had written his recantation) steadily in the flames...

Margaret looked at her own right hand – a couple of blue biro marks across the bottom of the thumb – and thought of the tortured atonement that Cranmer had sought, and welcomed, for his earlier weaknesses. A tear ran hurriedly down her cheek, and she took from her handbag a white paper handkerchief to dry her eyes.

The stairs – iron now, and no longer enclosed for the next two flights – led up and over the roof of the Lady Chapel, and she felt a sense of exhilaration in the cold air as she climbed higher still to the Bell Tower, where the man with the binoculars, his hair windswept, had just descended the stone spiral staircase that led to the top.

'Not much further!' he volunteered. 'Bit blowy up there, though. Bit slippery, too. Be careful!'

For several seconds as she emerged at the top of the tower, Margaret was conscious of a terrifying giddiness as her eyes glimpsed, just below her feet, the black iron ring that circled the golden-painted Roman numerals of the great clock adorning the north wall of the church. But the panic was soon gone, and she looked out across at the Radcliffe Camera; and then to the left of the Camera at the colleges along Broad Street; then the buildings of Balliol where Cranmer had redeemed his soul amid the burning brushwood; then she could see the leafless trees along St Giles', and the roads that led off from there into North Oxford; and then the giant yellow crane that stood at the Haworth Hotel in the Banbury Road. She took a few steps along the high-walk towards the north-western corner of the tower, and she suddenly felt a sense of elation, and the tears welled up again in her eyes as the wind blew back her hair, and as she held her head up to the elements with the same joyous carelessness she had shown as a young girl when the rain had showered down on her tip-tilted face . . .

At a point on the corner, her wholly inadequate and unsuitable shoes had slipped along the walkway, and a man standing below watched the black handbag as it plummeted to the earth and landed, neatly erect, in a drift of snow beneath the north-west angle of the tower.

Chapter Thirty-one

Monday, January 6th: p.m.

Everything comes to him who waits — among other things, death.

(F. H. BRADLEY)

MORSE WAS DISSATISFIED and restless – that much was obvious as they sat outside the Bowmans' house in Charlbury Drive. Ten minutes they waited, Morse just sitting there in the passenger seat, his safety-belt still on, staring out of the window. Then another ten minutes, with Morse occasionally clicking his tongue and taking sharp audible breaths of impatient frustration.

'Think she's coming back?' said Lewis.

'I dunno.'

'How long are we going to wait?'

'How do *I* know!'

'Just asked.'

'I tell you one thing, Lewis. I'm making one bloody marvellous mess of this case!'

'I don't know about that, sir.'

'Well you *should* know! We should never have let her out of our sight.'

Lewis nodded, but said nothing; and for a further ten minutes the pair of them sat in silence.

But there was no sign of Margaret Bowman.

'What do you suggest we do, Lewis?' asked Morse finally.

'I think we ought to go to the post office: see if we can find some of Bowman's handwriting – there must be something there; see if any of his mates know anything about where he is or where he's gone; that sort of thing.'

'And you'd like to get somebody from there to go and look at the body, wouldn't you? You think it *is* Bowman!'

'I'd just like to check, that's all. Check it *isn't* Bowman, if you like. But we haven't done anything at all yet, sir, about identification.'

'And you're telling me it's about bloody time we did!'

'Yessir.'

'All right. Let's do it your way. Waste of time but—' His voice was almost a snarl.

'Are you feeling all right, sir?'

'Course I'm not feeling all right! Can't you see I'm dying for a bloody cigarette, man?'

The visit to the post office produced little information that was not already known. Tom Bowman had worked on the Thursday, Friday and Saturday following Christmas Day, and then had taken a week's holiday. He should have been back at work that very day, the 6th; but as yet no one had seen or heard anything of him. It seemed he was a quiet, punctual, methodical

213

sort of fellow, who had been working there for six years now. No one knew his wife Margaret very well, though it was common knowledge that she had a job in Oxford and took quite a bit of trouble over her clothes and her personal appearance. There were two handwritten letters from Bowman in the personnel file: one dating back to his first application to join the PO; the second concerning itself with his options under the PO pension provisions. Clearly there had been little or no calligraphic variance in Bowman's penmanship over the years, and here seemed further evidence – if any were required – that the letter Margaret Bowman had produced from her handbag that morning was genuinely in her husband's hand. Mr Jeacock, the co-operative and neatly competent postmaster, could tell them little more; but, yes, he was perfectly happy for one of Bowman's colleagues to follow the police officers down into Oxford to look at the unidentified body.

'Let's hope to God it's *not* Tom! he said as Morse and Lewis got up and left his small office.

'I honestly don't think you need to worry about that, sir,' said Morse.

As always, the cars coming up in the immediate rear had all decelerated to the statutory speed limit; and by the time the police car reached the dual carriageway just after Blenheim Palace, with Mr Frederick Norris, sorter of Her Majesty's mail in Chipping Norton, immediately behind, there was an enormous tailback of vehicles. Morse, who had told Lewis to take things quietly, sat silent throughout the return journey, and Lewis too held his peace. At the bottom of the Woodstock Road he turned right into a narrow road at the Radcliffe Infirmary and stopped on an 'Ambulances Only' parking lot outside the mortuary to which the body found in the Haworth annexe had now been transferred. Norris got out of the car that pulled up behind them.

'You coming, sir?' asked Lewis.

But Morse shook his head.

Fred Norris stood stock-still for a few seconds, and then – somewhat to Lewis's bewilderment – nodded slowly, his own pallor only a degree less ghastly than the skin that backed the livid bruising of the murdered man's features. No words were spoken; but as the mortuary attendant replaced the white sheet, Lewis put a kindly, understanding hand on Norris's shoulder, and then gently urged him out of the grim building into the bright January air.

An ambulance had pulled in just ahead of the police car, and Lewis, as he stood fixing a time with Norris for an official statement, saw the ambulance driver unhurriedly get out and speak to one of the porters at the Accident entrance. From the general lack of urgency, Lewis gathered that the man was probably delivering some fussy octogenarian for her weekly dose of physiotherapy. But the back doors were suddenly opened to reveal the body of a woman covered in a red blanket, with only the shoeless stockinged feet protruding.

Lewis's throat was dry as he walked past the police car, and saw Morse (the latter still unaware of the dramatic news that Lewis was about to impart) point to the back of the ambulance.

'Who is she?' asked Lewis as the two ambulancemen prepared to fix the runners for the stretcher.

'Are you . . .?' The driver jerked his thumb towards the police car.

'Chief Inspector Morse – him! Not me!'

'Accident. They found her—'

'How old?'

The man shrugged. 'Forty?'

'You know who she is?'

The man shook his head. 'No one knows yet. No purse. No handbag.'

Lewis drew back the blanket and looked at the woman's face, his heart pounding in anticipatory dread – for such an eventuality, as he well knew, was exactly what Morse had feared.

But the ambulance driver was right in suggesting that no one knew who she was: Lewis didn't know, either. For the dead woman in the back of the ambulance was certainly not Mrs Margaret Bowman.

That same lunch-hour, some fifty minutes before Norris had positively identified the man murdered at the Haworth Hotel as Mr Thomas Bowman, Ronald Armitage, an idle, dirty, feckless, cold, hungry, semi-drunken sixty-three-year-old layabout – unemployed and unemployable – experienced a remarkable piece of good fortune. He had spent the previous night huddled up on a bench in the passage that leads from Radcliffe Square to the High, and had spent most of the morning on the same bench, with an empty flagon of Bulmer's Cider at his numbed feet, and one dirty five-pound note and a few 10p coins in the pocket of the ankle-length greatcoat that for many years had been his most treasured possession. When he had first seen the black handbag as it plummeted to the ground, and came to rest in a cushion of deep snow at the corner of the church, his instinctive reaction was to look sharply and suspiciously around him. But for the moment the square was empty; and he quickly grabbed the handbag, putting it beneath the front of his coat, and walked hurriedly off over the snow-covered cobbles outside Brasenose into the lane on the left that led through to the Turl. Here – with none of his cronies in sight – like a wolf which grabs a great gobbet of meat from the kill and takes it away from the envious eyes of the rest of the pack, he examined his exciting discovery. Inside the handbag he found a lipstick, a powder compact, a comb, a cheap cigarette lighter, a packet of white paper handkerchiefs, a leaflet about St Mary the Virgin, a small pair of nail scissors, a bunch of car keys, two other keys – and a brown leather purse-cum-wallet. The plastic cards – Visa, Access, Lloyds – he ignored, but he quickly pocketed the two beautifully crisp ten-pound notes and the three one-pound coins he found therein.

In mid-afternoon, he wandered slowly up the High

to Carfax, and then turned left down past Christ Church and into St Aldates Police Station where he handed the bag over to Lost Property.

'Where did you find it?'asked the sergeant on duty.

'Someone must have dropped it—'

'You better leave your name—'

'Nah! Don't fink so.'

'Might be a reward!'

'Cheers, mate!'

CHAPTER THIRTY-TWO

Monday, 6th January: p.m.

Wordsworth recalls in 'The Prelude' how he was soothed by the sound of the Derwent winding among grassy holms.

(*Literary Landscapes of the British Isles*)

IT WAS SELDOM that Morse ever asked for more personnel. Indeed, it was his private view that the sight (as so often witnessed on TV) of a hundred or so uniformed policemen crawling in echelon across a tract of heathland often brought the force into something approaching derision. He himself had once taken part in such a massive sweep across a field in North Staffordshire, ending up, as he had done, with one empty packet of Featherlite Durex, one empty can of alcohol-free lager – and (the next morning) a troublesome bout of lumbago.

But he *did* ask for more personnel on the afternoon of January 6th; and Lewis, for one, was glad that much needed help (in the shape of Sergeant Phillips and two detective constables) had been summoned to follow up all inquiries regarding Margaret Bowman.

Oddly enough (yet almost everything about him was

219

odd, as Lewis knew) Morse had shown no great surprise on hearing the news that the murdered man was Thomas Bowman; indeed, the only emotion he showed – and that of immense relief – was after learning that the other corpse on view that lunchtime was *not* Margaret Bowman's. In fact, Morse suddenly seemed much more at peace with himself as he sat with Lewis in the Royal Oak, just opposite the hospital – a circumstance (as Lewis rightly guessed) not wholly unconnected with the fact that after his Herculean efforts over Christmas and the New Year he had finally surrendered and bought himself a packet of cigarettes. At two-thirty, they were once more on the A34 to Chipping Norton, this time with a much firmer mission – to investigate the property at 6 Charlbury Drive, which had now quite definitely become the focus of the murder inquiry.

'Shall we break one of the front windows or one of the back ones?' Morse asked as they stood in front of the property, faces at a good many windows in the quiet cul-de-sac now watching the activity with avid curiosity. But such forcible ingress proved unnecessary. Lewis it was who suggested that most people ('Well, the missus does') leave a key with the neighbours: and so it proved in this case, with the elderly woman in number 5 promptly producing both a back-door and a front-door key. Mrs Bowman, it appeared, had gone out on Friday evening, saying she wouldn't be back until Monday after work; hadn't been back, either – as far as the woman knew.

Finding nothing of immediate interest in the downstairs rooms, Lewis went upstairs where he found Morse
in one of the two spare bedrooms looking into a
cumbrous dark mahogany wardrobe which (apart from
an old-fashioned armchair) was the only item of furniture there.

'Found anything, sir?'

Morse shook his head. 'Lots of shoes he had.'

'Not much help.'

'No help at all.'

'Can you smell anything, sir?'

'Such as?'

'Whisky?' suggested Lewis.

Morse's eyes lit up as he sniffed, and sniffed again.

'I reckon you're right, you know.'

There was a stack of white shoe boxes, and they
found the half-full bottle of Bell's in the third box from
the bottom.

'You think he was a secret drinker, sir?'

'What if he was? *I'm* a secret drinker – aren't you?'

'No, sir. And I wouldn't have got away with this. The
missus cleans all my shoes.'

The other spare room upstairs (little more than a
small boxroom) was similarly short on furniture, with
three sheets of newspaper spread out across the bare
floorboards on which ranks of large, green cooking
apples were neatly arranged. 'They take the *Sun*,'
observed Lewis, as his eye fell on a young lady leaning
forward to maximize the measurements of a mighty
bosom. 'You think he was a secret sex maniac?'

'*I'm* a secret—' But Morse broke off as he saw the

broad grin across his sergeant's face, and he found himself smiling in return.

The main bedroom, though furnished fully (even tastefully, as Morse saw it), seemed at first glance to offer little more of interest than the rest of the house. Twin beds, only a few inches apart, were neatly made, each covered with an olive-green quilt, each with a small bedside table – the feminine accoutrements on the one nearer the window clearly signifying 'hers'. On the right as one entered the room was a large white-wood wardrobe, again 'hers', and on the left a tallboy obviously 'his'. A composite piece of modern furniture, mirror in the middle, three shelves above (two of them full of books), with drawers below, stood just beyond the tallboy – at the bottom of Margaret Bowman's bed. Since there seemed about three times as much of her clothing as of his, Morse agreed that Lewis should concentrate on the former, he on the latter. But neither of them was able to come up with anything of value, and Morse soon found himself far more interested in the two shelves of books. The thick spines of four white paperbacks announced a sequence of the latest inter-national best-sellers by Jackie Collins, and beside these stood two apparently unopened Penguins, *Brideshead Revisited* and *A Passage to India*. Then two large, lavishly illustrated books on the life and times of Marilyn Monroe; an ancient impression of the Concise Oxford Dictionary; and, a very recent purchase by the look of things, a book in the 'Hollywood Greats' series covering the career of Robert Redford (a star – unlike Miss

Monroe – who had yet to swim into Morse's ken). On the wall beside this top shelf of books were two colour photographs cut from sporting periodicals: one of Steve Cram, the great middle-distance runner; the other of Ian Terence Botham, his blond locks almost reaching the top of his England cricket sweater. The title *Sex Parties*, on the lower shelf, caught Morse's eye and he took it out and opened a page a random:

> Her hand slid across the gear-lever and touched his leg below the tennis shorts. 'Let's go to my place – quick!' she murmured in his ear.
> 'I shan't argue with that, my love!' he replied huskily as the powerful Maserati swerved across the street...
> As they lay there together the next morning –

Such anti-climactic pianissimo porn had no attraction whatever for Morse and he was putting the book back in its slot when he noticed that there was something stuck in the middle of the large volume next to it, a work entitled *The Complete Crochet Manual*. It was a holiday postcard from Derwentwater, addressed to Mrs M. Bowman, the date stamp showing July 29th, the brief message reading:

> Greetings from Paradise
> Regained — I wish
> you were here
>   Edwina

Morse turned the card over and looked lovingly at the pale-green sweep of the hills before putting the card back in its place. An odd place, perhaps, his brain suggested gently. And not the sort of book, surely, that Tom Bowman would often dip into for amusement or instruction? Edwina was doubtless one of Margaret's friends – either a local woman or one of her colleagues at Oxford. For the moment, he thought no more about it.

Downstairs once more, Lewis collected up the pile of documents he'd already selected from the mass of letters and bills that appeared to have been stuffed haphazardly into the two drawers of the corner cabinet in the lounge – water, electricity, mortgage, HP, bank statements, car insurance. Morse, for his part, sat down in one of the two armchairs and lit a cigarette.

'They kept their accounts and things in one hell of a mess, sir!'

Morse nodded. 'Mm!'

'Looks almost as if someone has been looking through all this stuff pretty recently.'

Morse shot up in the armchair as if a silken-smooth car driver had suddenly, without warning, decided to practise an emergency stop. 'Lewis! You're a genius, my son! The paper! There's a pile of newspapers in the kitchen, and I glanced at them while you were in here. Do you know something? *I think today's copy's there!*'

Lewis felt the blood tingling in his own veins as he

followed Morse into the kitchen once more, where beneath a copy of the previous week's *Oxford Times* was the *Sun*, dated January 6th.

'She must have been here some time today, sir.'

Morse nodded. 'I think she came back here *after we saw her this morning*. She must have picked up the paper automatically from the doormat—'

'But surely somebody would have seen her?'

'Go and see if you can find out, Lewis.'

Two minutes later, whilst Morse had progressed no further than page three of the Bowmans' daily, Lewis came back: the woman still peeping at events from the window immediately opposite had seen Margaret Bowman get out of a taxi.

'A *taxi*?'

'That's what she said – and go into the house, about half-past one.'

'When we were on the way back to Oxford . . .'

'I wonder what she wanted, sir?'

'She probably wanted her building society book or something – get a bit of ready cash. I should think that's why those drawers are in such a mess.'

'We can check easily enough – at the building societies.'

'Like the beauty clinics, you mean?' Morse smiled. 'No! Let Phillips and his lads do that – tedious business, Lewis! I'm really more interested to know why she came in a taxi.'

'Shall we get Sergeant Phillips to check on the taxis, too?' grinned Lewis, as for the present the two men left

6 Charlbury Drive. The house had been icily cold, and they were glad to get away.

Margaret Bowman's Metro was located, parking ticket and all, in St Giles' at 4.45 p.m. that same day, and the news was immediately rung through to Kidlington. But a folding umbrella, a can of de-icing spray, and eight 'Scrabble' tokens from Esso garages did not appear to Morse to be of the slightest help in the murder inquiry.

It was not until ten thirty the following morning that Sergeant Vickers rang Kidlington from St Aldates with the quite extraordinary news that Margaret Bowman's handbag had been found. Morse himself, Vickers learned (not without a steady sinking of his heart), would be coming down immediately to view the prize exhibit.

CHAPTER THIRTY-THREE

Tuesday, 7th January: a.m.

JACK (gravely): In a handbag.
LADY BRACKNELL: A handbag?

(OSCAR WILDE)

'WHAA—?'

Morse's inarticulate utterance sounded like the death agonies of a wounded banshee, and Lewis felt his sympathy going out to whichever of the officers in St Aldates had been responsible the previous day for the Lost Property inventory.

'We get a whole lot of lost property in every day, sir—'

'—and not all of it' (Morse completed the sentence with withering scorn) 'I would humbly suggest, Sergeant, a prime item of evidence in a murder inquiry – and if I may say so, *not* an inquiry of which this particular station is wholly ignorant. In fact, only yesterday afternoon your colleague Sergeant Phillips and two of your own detective constables were specifically seconded from their duties here to assist in that very inquiry. Remember? And do you know who asked for them – me! And do you know why I'm so anxious to show some interest in this inquiry? Because this bloody station *asked* me to!'

Palely, Sergeant Vickers nodded, and Morse continued.

'You! – and you'll do it straight away, Sergeant – you'll get hold of the bloody nincompoop who sat in that chair of yours yesterday and you'll tell him I want to see him immediately. Christ! I've never known anything like it. There are rules in this profession of ours, Sergeant – didn't you know that? – and they tell us to get names and addresses and occupations and times and details and all the rest of it – and here we are without a bloody clue who brought it in, where it was found, when it was found – nothing!'

A constable had come through in the midst of this shrill tirade, waiting until the peroration before quietly informing Morse there was a telephone call for him.

After Morse had gone, Lewis looked across at his old pal, Sergeant Vickers.

'Was it you, Sam?'

Vickers nodded.

'Don't worry! He's always flying off the handle.'

'He's right, though. I tell everybody else to fill in the forms and follow the rules but . . .'

'Do you remember who brought it in?'

'Vaguely. One of the winos. We've probably got him on the books for pinching a bottle of cider from a supermarket or something. Poor sod! But the last thing we can cope with is having the likes of him here! I suppose he nicked the money when he "found" the bag and then just brought it in to square his conscience. I didn't discover where he found it, though – or when – or what his name was. I just thought – well, never mind!'

'He can't shoot you, Sam.'

'It's not as if there's much in it to help, I don't think.'

Lewis opened the expensive-looking handbag and looked through its contents: as Vickers had said, there seemed little enough of obvious interest. He pulled out the small sheaf of cards from the front compartment of the wallet: the usual bank and credit cards, two library tickets, two creased first-class stamps, a small rectangular card advertising the merits of an Indian restaurant in Walton Street, Oxford, and an identity pass-card for the Locals, with a coloured photograph of Margaret Bowman on the left. One by one, Lewis picked them up and examined them, and was putting them back into the wallet when he noticed the few words written in red biro on the back of the white restaurant card:

> M. I love you
> darling. T.

Obviously, thought Lewis, a memory from happier days, probably their first meal together, when Tom and Margaret Bowman had sat looking dreamily at each other over a Bombay curry, holding hands and crunching popadums.

*

A brighter-looking Morse returned.

An intelligent and resourceful Phillips, it appeared, had discovered that Margaret Bowman had gone back – not in her own car, of course – to Chipping Norton the previous lunchtime, and had withdrawn £920 of her savings in the Oxfordshire Building Society there – leaving only a nominal £10 in the account.

'It's all beginning to fit together, Lewis,' said Morse. 'She was obviously looking for her pay-in book when she got a taxi back there. And this clinches things of course' – he gestured to the handbag. 'Car keys there, I'd like to bet. But she must have had an extra house key on her ... Yes! Cheque card, I see, but I'd be surprised if she kept that *and* her chequebook together. Most people have more sense these days.'

Lewis, not overjoyed by the high praise bestowed upon his fellow sergeant, ventured his own comments on the one item in the handbag which had puzzled him – the (obviously very recently acquired) leaflet on St Mary the Virgin. 'I remember when I was a lad, sir, somebody jumped from the tower there, and I was wondering—'

'Nonsense, Lewis! You don't do that sort of thing these days. You take a couple of boxes of pills, don't you, Sergeant Vickers?'

The latter, so unexpectedly appealed to, decided to take this opportunity of putting the record straight. 'Er, about the handbag, sir. I wasn't exactly telling you the whole truth earlier—'

But Morse was not listening. His eyes were staring at the small oblong card which Lewis had just examined and which lay on top of the little pile of contents, the handwritten message uppermost.

'What's that?' he asked with such quietly massive authority in his voice that Vickers found the hairs rising up on his brawny forearms.

But neither of the two sergeants could answer, for neither knew what it was that the chief inspector had asked, nor why it was that his eyes were gleaming with such triumphant intensity.

Morse looked cursorily through the other items from the handbag, quickly deciding that nothing merited further attention. His face was still beaming as he clapped a hand on Lewis's shoulder. 'You are – not for the first time in your life – a bloody genius, Lewis! As for you, Vickers, we thank you for your help, my friend. Forget what I said about that idiot colleague of yours! Please, excuse us! We have work to do, have we not, Lewis?'

'The Indian restaurant, is it?' asked Lewis as they got into the car.

'You hungry, or something?'

'No, sir, but—'

'I wouldn't say no to a curry myself, but not just for the time being. Put your foot down, my son!'

'Er – where to, sir?'

'Chipping Norton! Where else?'

Lewis saw that the fascia clock showed a quarter past twelve as the car passed through Woodstock.

'Fancy a pint?' asked a cheerful Lewis.

Morse looked at him curiously. 'What's the matter with you this morning? I hope you're not becoming an alcoholic?'

Lewis shook his head lightly.

'You want to be like me, Lewis. I'm a dipsomaniac.'

'What's the difference?'

Morse pondered for a while. 'I think an alcoholic is always trying to *give up* drink.'

'Whereas such a thought has never crossed your mind, sir?'

'Well put!' said Morse, thereafter lapsing into the silence he habitually observed when being driven in a car.

As they neared the Chipping Norton turning off the A34, a woman driving a very ancient Ford Anglia passed them on her way down from Birmingham to spend a night at the Haworth Hotel.

Chapter Thirty-four

Tuesday, January 7th: p.m.

A certain document of the last importance has been purloined.

(EDGAR ALLAN POE)

'WELL, I'LL BE buggered!' Morse shook his head in bewildered disappointment as he stood, once again, in Margaret Bowman's bedroom – *The Complete Crochet Manual* in his hands. 'It's gone, Lewis!'

'*What's* gone?'

'The card I showed you – the card from the Lake District – the one signed "Edwina".'

'You never showed it to me,' protested Lewis.

'Of course I—. Perhaps I didn't. But the handwriting on that postcard was the same as the handwriting on the back of your whatsitsname Indian place in Walton Street. *Exactly the same!* I can swear to it! The postcard was from Ullswater or some place like that and' (Morse sought to bully his brain into a clearer remembrance) 'it said something like "It's Paradise Regained – I wish you were here". But, you know, it's a bit odd, on a postcard, to say "*I* wish you were here". Nineteen times out of twenty, people just say "*Wish* you were here",

233

don't they? Do you see what I mean? That postcard *didn't* say "It's Paradise Regained" – then a dash – "I wish you were here"; it said "It's Paradise Regained *minus one*. Wish you were here". That card was from Margaret Bowman's lover, telling her there was only one thing missing from his Paradise – *her*!'

'Not much use if it's gone,' said Lewis dubiously.

'It *is* though! Don't you see? The very fact that Margaret Bowman came back a second time shows exactly *how* important it is. And I *think* I remember the postmark – it was August. All we've got to do is to find out who spent his holidays up in the Lake District last August!'

'It might have been the August before.'

'Don't be so pessimistic, man!' snapped Morse.

'But we *ought* to be pessimistic,' persisted Lewis, remembering his recent experience with the beauty clinics. 'Millions of people go up to the Lakes every summer. And who's this "Edwina"?'

'He's the lover-boy. Tom Bowman would have been very suspicious, wanting to know who the fellow was if he'd signed his own name. But the man we're dealing with, Lewis – *the man who almost certainly murdered Bowman* – is pretty clever: he changed his name – but he didn't change it too much! And that gives us a whacking great clue. The fellow signs himself "T" on the Indian thing – and then signs himself "Edwina" on the postcard. *So we've already got his Christian name, Lewis!* The "T" doesn't stand for Tom – it stands for Ted. And "Ted" is an abbreviation of "Edward"; and he signs himself in the feminine form of it – "Edwina"! QE bloody D, Lewis – as we used to say in the Lower Fourth! All right! You say there are a few millions every year who look forward to hearing the rain drumming on their caravan roofs in Grasmere. But not all that many of them were christened "Edward", and about half of *them* would be too old – or too young – to woo our fair Margaret. And, what's more, he'll pretty certainly live in Oxford, this fellow we're looking for – or not too far outside. And if he can afford to spend a holiday in the Lake District, he's probably in work, rather than on the dole, agreed?'

'But—'

'*And* – just let me finish! – not everybody's all that familiar with *Paradise Regained*. Mr Milton's not everybody's cup of tea in these degenerate days, and I'm going to hazard a guess that our man was a grammar-school boy!'

'But they're all comprehensives now, sir.'

'You know what I mean! He's in the top 25 per cent of the IQ range.'

'The case seems to be closed, then, sir!'

'Don't be so bloody sarcastic, Lewis!'

'I'm sorry, sir, but—'

'I've not finished! What was the colour of Bowman's hair?'

'Well – blondish, sort of.'

'Correct! And what have Robert Redford, Steve Cram and Ian Botham got in common?'

'All the girls go for them.'

'No! Physical appearance, Lewis.'

'You mean, they've all got blond hair?'

'Yes! And if Margaret Bowman's running to form, this new beau of hers has got fair hair, too! And if only about a quarter of Englishmen have got fair hair—'

'He could be a Swede, sir.'

'What? A Swede who's read *Paradise Regained*?'

For Lewis, the whole thing was becoming progressively more improbable; yet he found himself following Morse's deductive logic with reluctant admiration. If Morse were right there couldn't be all that many employed, fair-haired people christened Edward, in the twenty-five to forty-five age range, living in or just outside Oxford, who had spent their most recent summer holidays in the Lake District, could there? And Lewis appreciated the force of one point Morse had just made: Margaret Bowman had been willing to make *two* extraordinarily risky visits to her house in Charlbury Drive over the last twenty-four hours. If the *first* had been to fetch her building society book (or whatever) and to get some ready cash out, it couldn't really be seen as all that incriminating. But if the overriding purpose of the *second*, as Morse was now suggesting, had been to remove from the house any pieces of vital evidence that might have been hidden in the most improbable places . . .

Lewis was conscious, as he sat there in the Bowmans' bedroom that afternoon, that he had not yet even dared to mention to Morse the thought that had so obstinately lodged itself at the back of his mind. At the time, he had dismissed the idea as utterly fanciful – and yet it would not wholly go away.

'I know it's ridiculous, sir, but – but I can't help worrying about that crane at the back of the hotel.'

'Go on!' said Morse, not without a hint of interest in his voice.

'Those cranes can land the end of a girder on a sixpence: they *have* to – match up with the bolts and everything. So if you wanted to, you could pick up a box, let's say, and you could move it wherever you wanted – *outside a window, perhaps*? It's only a thought, sir, but could it just be that Bowman was murdered *in the main part of the hotel*? If the murderer wraps up the body, say, and hooks it on to the crane, he can pinpoint it to just outside Annexe 3, where he can get an accomplice in the room to pull the box gently in. The murderer himself wouldn't be under any suspicion at all, because he's never been *near* the annexe. And if it had been snowing – like the forecast said – there wouldn't be any footprints *going in*, would there? There's so much mess and mud outside the back of the hotel, though, that nobody's going to notice anything out of the ordinary there; and nobody's going to hear anything, either – not with all the racket of a disco going on. I know it may be a lot of nonsense, but it does bring all those people staying in the hotel back into the reckoning, doesn't it? And I think you'll agree, sir, we *are* getting a bit short of suspects.'

Morse, who had been listening with quiet attention, now shook his head with perplexed amusement. 'What you're suggesting, Lewis, is that *the murderer's a crane-driver*, is that it?'

'It was only a thought, sir.'

'Narrows things down, though. A fair-haired crane-driver called Ted who spent a week in Windermere or somewhere . . .' Morse laughed. 'You're getting worse than I am, Lewis!'

Morse rang HQ from the Bowmans' house, and two men, Lewis learned, would immediately be on their way to help him undertake an exhaustive search of the whole premises at 6 Charlbury Drive.

Morse himself took the car keys and drove back thoughtfully into Oxford.

CHAPTER THIRTY-FIVE

Tuesday, January 7th: p.m.

No words beyond a murmured 'Good-evening' ever
passed between Hardy and Louisa Harding.

(The Early Life of Thomas Hardy)

INSTEAD OF GOING straight back to Kidlington HQ,
Morse drove down once more into Summertown and
turned into Ewert Place where he drove up to the front
steps and parked the police car. The Secretary, he
learned, was in and would be able to see him almost
immediately.

As he sat waiting on the long wall-seat in the foyer,
Morse was favourably struck (as he had been on his
previous visit) by the design and the furnishings of the
Delegacy. The building was surely one of the (few)
high spots of post-1950 architecture in Oxford, and he
found himself trying to give it a date: 1960? 1970? But
before he reached a verdict, he learned that the
Secretary awaited him.

Morse leaned back in the red leather armchair once
again. 'Lovely building, this!'

'We're very lucky, I agree.'

'When was it built?'

'Finished in 1965.'

'I was just comparing it to some of the hideous structures they've put up in Oxford since the war.'

'You mustn't think we don't have a few problems, though.'

'Really?'

'Oh, yes. We get floods in the basement fairly regularly. And then, of course, there's the flat roof: anyone who designs a building as big as this with a flat roof – in England! – hardly deserves the Queen's medal for architecture. Not in my book, anyway.'

The Secretary had spoken forcefully, and Morse found himself interested in her reaction. 'You've had trouble?'

'*Had?* Yes, we've had trouble, and we've got trouble now, and it'll be a great surprise if we don't have more trouble in the future. We've only just finished paying for a complete re-roofing repair – the *third* we've had!'

Morse nodded in half-hearted sympathy as she elaborated the point; but his interest in the Delegacy's roofing problems soon dissipated, and he moved to the reason for his visit. He told the Secretary, in the strictest confidence, almost everything he had discovered about the Bowmans, and he hinted at his deep concern for Margaret Bowman's life. He asked whether Margaret had any particular women friends in the Delegacy; whether she had any *men* friends; whether there might have been any gossip about her; whether there was anything at all that might be learned from interviewing any of Margaret's colleagues.

The result of this request was the summoning to the Secretary's office of Mrs Gladys Taylor, who disclaimed all knowledge of Margaret Bowman's married life, of any possible extramarital infidelity, and of her present whereabouts. After only a few minutes Morse realized he was getting nowhere with the woman; and he dismissed her. He was not at all surprised that she knew so little; and he was aware that his own abrupt interlocutory style had made the poor woman hopelessly nervous. What Morse was not aware of – and what, with a little less conceit, he might perhaps have divined – was that Gladys Taylor's nervousness had very little at all to do with the tone of Morse's questioning, but everything to do with the fact that, after spending the weekend at Gladys's council house on the Cutteslowe Estate in North Oxford, Margaret Bowman had turned up *again* – dramatically! – late the previous evening, begging Gladys to take her in and making her promise to say nothing to anyone about her whereabouts.

The former prison officer at Reception deferred his daily perusal of the Court Circular and saluted the Chief Inspector as Morse handed in the temporary badge he had been given – a plastic folder, with a metal clip, containing a buff-coloured card on which was printed VISITOR, in black capitals, and under which, in black felt tip pen, was written 'Insp. Morse'. A row of mailbags stood beside the front door, waiting for the post office van, and Morse was on the point of leaving the building when he turned back – struck by the appropriate juxtaposition of things – and spoke to the Security Officer.

'You must feel almost at home with all these mailbags around!'

'Yes! You don't forget things like that, sir. And I could still tell you where most of 'em were made – from the marks, I mean.'

'You can?' Morse fingered one of the grey bags and the Security Officer walked round to inspect it.

'From the Scrubs, that one.'

'Full of criminals, they tell me, the Scrubs.'

'Used to be – in my day.'

'You don't get many criminals here, though?'

'There's a lot of things here they'd *like* to get their hands on – especially all the question papers, of course.'

'And that's why you're here.'

'Can't be too careful, these days. We get so many people coming in – I'm not talking about the permanent staff – I'm talking about the tradesmen, builders, electricians, caterers—'

'And you give them all a pass – like the one you gave me?'

'Unless they're pretty regular. Then we give 'em a semi-permanent pass with a photograph and all that. Saves a lot of time and trouble.'

'I see,' said Morse.

A letter was awaiting Morse at Kidlington: a white envelope, with a London postmark, addressed to Chief

Inspector Morse (in as neat a piece of typewriting as one could wish to find) and marked 'Strictly Private and Personal'. Even before he opened the envelope, Morse was convinced that he was about to be apprised of some vital intelligence concerning the Bowman case. But he was wrong. The letter read as follows:

This is a love letter but please don't feel too embarassed about it because it doesn't really matter. You are now engaged on a murder inquiry and it was in connection with this that we met briefly. I don't know why but I think I've fallen genuinely and easily and happily in love with you. So there!

I wouldn't have written this silly letter but for the fact that I've been reading a biography of Thomas Hardy and he (so he said) could never forget the face of a girl who once smiled at him as she rode by on a horse. He knew the girl by name and in fact the pair of them lived quite close, but their relationship never progressed even to the point of speaking to each other. At least I've done that!

Tear this up now. I've told you what I feel about you. I almost wish I was the chief suspect in the case. Perhaps I *am* the murderer! Will you come and arrest me? Please!

The letter lacked both salutation and signature, and Morse's expression, as he read it, seemed to combine a dash of distaste with a curiously pleasurable fascination. But as the girl herself (whoever she was!) had said – it didn't really matter. Yet it would have been quite extraordinary for any man not to have pondered on the identity of such a correspondent. And, for several minutes, Morse did so ponder as he sat silently at his desk that winter's afternoon. She sounded a nice girl – and she'd only made the one spelling error . . .

The call from Lewis – a jubilant Lewis! – came in at 5.10 p.m. that day.

CHAPTER THIRTY-SIX

Tuesday, January 7th: p.m.

If you once understand an author's character, the comprehension of his writing becomes easy.

(LONGFELLOW)

IT HAD BEEN in the inside breast pocket of a rather ancient sports jacket that Lewis had finally found the copied letter. And such a discovery was so obviously what Morse had been hoping for that he was unable to conceal the high note of triumph in his voice as he reported his find. Equally, for his part, Morse had been unable to conceal his own delight; and when (only some half an hour later) Lewis delivered the four closely handwritten sheets, Morse handled them with the loving care of a biblical scholar privileged to view the *Codex Vaticanus*.

You are a selfish thankless bitch and if you think you can just back out of things when *you* like you'd better realize that you've got another big thick headaching think coming because it could be that I've got some ideas about what *I* like. You'd better understand what I'm saying. If you can act like a bitch you'd better know I can be a bit of a sod too. You were glad enough to get what you wanted from me and just because I wanted to give it to you you think that we can just drop everything and go back to square one. Well this letter is to tell you we can't and like I say you'd better understand what I'm telling you. You can be sure I'll get my own back on you. You always say you can't really talk on the phone much but you didn't have much trouble on Monday did you. Not much doubt about where you stood then. Not free this week, and perhaps not next week either, and the week after that is a bit busy too!! I know I've not been round *quite* as long as you but I'm not a fool and I think you know I'm not. You say you're not going to sign on next term for night classes and that was the one really long time we did have together. Well I don't want any Dear John letter thank you very much. But I do want one thing and I'm quite serious about saying that I'm going to get it. I must see you again – at least once again. If you've got any sense of fairness to me you'll agree to that. And if you've got just any plain *sense* – and forget any fairness – you'll still agree to see me because if you don't I shall get my own back. Don't drive me to anything like that. Nobody knows about us and I want to leave things like that like they were. You remember how careful I always was and how none of your colleagues ever knew. Not that it matters much to me, not a quarter of what it matters to you. Don't forget that. So do as I say and meet me next Monday. Tell them you've got a dental appointment and I'll pick you up as usual outside the Summertown Library at ten to one. Please make sure you're there for your sake as much as mine. Perhaps I ought to have suspected you were cooling off a bit. When I was at school I read a thing about there's always one who kisses and one who turns the cheek. Well I don't mind it that way but I must see you again. There were lots of times when you wanted me badly enough – lots of times when you nearly set a world record for getting your clothes off, and that wasn't just because we only had forty minutes. So be there for sure on Monday or you'll have to face the consequences. I've just thought that last sentence sounds like a threat but I don't really want to be nasty about all this. I suppose I've never said too much about what I really feel but I think I was in love with you the very first time I saw the top of your golden head in the summer sunshine. Monday – ten to one – or else!

Morse read the letter through twice – each time slowly, and (much to Lewis's delight) appeared to be highly satisfied.

'What do you make of it, sir?'

Morse put the letter down and leaned back in the old black leather chair, his elbows resting on the arms, the tips of his middle fingers tapping each other lightly in front of a well-pleased mouth. 'What would *you* say about that letter, Lewis, eh? What do *you* learn from it?'

Lewis usually hated moments such as this. But he had been asking himself exactly the same question since he'd first read the letter through, and he launched into what he hoped Morse would accept as an intelligent analysis.

'It's quite clear, sir, that Margaret Bowman was

unfaithful to her husband over quite a while. He talks in the letter about night classes and I think they were probably held in the autumn term – say, for about three or four months – after he first saw her, like he says, in the summer. I'd say from about July onwards. That's the first thing.' (Lewis was feeling not displeased with himself.) 'Second thing, sir, is this man's age. He says he's not been around quite as long as she has, and he's underlined the word "quite". He probably teased her a bit – like most people would – if she was a little bit older than he was: let's say, six months or a year, perhaps. Now, Margaret Bowman – I've found out, sir – was thirty-six last September. So let's put our prime suspect in the thirty-five age-bracket then, all right?' (Lewis could recall few occasions on which he had seemed to be speaking with such fluent authority.) 'Then there's a third point, sir. He asks her to meet him outside the library at ten minutes to one – so he must know it takes about five minutes for her to get there *from* the Locals – and five minutes to get back. That leaves us with fifty minutes from the hour they're given at the Locals for a lunch-break. But he mentions "*forty* minutes": so, as I see things' (how happy Lewis felt!) 'he must live only about five minutes' drive away from South Parade. I don't think they just went to a pub and held hands, sir. I think, too, that this fellow probably lives on the *west* side of Oxford – let's say off the Woodstock Road somewhere – because Summer-town Library would be a bit of a roundabout place to pick her up if he lived on the *east* side, especially with such a little time they've got together.'

Morse had nodded agreement at several points during this exposition; and had been on the point of congratulating his sergeant when Lewis resumed – still in full spate.

'Now if we add these new facts to what we've already discovered, sir, I reckon we're not all that far off from knowing exactly who he is. We can be far more precise about where he lives – within five minutes' drive, at the outside, from Summertown; and we can be far more precise about his age – pretty certainly thirty-four or thirty-five. So if we had a computerized file on every-body, I think we could spot our man straight away. But there's something else – something perhaps much more helpful than a computer, sir: that night-school class! It won't be difficult to trace the people in Mrs Bowman's class; and I'd like to bet we shall find somebody who had a vague sort of inkling about what Margaret Bowman was up to. Seems to me a good line of inquiry; and I can get on with it straight away if you agree.'

Morse was silent for a little while before replying. 'Yes, I think I *do* agree.'

Yet Lewis was conscious of a deeper undercurrent in Morse's tone: something was worrying the chief, pretty surely so.

'What's the matter, sir?'

'Matter? Nothing's the matter. It's just that – well, tell me what you make of that letter *as a whole*, Lewis. What *sort* of man is he, do you think?'

'Bit of mixture, I'd say. Sounds as if he's genuinely fond of the woman, doesn't it? At the same time it sounds as if he's got quite a cruel streak in him – bit of a coarse streak, too. As if he loved her – but always in a selfish sort of way: as if perhaps he might be prepared to do anything just to keep her.'

Morse nodded. 'I'm sure you're right. I think he *was* prepared to do almost anything to keep her.'

'Have you got any idea of what really happened?' asked Lewis quietly.

'Yes! – for what it's worth, I have. Clearly Bowman found this letter somewhere, and he realized that his wife was going with another fellow. I suspect he told her what he knew and gave her an ultimatum. Most men perhaps would have accepted the facts and called it a day – however much it hurt. But Bowman didn't! He loved his wife more than she could ever have known, and his first instinctive reactions mustered themselves – not against his wife – *but against her lover*. He probably told her all this, in his own vague way; and I think he decided that the best way to help Margaret and, at the same time, to save his own deeply injured pride, was *to get rid of her lover*! We've been on a lot of cases together, Lewis – with lots of people involved; but I don't reckon the motives are ever all *that* different – love, hate, jealousy, revenge ... Anyway, I think that Bowman got his wife to agree to collaborate with him in a plot to get rid of the man who – at least for the moment – was a threat to both of them. What *exactly* that plan involved, we may never know – unless Margaret Bowman decides to tell us. The only firm thing we know about it so far is that Bowman himself wrote a wholly genuine letter which would rather cleverly serve two purposes when lover-boy was found murdered – that is, if any suspicion were ever likely to fall on either of the Bowmans: first, it would put Margaret Bowman in a wholly sympathetic light; second, it would appear to put Tom Bowman some few hundreds of miles away from the scene of the immediate crime.'

'Didn't we know most of that already—'

'Let me finish, Lewis! At some particular point – I don't know when – *the plan was switched*, and it was switched by the only person who could switch it – by Margaret Bowman, who decided that if she had to take a profoundly important decision about life (as she did!) she would rather throw in her lot with her illicit lover than with her licit husband. Is that clear? Forget the details for the minute, Lewis! The key thing to bear in mind is this: instead of having a plot involving the death of a troublesome lover, we have a plot involving the death of an interfering husband!'

'You don't think the letter helps much at all, then?' Lewis's initial euphoria slipped a notch or two towards his wonted diffidence.

'My goodness, yes! And your own reading of that letter was a model of logic and lucidity! But . . .'

Lewis's heart sank. He knew what Morse was going to say, and he said it for him. 'But you mean I missed some vital clue in it – is that right?'

Morse waited awhile, and then smiled with what he trusted was sympathetic understanding: 'No, Lewis. You didn't miss one vital clue, at all. You missed two.'

Chapter Thirty-seven

Tuesday, January 7th: p.m.

Stand on the highest pavement of the stair –
Lean on a garden urn –
Weave, weave the sunlight in your hair

(T. S. ELIOT)

'APART FROM YOUR own admirable deductions, Lewis, there are, as I say, a couple of other things you could have noticed, perhaps. First' (Morse turned to the letter and found the appropriate reference) 'he says, "You remember how careful I always was and how none of your colleagues ever knew". Now that statement's very revealing. It suggests that this fellow *could* have been very careless about meeting Margaret Bowman; careless in the sense that, if he'd wanted to, he could easily have made Margaret's colleagues aware of what was going on between them – pretty certainly by others actually *seeing* the evidence. It means, I think, that the pair of them were very often *near* each other, and that he very sensibly agreed to avoid all contact with her *in the place where they found themselves*. And you don't need me to tell you where that might have been – *must* have been – do you? It was on the Locals site itself, where twenty-odd workmen were employed on various jobs – but mostly on the roof – between May and September last year.'

'Phew!' Lewis looked down at the letter again. If what Morse was saying were true . . .

'But there's a second thing,' continued Morse, 'that's more specific still. There's a rather nice little bit of English at the end of the letter – "but I think I was in love with you the very first time I saw the top of your golden head in the summer sunshine". Now you were right in saying that this tells us roughly when he first met her. But it also tells us something else, and something even more important. Don't you see? It tells us from which *angle* he first saw her, doesn't it, Lewis? *He saw her from above!*'

Lewis was weighing up what Morse had just said: 'You mean this fellow might have been *on the roof*, sir?'

'Could be!' Morse looked extremely pleased with himself. 'Yes, he could have been on the roof. Or he could have been – *higher*, perhaps? The flat roof at the Locals has been causing a lot of trouble, and last summer they had a complete new go at the whole thing.'

'So?'

'So they had quite a few workmen there, and they'd need something to lift all that stuff . . .'

'A crane!' The words were out of Lewis's excited lips in a flash.

'It makes sense, doesn't it?'

'Did they have a crane on the site?'

'Don't know, do I.'

'Do you remember,' said Lewis slowly, 'that it was *me* who suggested he might be a crane-driver?'

'Nonsense!' said Morse happily.

'But I—'

'You may have got the right answer, Lewis, but you got it for the wrong reasons, and you can't claim much credit for that.'

Lewis's smile was as happy as Morse's. 'Shall I give the Secretary a ring, sir?'

'Think she's still there? It's gone half-past five.'

'Some people stay on after office hours. Like I do!'

The Secretary was still at her desk. Yes, there had been a crane on the site – a big yellow thing – from May to October! And no, the Secretary had no objection at all to the police coming to look at the security passes kept all together in a filing cabinet in Reception.

Morse got up from his chair and pulled on his greatcoat. 'And there's something else, you know, Lewis. Something to crown the whole lot, really. They keep all their records carefully at the Locals – well, the chap on the desk does. All passes have to be shown and I'd like to bet that those workmen were given semi-permanent passes so that they could make use of the facilities there without having to get a badge every time they went to the lavatory or whatever. Just think of it! We sit here and rack our brains – and all the time the fellow we're looking for is sitting there on a little card – in a little drawer at the Locals – with a photograph of himself on it! By Jove, this is the simplest case we've ever handled, my old friend. Come on. On your feet!'

But for a while, Lewis sat where he was, a wistful expression across his square, honest face. 'You know, it's a pity in a way, isn't it? Like you say, we've done all this thinking – we've even given the fellow a name! The only thing we never got round to was deciding where he lives, that's all. And if we'd been able to work that out – well, we wouldn't need any photograph or anything, would we? We'd have, sort of, *thought* it all out.'

Morse sat on the edge of his desk nodding his balding head. 'Ye-es. 'Tis a pity, I agree. Amazing, you know, what feats of logic the human brain is capable of. But sometimes life eludes logic – and sometimes when you build a great big wonderful theory you find there's a fault in the foundations and the whole thing collapses round your ears at the slightest earth tremor.'

Morse's voice had sounded strangely earnest, and Lewis noticed how tired his chief looked. 'You don't think we're in for an earthquake, do you?'

'Hope not! Above all I hope we get a chance to save Margaret Bowman – save her from herself as much as anything. Nice looker, you know, that woman. Lovely head of hair!'

'Especially when viewed from the top of a crane,' said Lewis, as he finally rose to his feet and pulled on his coat.

*

As they were leaving the office, Morse paused to look at a large white map of Oxford City that was fastened on the wall to the left of the door. 'What do you think, Lewis? Here we are: South Parade – that's where he picked her up. Now we want somewhere no more than five minutes away, so you say. Well, one thing's certain – he either turned left or he turned right at the Woodstock Road, agreed?' Morse's finger slowly traced a route that led off to the south: it seemed most unlikely that the man would be living in any of the large villa-type residences that lined the road for most of the way down to St Giles', and Morse found himself looking at the map just below St John's College playing fields, and especially at the maze of little streets that criss-crossed the heart of Jericho. For his part, Lewis's eyes considered the putative route that might have been taken if the man had turned right and towards the north; and soon he spotted a small cluster of streets, between the Woodstock Road itself and, to the west of it, the canal and the railway. The writing on the map was very small but Lewis could just about read the names: St Peter's Road; Ulfgar Road; Pixey Place; Diamond Close . . . All council property, if Lewis recalled correctly – or used to be until, in the 1980s, the Tories remembered Anthony Eden's promises of a property-owning democracy.

CHAPTER THIRTY-EIGHT

Tuesday, January 7th: p.m.

I keep six honest serving-men
(They taught me all I knew):
Their names are What and Why and When
And How and Where and Who.

(RUDYARD KIPLING)

THE MOST OBVIOUS improvements effected by those
who had bought their own red-brick houses had been
to the doors and the windows: several of the old doors
were replaced completely by stout oaken affairs – or at
the very least painted some colour other than the
former regulation light blue: and most of the old
windows, with their former small oblong panes, were
now replaced by large horizontal sheets of glass set in
stainless-steel frames. In general, it seemed fairly clear,
the tone of the neighbourhood was on the 'up'; and
number 17 Diamond Close was no exception to this
pattern of improved properties. A storm door (behind
which no light was visible) had been built across the
small front porch; and the front fence and garden had
been redesigned to accommodate a medium-sized car
– like the light-green Maestro which stood there now.

Under the orange glare of the street-lamps, the close was strangely still.

The two police cars had moved slowly along St Peter's Road and then stopped at the junction with Diamond Close. Morse, Lewis and Phillips were in the first car; two uniformed constables and a plain-clothes detective in the second. Both Phillips and the plain-clothes man had been issued with regulation revolvers; and these two (as prearranged) got out of their cars and without slamming the doors behind them walked silently along the thirty or so yards to the front of number 17, where, with the plain-clothes man rather melodramatically pointing his revolver to the stars, Sergeant Phillips pushed the white button of the front-door bell. After a few seconds, a dull light appeared from somewhere at the back of the house, and then a fuller light and the silhouette of a figure seen through the glass of the outer door. At that moment the watching faces of Morse and Lewis betrayed a high degree of tension: yet, in retrospect, there had been nothing whatsoever to occasion such emotion.

From the outset the man in the thick green sweater had proved surprisingly co-operative. He had requested to be allowed to finish his baked beans (refused), to collect a packet of cigarettes (granted), to drive to Police HQ in his own car (refused), and to take his scarf and duffel coat (granted). At no stage had he mentioned writs, warrants, lawyers, solicitors, civil rights, unlawful arrest or Lord Longford, and Morse himself was beginning to feel a little shamefaced about the death-or-glory scenario of the arrest. But one never knew.

In the interview room it was Lewis who began the questioning.

'Your full name is Edward Wilkins?'

'Edward James Wilkins.'

'Your date of birth?'

'Twentieth September, 1951.'

'Place of birth?'

'17 Diamond Close.'

'The house you live in now?'

'Yes. My mother lived there.'

'Which school did you go to?'

'Hobson Road Primary – for a start.'

'And after that?'

'Oxford Boys' School.'

'You passed the eleven plus to go there?'

'Yes.'

'When did you leave?'

'In 1967.'

'You took your O levels?'

'Yes. I passed in Maths, Physics and Engineering Drawing.'

'You didn't take English Literature?'

'Yes, I did. But I failed.'

'Did you read any Milton?' interrupted Morse.

'Yes, we read *Comus*.'

'What did you do after you left school?' (Lewis had taken up the questioning once more.)

'I got an apprenticeship at Lucy's Ironworks in Jericho.'

'And then?'

'I didn't finish it. I stuck it for eighteen months and then I got offered a much better job with Mackenzie Construction.'

'You still work for them?'

'Yes.'

'What's your job, exactly?'

'I'm a crane-driver.'

'You mean you sit up in the cabin and swing all the loads round the site?'

'That's one way of putting it.'

'This company – Mackenzie Construction – they did some re-roofing last year at the Oxford Delegacy – Oxford Locals, I think you call it. Is that right?'

'Yes. About April to September.'

'You worked there all that time?'

'Yes.'

'Not *all* that time, surely?'

'Pardon?'

'Didn't you have any summer holiday?'

'Oh yes, I'm sorry. I was off a fortnight.'

'When was that?'

'Late July.'

'Where did you go?'

'Up to the north of England.'

'Whereabouts exactly?'

'The Lake District.'

'And where in the Lake District?'

'Derwentwater.'

'Did you send any postcards from there?'

'A few. Yes.'

'To some of your friends here – in Oxford?'

'Who else?'

'Oh, I don't know, Mr Wilkins. If I'd known I wouldn't have asked, would I?'

It was the first moment of tension in the interview, and Lewis (as Morse had instructed him) left things there for a while, saying nothing; and for a little while the silence hung heavily over the bare, rather chilly room at the rear of Police HQ in Kidlington.

From the doorway Sergeant Phillips, who had never previously been present at such an interrogation, watched events with a touch of embarrassment. The prolonged period of silence seemed (as Phillips saw things) particularly to affect Wilkins, whose hands twice twitched at his hip pocket as if seeking the solace of a cigarette, but whose will-power appeared for the minute in adequate control. He was a large-boned, fairish-haired, pleasantly spoken man who seemed to Phillips about the last person in the world who would suddenly display any symptoms of homicidal ferocity. Yet Phillips was also aware that the two men in charge of the case, Morse and Lewis, had great experience in these affairs, and he listened to Lewis's further questions with absorbed fascination.

'When did you first meet Mrs Margaret Bowman?'

'You know all about that?'

'Yes.'

'I met her when I was working at the Locals. We had the use of the canteen and some of us used to have a meal there and that's when I met her.'

'When did you first meet her outside working hours?'

'She had a night-school class, and I used to meet her for a drink afterwards.'

'Quite regularly, you did this?'

'Yes.'

'And you invited her back to your house?'

'Yes.'

'And you made love to each other?'

'Yes.'

'And then she got a bit fed up with you and wanted the affair to stop – is that right, Mr Wilkins?'

'That's not true.'

'You were in love with her?'

'Yes.'

'You still in love with her?'

'Yes.'

'Is she in love with you?' (Morse was delighted with such a beautifully modulated question.)

'I didn't force her along, did I?' (For the first time a little hesitancy – and a little coarseness – had crept into Wilkins's manner.)

'Did you write this?' Lewis handed over a Xeroxed copy of the letter found in Bowman's jacket.

'I wrote it, yes,' said Wilkins.

'And you still say you weren't forcing her along a bit?'

'I just wanted to see her again, that's all.'

'To make love to her again, you mean?'

'Not just that, no.'

'Did you actually see her that day – in South Parade?'

'Yes.'

'And you took her to your house?'

'Yes.'

'Was anyone following you – in a car?'

'What do you mean?'

'Mr Bowman knew all about you – we found that copy of the letter in one of his jackets.'

Wilkins shook his head, as if with regret. 'I didn't know that – honestly, I didn't. I always said to Margaret that whatever happened I never wanted to – well, to *hurt* anybody else.'

'You didn't know that Mr Bowman knew all about you?'

'No.'

'She didn't tell you?'

'No. I stopped seeing her after that day I met her in South Parade. She said she couldn't cope with the strain and everything, and that she'd decided to stay with him. It was a bit hard to take, but I tried to accept it. I hadn't got much option, had I?'

'When did you last see her?'

For the first time in the interview, Wilkins allowed himself a ghost of a smile, showing regular though nicotine-stained teeth. 'I saw her,' he looked at his wrist-watch, 'just over an hour ago. She was in the house when you called to bring me here.'

Morse closed his eyes momentarily in what looked like a twinge of intolerable pain; and Lewis began 'You mean . . .?'

'She came about a quarter to six. She just said she didn't know what to do – she wanted help.'

'Did she want money?'

'No. Well, she didn't mention it. Not much good asking *me* for money, in any case – and she knew that.'

'Did she say where she was going?'

'Not really, but I think she'd been in touch with her sister.'

'She lives where?'

'Near Newcastle, I think.'

'You didn't tell her she could stay with you?'

'That would have been a mad thing to do, wouldn't it?'

'Do you think she's still in your house?'

'She'd be out of there like a bat out of hell immediately we'd gone.'

(Morse gestured to Sergeant Phillips, spoke a few words in his ear and dismissed him.)

'So you think she's off north somewhere?' continued Lewis.

'I don't know. I honestly don't know. I advised her to get on a boat or something and sail off to the continent – away from everything.'

'But she didn't take your advice?'

'No. She couldn't. She hadn't got a passport, and she was frightened of applying for one because she knew everybody was trying to find her.'

'Did she know that everybody was trying to find *you*, as well?'

'Of course she didn't! I don't know what you mean.'

'I'm sure you know why we've brought you here,' said Lewis, looking directly across into Wilkins's eyes.

'Really? I'm afraid you're wrong there.'

'Well she *did* know that everybody was looking for you. You see, Mr Wilkins, she went back to her own house in Chipping Norton, at considerable risk to herself, to remove any incriminating evidence that she thought might be lying around. For example, she took the postcard you wrote to her from the Lake District.'

There was a sudden dramatic silence in the interview room, as though everybody there had taken a sharp intake of breath – and was holding it.

'It's my duty as a police officer,' continued Lewis, 'to tell you formally that you are under arrest for the murder of Thomas Bowman.'

Wilkins slumped back in his chair, his face ashen-pale and his upper lip trembling. 'You're making the most terrible mistake,' he said very quietly.

CHAPTER THIRTY-NINE

Tuesday, January 7th: p.m.

When angry, count four; when very angry, swear.

(MARK TWAIN)

'AM I DOING all right?' asked a slightly subdued Lewis as, five minutes after this preliminary interview, he sat in the canteen drinking coffee with Morse.

'Very good – *very* good,' said Morse. 'But we've got to tread a bit carefully from now on because we're getting to the point where we're not *quite* sure of the ground – by which I mean it's going to be difficult to *prove* one or two things. So let's just recap a minute. Let's go back to the beginning of things – Plan One, let's call it. Bowman follows his wife up to Diamond Close that day, and later he confronts her with the evidence. She's getting desperate anyway, and she goes along with the quite extraordinary plan he's concocted. As we've seen he fixes up the phoney address and books a New-Year-Package-for-Two at the Haworth Hotel. She tells Wilkins that her husband's gone off on a course and that they can spend all that time together; and he jumps at the chance. Once she's safely in her room, she rings Wilkins – we still haven't checked on that, Lewis –

to give him the room number and soon she's giving him the happy hour between the sheets. Then they both get ready for the fancy dress – which she's already told Wilkins about, and which he's already agreed to. If he *hadn't*, Lewis, the plan couldn't have worked. At about seven o'clock she makes some excuse to go out, when she gives the key to Bowman himself, who's waiting somewhere near the annexe, and who's dressed up in exactly the same sort of garb as Wilkins. Now Wilkins is a stronger man, I suspect, than Bowman ever was, and I should think that Bowman wouldn't have taken any chance about letting the whole thing develop into a brawl – he's probably got a knife or a revolver or something. Then the deed is done, and the next part of the deception begins. They could disappear from the scene straight away, but they agree that's far too risky. Somebody's going to find the body immediately if they do, because the "Ballards" as they called themselves won't be there for the party. There's virtually no risk in their being recognized anyway: they're both in fancy dress for the rest of the evening – he's got his face blacked, she's wearing a veil; and the only time a busy receptionist had seen Margaret Bowman was when she'd been muffled up in a scarf and hood – with a pair of dark skiing glasses on, for all we know.'

Lewis nodded.

'That was the original plan – and it must have been very much as I've described it, Lewis; otherwise it's impossible to account for several facts in the case – for instance, the fact that Bowman wrote a letter to his wife that would give them both a reasonable alibi – if the worse came to the worst. It wasn't a bad plan, either – except in one vital respect. Bowman was beginning to know quite a bit about Wilkins, but he never quite knew *enough*. Above all, he didn't know that Wilkins was beginning to dominate his wife in an ever increasing way, and that she'd become so sexually and emotionally dependent on him that she came to realize, at some point, that it was her husband, Tom Bowman, she wanted out of her life for good – not her lover. Maybe Bowman had become so obsessed with this revenge idea of his that she saw, perhaps for the first time, what a crudely devious man he really was. But for whatever reason, we can know one thing for certain: *she told Wilkins what they were planning.* Now you don't need to be a genius – and I don't think Wilkins *is* a genius – to spot an almost incredible opportunity here: the plan can go ahead as Bowman had devised it – exactly so! – but only up to the point when Bowman would let himself into the room. This time it would be *Wilkins* who's waiting behind the door *for Bowman* with a bottle of whatever it was to smash down on the back of his head.'

'Front, sir,' murmured Lewis if only, for conscience' sake, to put the unofficial record straight.

'So that's what happened, Lewis; and it's Plan Two that's now in operation. After murdering Bowman, Wilkins is all ready to go along to the party in exactly the same outlandish clothes as the murdered man would be found in. The two men were roughly the same height and everybody is going to assume that the man in the Rastafarian rig-out at the party is the same as the man in the Rastafarian rig-out later found dead on the bed in Annexe 3. Almost certainly – and this is in fact what happened – the corpse isn't going to be found until pretty late the next day; and if the heating is turned off – as it was – and if the window's left half-open – as it was – then any cautious clown like Max is going to be even cagier than usual about giving any categorical ruling on the time of death, because of the unusual room temperature. I'm not sure, myself, that it wouldn't have been far more sensible to turn the radiator on full and close all the windows. But, be that as it may, Wilkins clearly wanted to give the impression that the murder had taken place *as late as possible*. Agreed?'

'I can't quite see *why* though, sir.'

'You will do, in due course. Have faith!'

Lewis, however, looked rather less than full of faith. 'It's getting a bit too complicated for my brain, sir. I keep forgetting who's dressed up for what and who's planning to kill who—'

'"Whom", Lewis. Your grammar's as bad as Miss Jonstone's.'

'You're sure he *is* the murderer? – Wilkins?'

'My son, the case is over! There are bound to be one or two details—'

'Do you mind if we just go over one or two things again?'

'I can't spell things out *much* more simply, you know.'

'You say Wilkins wanted the murder to look as if it took place as late as possible. But I don't see the point of that. It doesn't give him an alibi, does it? I mean, whether Bowman's murdered at seven o'clock or after midnight – what does it matter? Wilkins and Margaret Bowman were there *all the time*, weren't they?'

'Yes! But who said they'd got an alibi? *I* didn't mention an alibi. All I'm saying is that Wilkins had a reason for wanting to mislead everyone into believing that the murder was committed after the party was over. That's obvious enough, isn't it?'

'But going back a minute, don't you think that in Bowman's original plan – Plan One, as you call it – it would have been far more sensible to have committed the murder – murder Wilkins, that is – and then to get out of the place double quick? With any luck, no one's going to suspect a married couple from Chipping Norton – even if the body's found very soon afterwards.'

Morse nodded, but with obvious frustration.

'I *agree* with you. But somehow or other we've got to explain how it came about that Bowman was found dressed up in identically the same sort of outfit as Wilkins was wearing at the party. Don't you *see* that, Lewis? We've got to explain the facts! And I refuse to believe that anyone could have dressed up Bowman in all that stuff *after* he'd been murdered.'

'There's one other thing, sir. You know from Max's report it says that Bowman could have been eating some of the things they had at the party?'

'What about it?'

'Well – was it just coincidence he'd been eating the same sort of meal?'

'No. Margaret Bowman must have known – she must

have found out – what the menu was and then cooked her husband some of it. Then all Wilkins had to do was just eat a bit of the same stuff—'

'But how did Margaret Bowman know?'

'How the hell do I know, Lewis? But it *happened*, didn't it? I'm not making up this bloody corpse you know! I'm not making up all these people in their fancy dress! You do realize that, don't you?'

'No need to get cross, sir!'

'I'm *not* bloody cross! If somebody decides to make some elaborate plan to rub out one side of the semi-eternal triangle – we've got to have some equally elaborate explanation! Surely you can see that?'

Lewis nodded. 'I agree. But just let me make my main point once again, sir – and then we'll forget it. It's this business of *staying on after the murder* that worries me: it must have been a dreadfully nerve-racking time for the two of them; it was very complicated; and it was a bit chancy. And all I say is that I can't *really* see the whole point of it. It just keeps the pair of them on the hotel premises the whole of the evening, and whatever time the murder was committed they haven't got any chance of an alibi—'

'There you go again, Lewis! For Christ's sake, come off it! *Nobody's got a bloody alibi.*'

The two men were silent for several minutes.

'Cup more coffee, sir?' asked Lewis.

'Augh! I'm sorry, Lewis. You just take the wind out of my sails, that's all.'

'We've got him, sir. That's the only thing that matters.'

Morse nodded.

'And you're absolutely sure that we've got the right man?'

'It's a big word – "absolutely" – isn't it?' said Morse.

CHAPTER FORTY

Tuesday, January 7th: p.m.

Alibi (n.) – the plea in a criminal charge of having been elsewhere at the material time.

(*Chambers 20th Century Dictionary*)

IT WAS, IN all, to be an hour or so before the interrogation of Wilkins was resumed. Morse had telephoned Max, but had learned only that if he, Morse, continued to supply the lab with corpses about twenty-four hours old, he, Max, was not going to make too many fanciful speculations: he was a forensic scientist, not a fortune teller. Lewis had contacted the Haworth Hotel to discover that one local call had in fact been made – untraceable, though – from Annexe 3 on New Year's Eve. Phillips, who had returned from Diamond Close with the not unexpected news that Margaret Bowman (if she *had* been there) had flown, now resumed his duties in the interview room, standing by the door, his feet aching a good deal, his eyes idly scanning the bare room once again: the wooden trestle-table, on which stood two white polystyrene cups (empty now) and an ash-tray (rapidly filling); and behind the table, the fairish-haired, fresh-complexioned man accused of a terrible murder, who seemed to Phillips to look perhaps rather less dramatically perturbed than should have been expected.

'What time did you get to the Haworth Hotel on New Year's Eve?'

'Say that again?'

'What time did you get to the hotel?'

'I didn't go to any hotel that night—'

'You were at the Haworth Hotel and you got there at—'

'I've never played there.'

'Never played what?'

'Never *played* there!'

'I'm not quite with you, Mr Wilkins.'

'We go round the pubs – the group – we don't often go to hotels.'

'You play in a pop group?'

'A jazz group – I play tenor sax.'

'So what?'

'Look, Sergeant. You say you're not with *me*: I'm not with *you*, either.'

'You were at the Haworth Hotel on New Year's Eve. What time did you get there?'

'I was at the Friar up in North Oxford on New Year's Eve!'

'Really?'

'Yes, really!'

'Can you prove it?'

'Not offhand, I suppose, but—'

'Would the landlord remember you there?'

'Course he would! He paid us, didn't he?'

'The group you're in – was playing there?'

'Yes.'

'And you were there *all the evening*?'

'Till about two o'clock the next morning.'

'How many others in the group?'

'Four.'

'And how many people were there at the Friar that night?'

'Sixty? – seventy? on and off.'

'Which bar were you in?'

'Lounge bar.'

'And you didn't leave the bar all night?'

'Well, we had steak and chips in the back room at about – half-past nine, I suppose it was.'

'With the rest of the group?'

'*And* the landlord – *and* the landlady.'

'This is New Year's Eve you're talking about?'

'Look, Sergeant, I've been here a long time already tonight, haven't I? Can you please ring up the Friar and get someone here straight away? Or ring up any of the group? I'm getting awfully tired – and it's been one hell of an evening for me – you can understand that, can't you?'

There was a silence in the room – a silence that seemed to Phillips to take on an almost palpable tautness, as the import of Wilkins's claim slowly sank into the minds of the detectives there.

'What does your group call itself, Mr Wilkins?' It was Morse himself who quietly asked the final question.

'The "Oxford Blues",' said Wilkins, his face hard and unamused.

Charlie Freeman ('Fingers' Freeman to his musical colleagues) was surprised to find a uniformed constable standing on his Kidlington doorstep that evening. Yes, the 'Oxford Blues' had played the Friar on New Year's Eve; yes, *he'd* played there that night, with Ted Wilkins, for about five or six hours; yes, he'd be more than willing to go along to Police HQ immediately and make a statement to that effect. No great hardship for him, was it? After all, it was only a couple of minutes' walk away.

By 9.30 p.m. Mr Edward Wilkins had been driven back to his home in Diamond Close; Phillips, at long last, had been given permission to call it a day; and Lewis, tired and dejected, sat in Morse's office, wondering where they had all gone so sadly wrong. Perhaps he might have suspected – and he'd actually *said* so – that Morse's ideas had all been a bit too bizarre: a man murdered in fancy-dress outfit; and then another man spending the night of the party pretending he *was* the murdered man and dressed in a virtually identical outfit. Surely, surely, the simple truth was that *Thomas Bowman* had been the man at the party, as well as the man who'd been murdered! There would be (as Lewis knew) lots of difficulties in substantiating such a view;

but none of them were anywhere near as insurmountable as trying to break Wilkins's alibi – an alibi which could be vouched for by sixty or seventy wholly disinterested witnesses. Gently, quietly, Lewis mentioned his thoughts to Morse – the latter sitting silent and morose in the old black leather armchair. 'You could be right, Lewis.' Morse rubbed his left hand across his eyes. 'Anyway, it's no good worrying about it tonight. My judgement's gone! I need a drink. You coming?'

'No. I'll get straight home, if you don't mind, sir. It's been a long day, and I should think the missus'll have something cooking for me.'

'I should be surprised if she hasn't.'

'You're looking tired, sir. Do you want me to give you a lift?'

Morse nodded wearily. 'Just drop me at the Friar, if you will.'

As he walked up to the entrance, Morse stopped. Red, blue, green and orange lights were flashing through the lounge windows, and the place was athrob with the live music of what sounded like some Caribbean delirium at the Oval greeting a test century from Vivian Richards. Morse checked his step and walked round to the public bar, where in comparative peace he sat and drank two pints of Morrell's bitter and watched a couple of incompetent pool-players pretending to be Steve Davises. On the wall beside the dartboard he saw the notice:

7th January
LIVE MUSIC 7–11 p.m.
Admission Free!!
The fabulous
CALYPSO QUARTET

Morse pondered a quick third pint; but it wanted only a couple of minutes to eleven, and he decided to get home – just a few minutes' walk away, along Carlton Road and thence just a little way down the Banbury Road to his bachelor flat. But something thwarted this decision, and he ordered another pint, a large Bell's Scotch and a packet of plain crisps.

At twenty minutes past eleven he was the last one in the public bar, and the young barman wiping the table-tops suggested that he should finish his drink and leave: it was not unknown (Morse learned) for the police to check up on over-liquored loiterers after a live music evening.

As he left, Morse saw the Calypso Quartet packing away its collection of steel drums and sundry other Caribbean instruments into the back of an old, oft-dented Dormobile. And suddenly Morse stopped. He stopped dead. He stopped as if petrified, staring at the man who had just closed the back door of the vehicle and who was languidly lolling round to the driving seat. Even in the bitter late-night air this man wore only a blood-red, open-necked shirt on the upper part of his loose-limbed body; whilst on his head he had a baggy black-and-white checked cap that covered all his hair apart from the beaded dreadlocks which dangled on either side of his face like the snakes that once wreathed the head of the stone-eyed Gorgon.

'You all right, man?' enquired the coloured musician, holding both hands up in a mock gesture of concern about a fellow mortal who seemed to have imbibed too freely perhaps and too well. And Morse noticed the hands – hands that were almost like the hands of a white man, as though the Almighty had just about run out of pigment when he came to the palms.

'You all right, man?' repeated the musician.

Morse nodded, and there appeared on his face a stupidly beatific smile such as was seldom seen there – save when he listened to the love duet from Act One of *Die Walküre*.

Morse should (he knew it!) not have left things where they were that night. But his eyelids drooped heavily over his prickly-tired eyes as he walked back to his flat and in spite of his elation, he had little enough strength left, little appetite for anything more that day. But before throwing himself on the longed-for bed, he did ring Lewis; and prevailed upon Mrs Lewis (still up) to rouse her husband (an hour abed) for a few quick words before January 7th drew to its seemingly interminable close. And when, after only a brief monologue from Morse, a weary-brained Lewis put his receiver down, he, too, knew the identity of the man who on New Year's Eve had walked back to the annexe of the Haworth Hotel with Helen Smith on the one side and Philippa Palmer on the other.

CHAPTER FORTY-ONE

Wednesday, January 8th: a.m.

Matrimony is a bargain, and somebody has to get the worst of the bargain.

(HELEN ROWLAND)

AT THE DESK of the Haworth Hotel the following morning, Sarah Jonstone greeted Sergeant Lewis as if she were glad to see him; which indeed she was, since she had at last remembered the little thing that had been troubling her. So early in the day (it was only eight thirty), her excessively circumferenced spectacles were still riding high upon her pretty little nose, and it could hardly be claimed, at least for the present, that she was being hectically overworked; in fact Lewis had already observed her none-too-convincing attempt to conceal beneath a pile of correspondence the book she had been reading when he had so unexpectedly walked in – on Morse's instruction – to interview her once again.

It was just a little corroboration (Lewis had pointed out) that was needed; and Sarah found herself once again seeking to stress the few unequivocally certain points she had made in her earlier statement. Yes, she *did* remember, and very clearly, the man coming out of the Gentlemen's lavatory just before the New Year's Eve party was due to begin; yes (now that Lewis mentioned it) perhaps his hands *hadn't* been blackened-over as convincingly as the rest of him; yes, the two of them, 'Mr and Mrs Ballard', *had* kept themselves very much to themselves for the greater part of the evening – certainly until that hour or so before midnight when a series of eightsome reels, general excuse-mes and old-time barn-dances had severed the last ties of self-consciousness and timidity; and when 'Mr Ballard' had danced with her, his sweaty fingers leaving some of their dark stain on her own hands, *and* on her blouse; yes, without a shadow of doubt that last fact *was* true, because she remembered with a sweet clarity how she had washed her hands in the bedroom washbasin before going to bed that night, and how she had tried to sponge the stain off her blouse the following morning.

A middle-aged couple stood waiting to pay their bill; and while Sarah fetched the account from the small room at the back of Reception, Lewis turned his head to one side and was thus able to make out the title on the white spine of the book she had been reading: MILLGATE: *Thomas Hardy – A Biography*. O.U.P.

The bill settled, Sarah resumed her seat and told Lewis what she had remembered. It had been odd, though it didn't really seem all that important now. What had happened was that someone – a woman – had rung up and asked what the New Year's Eve menu was: that was all. As far as she could recall, the little incident had taken place on the Monday before – that would be December 30th.

Knowing how pleased Morse would be to have one of his hunches confirmed, Lewis was on the point of taking down some firm statement from Sarah Jonstone when he became aware of an extraordinarily attractive brunette standing beside him, shifting the weight of her beautifully moulded figure from one black-stockinged leg to the other.

'Can I have my bill, please?' she asked. Although the marked Birmingham accent was not, as he heard it, exactly the music of the spheres, Lewis found himself staring at the woman with an almost riveted fascination.

The whispered voice in his ear was totally unexpected: 'Take your lecherous eyes off her, Lewis!'

'Thank you very much, Miss Arkwright!' said Sarah Jonstone, as the woman turned and left, flashing a brief, but almost interested, glance at the man who had just come in.

'Good morning, Miss Jonstone!' said Morse.

'Oh, hello!' There was nothing about her greeting that could be construed as even wanly welcoming.

'Is she the same one?' asked Morse, gesturing after the departed beauty. 'The one who was due for the New Year?'

'Yes!'

'Well, well!' said Morse, looking quite extraordinarily pleased with himself and with life in general; and quite clearly pleased with the sight of Miss Doris Arkwright in particular. 'Could you please ask *Mrs*

Binyon to come along to Reception, Miss Jonstone? There's something rather important—'

'She's not here, I'm afraid. She's gone up to Leeds. She *was* going there for the New Year, but—'

'Really? How *very* interesting! Well thank you very much, Miss Jonstone. Come on, Lewis! We've a busy morning ahead.'

'Miss Jonstone remembered something—' started Lewis.

'Forget it for the minute! Bigger things to worry about just now! Goodbye, Miss Jonstone!'

Morse was still smirking to himself with infinite self-satisfaction as, for the last time, the two men walked from the Haworth Hotel.

An hour later, a man was arrested at his home in south-east Oxford. This time, there were no revolvers on view; and the man in question, promptly cautioned by Sergeant Lewis of the Oxfordshire CID, made no show of resistance whatsoever.

CHAPTER FORTY-TWO

Wednesday, January 8th: noon

Lovers of air travel find it exhilarating to hang poised between the illusion of immortality and the fact of death.

(ALEXANDER CHASE)

THE BOEING 737 scheduled to take off from Gatwick at 12.05 hours was almost fully booked, with only four or five empty seats visible as the air hostesses went through their dumb-shows with the oxygen masks and the inflatable life-jackets. It was noticeable that almost all the passengers were paying the most careful attention to the advice being offered: several tragic air crashes during the previous months had engendered a sort of collective pterophobia, and airport lounges throughout the world were reporting a dramatic rise in the sales of tranquillizing pills and alcoholic spirits. But quite certainly there were two persons on the aircraft (and there may have been others) who listened only perfunctorily to the safety instructions being rehearsed that lunchtime. For one of these two persons, the transit through the terminal had been a nightmare: and yet, as it now seemed, there had been no real cause for anxiety. Documentation, baggage, passport – none had brought any problem at all. For the second of these two persons, worries had sprung from a slightly different source; yet he, too, was now beginning to feel more relaxed. As he looked down from his window-seat on to the wet tarmac, his left hand quietly slid the half-bottle of brandy from his anorak pocket, allowing his right hand to unscrew the cap. The attention of those passengers sitting immediately around him was still focused on the slim-waisted stewardesses, and he was able to pour for himself a couple of tots without his imbibings being too obvious. And already he felt slightly better! It had been a damnably close-run thing – but he'd made it! A sign came on just above him, bidding all passengers to fasten their seatbelts and to refrain from smoking until further notice; the engines vibrated anew along the fuselage; and the stewardesses took their seats, facing the passengers, and smiling perhaps with slightly spurious confidence upon their latest charges. Gradually the giant plane moved forward in a quarter-turn, took up its proper station, and stood there for a minute or two preparing, like a long-jump finalist in the Olympic Games, to accelerate along the runway. The man seated by the window knew that any second now he would be able to relax – almost completely. Like so many fellow criminals, he was under the happy delusion that there was no extradition treaty between Spain and the United Kingdom, and he had read of so many criminals – bank robbers, embezzlers, drug-peddlers and pederasts – who were even now lounging lazily at various resorts along the Costa del Sol.

Suddenly the aircraft's throttles were opened completely and the mighty power seemed almost a tangible entity.

Then the engines seemed to die a little.

And then they seemed to die completely.

And two members of Gatwick Security Police boarded the aircraft.

For the man in the window-seat, beside whom these men stopped, there appeared little point in even thinking of escape. Where was there to escape to?

The Boeing was only very slightly delayed; and five minutes behind schedule it was shooting off the earth at an angle of forty-five degrees and heading for its appointed destination. Very soon, passengers were told that they could unfasten their seatbelts: everything was fine. And six rows behind the now-empty window-seat, a woman lit a cigarette and inhaled very deeply.

CHAPTER FORTY-THREE

Wednesday, January 8th: p.m.

No mask like open truth to cover lies,
As to go naked is the best disguise.

(WILLIAM CONGREVE)

MORSE SAT IN Superintendent Bell's office in St Aldates awaiting Lewis – the latter having been deputed the task of taking down in his rather laborious longhand the statement from the man arrested earlier that day at his home in south-east Oxford.

'Damned clever, you know!' reiterated Bell.

Morse nodded: he liked Bell well enough perhaps – though not overmuch – and he found himself wishing that Lewis would get a move on.

'Well done, anyway!' said Bell. 'The Chief Constable'll be pleased.'

'Perhaps he'll let me have a day or two's holiday before the end of the decade.'

'We're *very* grateful, though – you know that, don't you?'

'Yes,' said Morse, honestly enough.

*

It was a highly euphoric Lewis who came in at a quarter past one, thrusting a statement – four pages of it – on the desk in front of Morse. 'Maybe a few little errors in English usage here and there, sir; but on the whole a splendid piece of prose, I think you'll find.'

Morse took the statement and scanned the last page:

in the normal way, but we were hard up and I lost my job in November and there was only playing in the group left with a wife and my four little children to feed and look after. We'd got the Social Security but the HP was getting bad, and then this came along. All I had to do was what he told me and that wasn't very difficult. I didn't really have any choice because I needed the money bad and it wasn't because I wanted to do anything that was wrong. I know what happened because I saw it in the *Oxford Mail* but when I agreed I just did what I was told and I never knew what things were all about at the time. I'm very sorry about it. Please remember I said that, because I love my wife and my little children.

As dictated to Sergeant Lewis, Kidlington CID, by Mr Winston Grant, labourer (unemployed), of 29 Rose Hill Gardens, Rose Hill, Oxford. 8 Jan.

'The adverb from "bad" is "badly",' mumbled Morse.

'Shall we keep him here?' asked Bell.

'He's your man,' said Morse.

'And the charge – officially?'

'"Accessory to murder", I suppose – but I'm not a legal man.'

'"Party to murder", perhaps?' suggested Lewis, who had seldom looked so happy since his elder daughter announced her first pregnancy.

Back at Kidlington HQ, Morse sat back in the old black leather armchair, looking (for the while) imperturbably expansive. The man arrested at Gatwick, almost two hours earlier, was well on his way to Oxfordshire, expected (Morse learned) within the next fifteen minutes. It was a time to savour.

Lewis himself now knew exactly what had happened on New Year's Eve in Annexe 3; knew, too, that the murderer of Thomas Bowman had neither set foot inside the main hotel building, nor bedecked himself in a single item of fancy dress. And yet, as to how Morse had arrived at the truth, he felt as puzzled as a small boy witnessing his first conjuring performance. 'What really put you on to it, sir?'

'The *key* point was, as I told you, that the murderer tried desperately hard to persuade us that the crime was committed *as late as possible*: after midnight. But as you yourself rightly observed, Lewis, there would seem to be little point in such a deception if the murderer stayed on the scene the whole time from about eight that night to one o'clock the next morning. But there was every point if he *wasn't* on the scene in the latter part of the evening – a time for which he had an *alibi*.'

'But, sir—'

'There were three clues in this case which should

have put us on to the truth much earlier than they did. Each of these three clues, in itself, looks like a pedestrian little piece of information; but taken together – well ... The *first* vital clue came largely from Sarah Jonstone – the only really valuable and coherent witness in the whole case – and it was this: that the man posing as "Mr Ballard" ate virtually nothing that evening! The *second* vital clue – also brought to our notice, among others, by Miss Jonstone – was the fact that the man posing as "Mr Ballard" was still staining whatever he touched late that evening! Then there was the *third* vital clue – the simplest clue of the lot, and one which was staring all of us in the face from the very beginning. So obvious a clue that none of us – none of us! – paid the slightest attention to it: the fact that the man posing as "Mr Ballard" won the fancy-dress competition!

'You see, Lewis, there are two ways of looking at each of these clues – the complex way, and the simple way. And we'd been looking at them the wrong way – we've been looking at them the *complex* way.'

'I see,' said Lewis, unseeing.

'Take the food business,' continued Morse. 'We almost got in some hopelessly complex muddle about it, didn't we? I read carefully what dear old Max said in his report about what had been floating up and down in the ascending and descending colons. You, Lewis, were bemused enough to listen to what Miss Jonstone said about someone ringing up to ask what the menu was. Why the hell *shouldn't* someone ring up and ask if they're in for another few slices of the virtually inevitable turkey? And do you know what we didn't do amid all this cerebration, Lewis? We didn't ask ourselves a very simple question: if our man had eaten nothing of the first two courses, shouldn't we assume he might be getting a little *hungry*? And even if he's been told he'd better go through the evening secretly sticking all the goodies into a doggie-bag, you might have thought he'd be tempted when he came to the next two courses on the menu – especially a couple of succulent pork chops. So why, Lewis – just think simply! – why didn't he have a mouthful or two?'

'Like you say, sir, he was told not to, because it was vital—'

'No! You're still getting too *complicated*, Lewis. There's a very *simple* answer, you see! Rastafarians aren't allowed to eat pork!

'Now let's come to this business of the stains this man was leaving behind on whatever he touched – even after midnight! We took down all the evidence, didn't we – we got statements from Miss Palmer, and Mrs Smith, and Sarah Jonstone – about how the wretched fellow went round ruining their coats and their blouses. And we almost came to the point – well, *I* did, Lewis – of getting them all analysed and seeing if the stains were the same, and trying to find out where the original theatre-black came from and – well, we were getting too *complex* again! The simple truth is that any make-up *dries* after a few hours; it comes off at first, of course, on anything that's touched – but after a while it's no problem at all. Yet in this case it *remained* a problem.

And the *simple* answer to this particular mystery is that our man *wanted* to leave his marks late that evening; he deliberately put *more* stain on his hands; and he deliberately put his hands where they *would* leave marks. All right, Lewis? He had a stick of theatre-black in his pocket and he smeared it all over the palms of his hands in the final hour or so of the New Year party.

'And then there's the last point. The man won a prize, and we made all sorts of complex assumptions about it; he'd been the most painstaking and imaginative competitor of the lot; he'd been so successful with his make-up that no one could recognize him; he'd been anxious for some reason to carry off the first prize in the fancy-dress competition. And all a load of *complex* nonsense, Lewis. The fact is that the very last thing he wanted was to draw any attention to himself by winning the first prize that evening. And the almost childishly *simple* fact of the matter is that if you want to dress up and win first prize *as*, let's say, Prince Charles, well, the best way to do it is to *be* Prince Charles. And we all ought to have suspected, perhaps, that the man who dressed up in that Rastafarian rig-out and who put on such a convincing and successful performance that night *as* a Rastafarian, might perhaps have owed his success to the simple fact that he *was* a Rastafarian!'

'Mr Winston Grant.'

'Yes, Mr Winston Grant! A man, in fact, I met outside the Friar only last night! And if anyone ever tells you, Lewis, that there isn't a quite extraordinary degree of coincidence in this world of ours – then you tell him to come to see me, and I'll tell him different!'

'Should you perhaps say "differently"?' asked Lewis.

'This man had been a builder's labourer; he'd worked on several sites in Oxford – including the Locals; he'd lost his job because of cutbacks in the building industry; he was getting short of money for himself and his family; he was made an extraordinarily generous offer – we still don't know *how* generous; and he agreed to accept that offer in return for playing – as he saw things – a minor role for a few hours at a New Year's party in an Oxford hotel. I doubt we shall ever know all the ins and outs of the matter but—'

Sergeant Phillips knocked and announced that the prisoner was now in the interview room.

And Morse smiled.

And Lewis smiled.

'Just finish off what you were saying, will you, sir?'

'Nothing more to say, really. Winston Grant must have been pretty carefully briefed, that's for sure. In the first place he'd be coming into the hotel directly from the street, and it was absolutely essential that he should wait his time, to the second almost, until Margaret Bowman had created the clever little distraction of taking Sarah Jonstone away from the reception desk to inspect the graffito in the Ladies' – a graffito which she, Margaret Bowman, had herself just scrawled across the wall. Then, I'm sure he must have been told to say as little as possible to anyone else all the evening and to stick close to Margaret Bowman, as if they were far

COLIN DEXTER

more interested in each other than in the goings-on around them. *But there was no chance of him opting out of the fancy-dress competition!* I suspect, too, that he was told not to eat anything – if he could manage not to without drawing too much attention to himself; and remember, he was helped in this by the way Binyon had scheduled the various courses at different tables. But it may well be, Lewis, that we're overestimating the extent to which the plan was completely thought out. Above all, though, he had to carry through that final, extraordinarily clever, little deception: he was to make every effort to *pretend* that he was a black man – even though he *was* a black man. And there was one wonderfully simple way in which such a pretence could be sustained, and that was by rubbing dark-stain on to his hands – *hands that were already black* – so that everyone who came into physical contact with him should believe that he was *not* a black man – but a white man. And that, Lewis, in the later stages of that New Year's party is what he did, making sure he left a few indelible marks on the most obvious places – like the shoulders of the light-coloured winter mackintoshes worn by both Miss Palmer and Mrs Smith—'

'—and the white blouse of Sarah Jonstone.'

'Cream-coloured actually,' said Morse.

For Sergeant Phillips it was all somewhat *déjà vu* as he resumed his vigil at the door of the interview room, his feet still aching, his eyes scanning the bare room once again: the wooden trestle-table on which stood a white

294

polystyrene coffee cup (full) and an ash-tray (as yet empty); and behind the table, the same fairish-haired, fresh-complexioned man who had sat there the previous evening – Mr Edward Wilkins.

CHAPTER FORTY-FOUR

Wednesday, January 8th: p.m.

Felix qui potuit rerum cognoscere causas.

(VIRGIL, *Georgics*)

AT 5 P.M., Mr James Prior, Security Officer at the Locals, put on his bicycle clips and prepared to leave. Before he did so he had a final look round Reception to make sure that everything that should be locked up *was* locked up. It was odd though, really, to think that the only thing the police had been interested in was the one drawer that *wasn't* locked up – the drawer in which he kept all the out-of-date security passes, elastic-banded into their various bundles. Like the bundle for the last lot of building workers from which the police had already taken two passes away: that of Winston Grant, a Rastafarian fellow whom Prior remembered very well; and that of a man called Wilkins, who'd operated the giant yellow crane that had towered over the Delegacy building throughout the summer months. After Morse's call early that morning, Prior had looked briefly through the rest of that particular bundle, and had wondered whether there were any other criminals lurking among those very ordinary-looking faces. But the truth was that one could never tell: he, far more than most people, was fully aware of that.

That afternoon, Wilkins had been resignedly co-operative about every detail of the whole case – with the exception of the act of murder itself, which he stubbornly and categorically refused to discuss in any respect whatsoever: it was as if that single, swift dispatch (to which he now confessed) had paralysed his capacity to accept it as in any way a piece of voluntary, responsible behaviour. But for the rest, he spoke fully and freely; and there was nothing surprising, nothing new, that emerged from his statement. Naturally enough, perhaps, he expressed the hope that Winston Grant should be treated with appropriate leniency, although it seemed to others (certainly to Lewis) that such an accomplice must have been rather more aware of the nature of his assignment than either Grant or Wilkins was prepared to admit.

About Margaret Bowman, the only piece of new information Wilkins was able to give was that he had more than once picked her up from a beauty clinic in Oxford, and Lewis shook his head ruefully as he learned that this clinic was the very first one he had rung – the one refusing to divulge any confidential details. About Margaret's present fate Wilkins appeared strangely indifferent. He hadn't (he said) the faintest idea where she'd finally drifted off to; but presumably the police would be concentrating on her various relatives up around Alnwick or Berwick or Newcastle or wherever they were. For his part, he was perhaps glad to get shot of the woman. She'd brought him nothing but trouble, although he fully accepted that it had been far more his fault than hers that things had finally . . . But that was all over now. And in an odd sort of way (he'd said) he felt relieved.

It was just after 6.30 p.m. when Sergeant Phillips escorted Wilkins down to St Aldates where temporarily, together with Grant, he would be held, awaiting (in the short term) the provision of alternative custodial arrangements and (in the long term) the pleasure of Her Majesty.

Morse insisted that both he himself and Lewis should call it a day; and Lewis was just closing the box-file on the Haworth Hotel case when he noticed a letter which he had never been shown: one beginning 'This is a love letter . . .' He read the first few lines with some mystification – until he came to the quite extraordinary statement that the anonymous correspondent had been 'reading a biography of Thomas Hardy . . .'!

Should he tell Morse? He read the letter through again with the greatest interest.

Well, well, well!

At 7 p.m. Morse (Lewis thought he had gone) came back into his office once more. 'Listen, Lewis! This Wilkins is one of the cleverest buggers we've ever had! You realize that? He's pulled the wool over my eyes about the most central, central, central issue of the lot! And you know what that is? That he, Wilkins, was – is!

– hopelessly in love with this woman, Margaret Bowman; and that he'd do anything – *did* do anything – to keep her. In fact, he murdered her husband to keep her! And likewise, Lewis, the fact that he'd do anything to protect her *now*! You remember what he said last night? Just get the transcript, Lewis – the bit about the passport!'

Lewis found the document and read aloud:

'I advised her to get on a boat or something and sail off to the continent – away from everything.'

'But she didn't take your advice?'

'No, she couldn't. She hadn't got a passport and she was frightened of applying for one because she knew everybody was trying to find her ...'

'God, I'm a fool, Lewis! I wonder how many lies he *has* told us? That she was at his house last night? That she was up with her sister in Newcastle? Has she *got* a sister, Lewis? Oh dear! She hasn't got a passport, he says? And we believe him! So we don't watch all the boats—'

'Or the planes,' added Lewis quietly.

'I don't believe it!' said Morse softly, after a pause.

'What's worrying you, sir?'

'Get a telex off to Gatwick straight away! Get the passenger list of flight number whatever-it-was!'

'You don't think—?'

'*Think?* I'm almost *sure*, Lewis!'

*

When Lewis returned from the telex office, Morse already had his greatcoat on and was ready to leave.

'You know that letter you had from one of your admirers, sir?'

'How do you know about that?'

'You left it in the box.'

'Oh!'

'Did you notice the postmark on the original letter?'

'London. So what?'

'London? Really?' (Lewis sounded like a man who knows all the answers.) 'You get a lot of people going up to the London sales from all over the country, don't you? I mean anyone from anywhere – from Oxford, say – could go up to the January sales and drop a letter in a postbox outside Paddington.'

Morse was frowning. 'What exactly are you trying to tell me, Lewis?'

'I just wondered if you had any idea of who'd written that letter to you, that's all.'

Morse's hand was on the doorknob. 'Look, Lewis! You know the difference between you and me, don't you? You don't use your *eyes* enough! If you *had* done – and very recently, too! – you'd know perfectly well who wrote that letter.'

'Yes?'

'Yes! And it so happens – since you're suddenly so very interested in my private affairs, Lewis – that I'm going to take the particular lady who wrote that particular letter out for a particularly fine meal tonight – that's if you've no objections?'

'Where are you taking her, sir?'

'If you must know, we're going out to Springs Hotel near Wallingford.'

'Pretty expensive, so they say, sir.'

'We shall go halves – you realize that, of course?' Morse winked happily at Lewis – and was gone.

Lewis, too, was smiling happily as he rang his wife and told her that he wouldn't be long.

At 7.50 p.m. the telex reply came through from Gatwick: on the scheduled 12.05 flight that had left that morning for Barcelona, the passenger list had included, apart from a Mr Edward Wilkins, a Mrs Margaret Bowman, the latter giving an address in Chipping Norton, Oxfordshire.

At 8.00 p.m., Lewis pulled on his overcoat and left Kidlington HQ. He wasn't at all sure whether Morse would be pleased, or displeased, with the news he had just received. But the last thing he was going to do was to ring Springs Hotel. He just hoped – very much he hoped – that Morse would have an enjoyable evening, and an enjoyable meal. As for himself, the missus would have the egg and chips ready; and he felt very happy with life.